TO ALL THE MEN I'VE KILLED BEFORE

KATY BRENT

HQ

ONE PLACE. MANY STORIES

HQ
An imprint of HarperCollins*Publishers* Ltd
1 London Bridge Street
London SE1 9GF

www.harpercollins.co.uk

HarperCollins*Publishers*
Macken House, 39/40 Mayor Street Upper
Dublin 1, D01 C9W8, Ireland

This edition 2026

1
First published in Great Britain by HQ,
an imprint of HarperCollins*Publishers* Ltd 2026

A catalogue record for this book is available from the British Library.

ISBN: 9780008656720

Set in Sabon LT Pro by HarperCollins*Publishers* India

Printed and bound in the UK using 100%
Renewable Electricity at CPI Group (UK) Ltd

MIX
Paper | Supporting responsible forestry
FSC® C013604

Praise for *To All The Men I've Killed Before*

'*To All the Men I've Killed Before* is sharp in wit and blunt in murder weapon. I had a bloody good time rooting for my fave vegan serial killer as she strutted her gloriously gory way around Hollywood.'
Charlotte Vassell, author of *The In Crowd*

'All the twists, all the drama, and wit sharp enough to slit throats. Kitty Collins has conquered America.'
Tam Barnett, author of *How to Get Away With Murder*

'Kitty Collins has sealed her place as my favourite serial killer! Another sharply written, darkly funny take-down of toxic masculinity, with the added bonus of the spectacular Antoinette.'
Sarah Clarke, author of *Someone in the Water*

'The perfect conclusion to the Kitty Collins series. Brent delivers a glamorous and deadly finale with everything fans have come to love. Devilishly smart and funny.'
Rhiannon Barnsley, author of *Slander*

'Kitty Collins is back and as sharp, funny and dangerous as ever and, with the arrival of her sibling sidekick, dare I say, endearingly tender too. When it comes to the patriarchy, Brent is killing it. Brava!'
Amy Beashel, author of *Bad Manners*

'Prepare for a riotous rollercoaster of revenge! Whip smart and deliciously dark. Katy Brent perfectly balances the gore and the glamour as Kitty and Antoinette make their mark in Hollywood. I absolutely loved it!'
Kate Gray, author of *Welcome to the Family*

KATY BRENT is the author of four novels. Previously an award-winning journalist, she always dreamed of writing a book and lockdown finally gave her the excuse to do it.

Also by Katy Brent

Kitty Collins series
How to Kill Men and Get Away With It
I Bet You'd Look Good in a Coffin

The Murder After the Night Before

For Seb

Revenge is a kind of wild justice

—FRANCIS BACON

Revenge is sweet and not fattening

—ALFRED HITCHCOCK

Prologue

UNDISCLOSED LOCATION, LOS ANGELES, CALIFORNIA

They all look the same in this moment.

Men.

When they're about to die.

I'm not talking about the blood, or the sweat that gathers on their upper lip. I'm not even talking about the *smell* they make when they're about to meet their maker.

It's the expression.

That slow, creeping recognition that their strength, their size, their privilege of simply being born a man suddenly mean nothing.

The moment they realise they're on the ground.

At my feet.

And it's all about to be over.

He blinks up at me, his body jerking with fast, shallow breaths. I almost want to tell him to take his time with them, they're some of his very last ones. He should be savouring his oxygen. But he's too busy fighting against the zip ties, straining his wrists against them even though it's so obviously futile.

They always do this too.

Hope that some last burst of violence will get them out of their restraints so then they can overpower me.

But there's something different this time.

He's not just facing one of us.

He's facing two.

My sister steps into his eyeline and I see the moment he registers her. His pupils dilate in fear.

'You,' he says.

'Yes,' she says, sweetly. 'Me.'

His Adam's apple bobs as he tries to swallow down his panic. But he doesn't say anything else. I crouch beside him, letting the knife sparkle in the light of the single naked bulb.

'Any last words?' I say.

Still nothing.

But he looks up at me now, his eyes pleading with me.

'What is it?' I say. 'You didn't seriously think I was going to let you off the hook because we bonded a bit, did you? As if *that* makes up for what you've done. It was always going to end like this.'

His eyes flicker now, a spark of panic.

Good.

And now . . . now it's showtime.

As they say in Hollywood, *action.*

1

TERMINAL B, LAX AIRPORT, LOS ANGELES, TWELVE DAYS EARLIER

Okay, this is fine.

I don't need to get stressed about it.

It's just a bag. Just a missing bag.

With all my fucking stuff in it.

'Sorry, ma'am,' the member of staff at the Baggage Service Office who looks like a Victoria's Secret model is saying. 'You're absolutely certain the bag was not on the luggage carousel?'

I grit my teeth.

'Yes,' I say, trying to move my rictus lips into a smile, because this is about the fourth time I've explained this to her. 'I'm absolutely certain that after standing at the carousel for over an hour and watching people collect their bags until it was completely empty, that mine was not there.'

She frowns hard at me, her perfect brows almost touching. She's trying to decide if I'm being an arsehole or not.

I'm trying to not be.

I'm really trying.

'Okay, ma'am, well, as I explained, you'll need to fill out a

Property Irregularity Report and then I'll be able to give you a reference number.'

A reference number? I don't want a fucking reference number. What I want is my suitcase.

'Okay,' I say through my teeth. 'That's great.'

She hands me a form and gives me a tight little smile of her own.

'We do ask you to be patient,' she says, 'as it can take some time to locate lost luggage.'

I hear my half-sister Antoinette next to me make a noise like she's choking when the woman says 'patient'. I ignore her.

I have loads of patience.

I fill out the form and hand it back to the desk clerk, who then gives me this all-important *reference number* even though I'm pretty sure I'll never see my bag again. There's a little pang of pain in my heart when I think about the beautiful tiered Chloé dress that is probably being pawed over by some errant baggage handler as we speak.

'We'll be in touch,' the model-slash-airport-staffer tells me. 'Have a great stay in Los Angeles.'

Well, how could it not be? It's already off to a *brilliant* start.

'Look on the bright side,' Antoinette says as we shuffle out of the airport and ready ourselves to fight our way through the arrivals crowds to find our Uber driver. 'At least you've got an excuse to go shopping now.'

'We're not here to go shopping,' I say as we push through a gaggle of young women dressed in fluffy boots and pink cowboy hats, one with a white sash, the word 'Bride' bejewelled on it. 'You know that.'

We're here for revenge.

And the revenge I have in mind isn't just going to be sweet.

It will be brutal.

'I know, I know,' Antoinette says. 'We're here to find and kill Aidan Ward.'

I smile at her, pleased that she hasn't forgotten the purpose of our trip.

Aidan Ward is a therapist who beat my friend Tor half to death in London before fleeing to LA. I mistakenly gave him the benefit of the doubt when they started dating. I mean, what kind of therapist hits on their vulnerable patient? So we're here to fix my fuck-up.

Out of all the men I've killed before, he is going to be my favourite.

I spot a middle-aged man in a grey T-shirt and khaki shorts holding a tablet with the name Collins on it.

'There's our ride,' I say to my sister as we make our way past a group of men who look to be in their early twenties. As we pass them a wolf-whistle pierces the air like a siren and I feel Antoinette tense up. She stops walking and spins round to face the men. One of them, a guy in a fitted white top, tight joggers that could be described as 'skinny' and a *backwards* baseball cap, gives us a grin.

Antoinette bristles.

Oh God.

Oh God.

But instead of shouting something back at them, which is what I think she's gearing up to do, she points her phone at the group and snaps a picture, before slipping her arm through mine and continuing to walk.

'What was that for?' I ask. 'Why did you take a photo?'

'It's so I can do an image search later and find out exactly who that fucker is,' she says with a smile.

'And why would you want to do that?'

She gives me a look like I've said something stupid and says, 'So we can find him and kill him, of course.'

I look at her to see if she's joking but her face is deadly serious. 'We're not doing that, Antoinette.'

'He blatantly disrespected us,' she says. 'He *whistled* at us like we're just bits of meat or something. He deserves to die.'

'It was just a whistle,' I say. 'He didn't hurt anyone. It's okay.'

She stops walking again.

'It's not *okay*, Kitty,' she says. 'It might be just a whistle to you but it's actually much more than that. He's a misogynist. He doesn't respect women. It might start with just a whistle but if he carries on unchecked his next move could be a sexual assault. This shit doesn't happen in isolation.'

'I know it's not nice but he was probably just showing off in front of his friends,' I say.

'Who cares,' she says. 'He still did it. It's sexual harassment. What if it wasn't us that he whistled at? What if it was some other woman, a woman dealing with PTSD or something? What if that one whistle was the thing to push her over the edge?'

She's got a point.

But still.

'And,' she continues vehemently, 'a guy who catcalls you isn't trying to date you. He knows that no woman is going to immediately have sex with him because he shouted "nice tits" at her or whatever. Catcalling is about humiliating us. It's not a compliment. It's a threat.'

'Antoinette,' I say patiently. 'You're absolutely and completely right but we can't kill every man on the planet who catcalls someone.'

'Why not?' she asks. 'It's stuff like this, Kitty, the everyday harassment, the whistles, the slut-shaming that underpin the rest of it. That makes men think they can get away with the bigger stuff too.'

'I agree,' I say, 'I do. But it's just not physically possible to murder every man who's been a bit of a dick. I've only got one pair of hands, for a start.'

'Well, you've got me now,' she says.

'We're still not killing him,' I say and Antoinette gives me a sly look.

'Maybe.'

'No maybe. We're not!'

She shrugs. 'Whatever. But there's more than one way to skin a cat.'

I want to ask her what she means but our driver has spotted us walking towards him and is waving frantically.

I wave back.

2

CHATEAU MARMONT, WEST HOLLYWOOD, LOS ANGELES

Okay.

So this is impressive.

Like *really* impressive.

I stare up at the huge white building and blink a few times as I take it in. There might even be tears in my eyes.

This place.

The history.

It's beautiful.

I can't believe I haven't actually been here before.

And where else could we possibly stay while in LA than here, a place renowned for two of the most important things for murder: privacy and discretion. After all, that's why we're here.

I turn to look at Antoinette to see the same stars twinkling in her eyes. But she just looks . . . underwhelmed.

'Is this it?' she asks me with absolutely no irony in her voice.

'What do you mean, is this it?'

She shrugs and stares at the building. 'I don't know. I was just expecting something else. It looks like the Hollywood Tower ride at Disneyland.'

I stare at the building with her and, yes, okay, it does maybe look a *little* bit on the dilapidated side, but that's part of its charm.

It's the fucking *Chateau*.

'It's Hollywood history,' I tell her. 'So much has gone on in between those walls. Parties, affairs, deaths. It's actually haunted.'

'Urgh, imagine being stuck here for eternity,' she says with a sigh as she grabs the handle on her suitcase and begins to wheel it towards the entrance where a concierge is waiting to greet us.

I stare after her.

How can a sister of mine be *disappointed* by the Chateau Marmont?

I suppose I'm only just getting to know her properly though. I actually know very little about this twenty-year-old who is suddenly my flesh and blood.

I only discovered she was my half-sister a few weeks ago, even though I've known her since she was born. Turns out she was the product of an affair between my father and her mother. Since then I've discovered that, while blood may well be thicker than water, it's also very . . . different.

But it's going to be fine.

I'm sure we'll discover that we have loads of other things in common.

Apart from our father's passion for killing.

And where better to build our sisterly bond than here, in Hollywood, tied by blood and our mission – to find Aidan Ward.

* * *

Inside, the lobby is elegant and dimly lit and I feel my heart quicken. It even smells of glamour. Like skin, the ghost of cigarettes and leather.

It's perfect.

We're booked into one of the (in)famous bungalows, which should give us the privacy we need.

Antoinette is looking around. 'It's a bit dingy.'

Dingy?

Dingy?

'It's the Chateau Marmont, Antoinette,' I say. 'It's iconic.'

'Beyoncé is iconic,' Antoinette says, 'but she is also old and in need of modernisation.'

I have no words. I am now just standing here, my jaw by my knees as she looks around the beautiful lobby like I've dragged her into a derelict woodshed.

She takes a big breath like she's being *very brave* and moves forward, avoiding touching the furniture like it might infect her.

After we check in we make our way past the world-famous pool – which is surrounded by swimwear-clad people all pretending not to be checking each other out – towards our bungalow.

I slide the key into the lock, and as the door swings open, I feel the excitement that has been bubbling in my veins reach boiling point.

Antoinette touches my arm. 'Kitty,' she says in a whisper. 'Are you short on money or something? I can cover accommodation if it's an issue.'

While we both grew up in Chelsea, London, and are what would be called 'trust-fund babies', Antoinette's family are quite a bit richer than mine. Her dad – or the man she believed to be her dad – is, *was* James Pemberton, one of the biggest music producers in the world. Meanwhile, my dad – *our* dad – owned a chain of abattoirs and meat-processing plants. A bit of an empire actually. I have money. Rather a lot of money. But Antoinette has more – 'pedo island money' as she once charmingly referred to it. And, since James's death last year, she's inherited most of it.

I ignore her and take a step inside and it is like going back in time to the 1950s. I feel like a Hollywood starlet. I take a deep breath in, wondering if some remnants of stardust are making their way into my lungs. I wish the walls could talk so they could tell me some of the no doubt *insane* things that have happened in this room. The parties, the secret trysts. Actually, considering what *I'm* planning on doing in this room, it's a good thing the walls can't speak. There's a private terrace and patio just outside the huge living area. I bet that's seen some wild times too.

I turn to Antoinette, excited, but I feel my face drop when I see her expression.

'It might have been nice if there was a spa here,' she says.

'You can get treatments in the room,' I say, 'if it's that important to you.'

Antoinette just shrugs and wheels her suitcase through to the bedrooms. 'I'll be taking the master bedroom,' she calls through to me. 'Seeing as how you're making me slum it.'

I stare after her, my jaw on the floor.

I can't believe I'm related to someone who thinks the Chateau Marmont is 'slumming it'.

3

BUNGALOW THREE, CHATEAU MARMONT, WEST HOLLYWOOD, LOS ANGELES

'So, what do you want to do first?' Antoinette asks when she's finished unpacking while I watched, looking on mournfully at all her clothes, wondering where mine are at this moment. I'm sitting on the sofa with my laptop open.

'I want to find Aidan Ward,' I say. 'I thought we'd start by going online and checking out therapists, especially any new, British ones. I've already started a spreadsheet.'

Antoinette sits down next to me and peers at the Excel document I've got open.

'Oh, wow,' she says. 'You really did.'

'So I think the best way to do this is to make some burner accounts on Reddit and Facebook, join some local groups and ask if anyone knows of recently arrived guys. I thought you could take Reddit and I'll do Facebook?'

Antoinette nods. 'Makes sense,' she says. 'Because you're old.' I give her a look. '. . . -der, than me,' she adds, quickly.

'When we've got some possibilities, we'll make appointments so we can find out if it's Aidan Ward.'

‘Sounds good,’ Antoinette says with a yawn. ‘Don’t you think that you should go shopping first though? Unless you’re planning on wearing your plane outfit to dinner.’

I look down at the cherry-coloured cashmere Loro Piana co-ord set I’ve been wearing for at least the last eighteen hours and give it a sniff. It smells of plane-cabin air and stale sweat.

She’s got a point.

And, actually, what better than a shopping trip for some sisterly bonding?

‘We could both go,’ I say excitedly. ‘We could hit up Rodeo Drive, grab me some basics, get some food?’

Antoinette has sprawled herself across the couch, her long, tanned limbs askew. ‘I might skip it,’ she says, ‘if you don’t mind. I think the jet lag is hitting me.’

Disappointment thumps in my chest. ‘Shopping is good for jet lag,’ I say with a weak laugh but Antoinette just closes her eyes.

‘I don’t really enjoy shopping.’

I think of her now-full wardrobe jammed with clothes, some with labels still attached. ‘You don’t?’

She opens one eye. ‘Not *shopping* shopping,’ she says. ‘I prefer to do it online. It’s a much more Zen experience.’

‘But Antoinette,’ I say, ‘I’m not suggesting we go and hang out at some outlet mall. These are designer shops. With VIP rooms and champagne.’

‘I just prefer the apps,’ she says with a shrug. ‘But you should go! I think I’ll stay here and take a look at Reddit, maybe have a nap.’

‘Okay,’ I say, crestfallen. ‘I guess I’ll see you later then?’

But Antoinette is already asleep.

4

RODEO DRIVE, BEVERLY HILLS, LOS ANGELES

It's okay that Antoinette didn't want to come shopping.

And that she doesn't even *like* shopping.

It really is.

She'd probably just slow me down anyway.

And we're not actually here for shopping and sightseeing, after all.

This isn't a girls' trip. It's a murder mission.

Hopefully we won't even be here very long so all I need to do is pop into a couple of shops and grab a few outfits.

We can get dinner and drinks this evening instead.

Yes, we can have a lovely time while we work out where to start our hunt for Aidan Ward.

In the Uber, my phone starts buzzing with an incoming FaceTime call.

It's Tor.

I haven't seen Tor since I visited her in hospital a few days before we flew out here. She messaged earlier to tell me that she had been sent home to recuperate and that her mother and our friend Maisie were taking it in turns to look after her. I don't know why but I'd assumed that because she'd been sent home, she'd look better than she did when I last saw her. I'm shocked to see that she doesn't.

Her face still looks swollen and her left eye is still partially closed underneath the fan of bruises. She winces as she tries to move her mouth into a smile to greet me.

'Hey,' I say, hoping that my face is doing a good job of hiding how shocked I am at her appearance. 'I'm in an Uber.' I don't want her grilling me about Aidan Ward and my mission with an eye-, or would it be ear-, witness.

She understands the assignment. 'Okay,' she says, 'I was just calling to check that you'd landed safely.'

'Safe and sound,' I say. 'Although the same can't be said about my luggage.' Tor pulls a puzzled expression which seems to cause her pain. 'My bag didn't arrive at LAX when I did.'

'Oh Kits, no,' she says.

'I know, but I'm on my way to Rodeo Drive, so, you know, silver linings.' I try for a smile but a wave of tiredness and nausea washes over me and almost takes me out.

'Kits? Are you okay? You look really pale.'

I look at the small version of my face at the bottom of the screen. She's not wrong. I look like Death. But with an expensive haircut.

'Jet lag,' I say, swallowing down a mouthful of bile. 'I'll be fine when I've had some sleep. And I won't be pale for long out here.' I spin the view around so she can see the unending blue sky.

'Okay . . .' Tor says as I turn the camera back. 'Just, you know, don't get sick.'

'I won't,' I say. 'I've got something very important to do out here.'

She smiles again, winces again. 'Love you.'

'Love you too,' I say. 'Speak soon.'

My Uber takes me to Rodeo Drive and I feel the underlying anxiety that's been niggling me since my baggage failed to arrive at its destination ebb away as I walk into the Gucci flagship store. I instantly feel relaxed as I breathe in the air-conditioned air and see rows of gorgeous clothes in the softest fabrics. Retail therapy is a real thing and I will die on that hill.

'Can I help you?' The voice belongs to a shop assistant who, like the airport worker, looks like she should actually be on a catwalk rather than working in a store. I've been to Beverly Hills before, of course, but I always forget just how beautiful everyone here is. It makes me a bit homesick for London and how there's such an eclectic mix of people there. I don't usually feel imposter syndrome when I'm shopping in Knightsbridge.

'Um, yes please,' I say. 'My bag was lost at the airport so I'm looking for a few pieces for my stay.'

The girl gives me a sympathetic look. 'I'm sorry,' she says. 'The same thing happened to a friend of mine a little while ago. It was a nightmare.'

'How long did it take for them to get their things back?' I ask, but the assistant just shakes her sleek head.

'No,' she says ominously. 'She didn't ever get it back.'

'Oh,' I say. 'Right.' My clothes are probably being sold on Vinted or something at this very moment.

She claps her hands together so suddenly, it makes me jump. 'So what you need is a capsule wardrobe?'

The words perk me up again. 'Yes,' I say. 'Exactly that.'

'How long are you here for?' she asks. 'What's the purpose of your trip?'

I can't really tell her that I'm here to hunt and kill a British therapist who went rogue. Although I'm quite curious as to how she might style that particular look.

Instead I say, 'It's a post-break-up trip,' which is at least kind of true. My boyfriend Charlie dumped me in France a few weeks ago. In his defence, he *had* just been held captive by Antoinette's insane brother – half-brother to be precise, that creep was *not* in my bloodline – and discovered that I'm a serial killer.

But still.

It stings.

A lot, actually.

Especially when I tried explaining to him that I only ever kill bad men.

The worst men who absolutely deserve it.

'Say less,' the assistant says and leads me to some dressing rooms. 'So let's find you some pretty day dresses and some *killer* night dresses.' She appraises me. 'You're a size four, right?'

I nod and she disappears back into the store.

While she's gone, I take my phone out of my bag and open Instagram. Thinking about Charlie has made me start missing him all over again. I scroll through until I find his profile. He's not a big social media user so I'm not surprised to find that he hasn't posted any new pictures, although I was hoping to get a snippet of what he's up to. I sigh and open Facebook instead. Again, there aren't any new photos but one thing has changed. And it makes my heart sink right into my shoes. In the little box where he previously declared to be 'in a relationship with Kitty Collins', it now says just one word – 'single'.

I try to swallow down the lump that has suddenly developed in my throat.

The assistant comes back in, her arms laden with clothes. She sees my face and gives me a sad smile.

'Put your phone away, girl,' she says. 'He is not worth your tears.'

I smile back, even though she's wrong. Charlie is absolutely worth my tears. He's the best person in the world. And he's *my* world. Was. He *was* my world. My soul mate. My twin flame. The man I wanted to grow old with.

The man I *still* want to grow old with.

And as soon as I've dealt with Aidan Ward, I need to get back to London to convince him to give me, us, another chance.

But for now I need to put him out of my mind. I can't be distracted from my mission. I take a deep breath and give the assistant one of my very best smiles, one of the ones that gained me over a million followers on Insta back in my influencer days. I try on the clothes she's picked out for me with an enthusiasm I'm faking at first but that soon becomes genuine. She's done a great job and I leave with most of them, before popping into some other shops for a few more casual pieces and shoes.

In one little boutique I see a gorgeous pale pink silk scarf. It's the colour of the inside of a seashell and as soft as dreams. I pick it up and hold it against my face in front of a mirror. It would look beautiful on me. Which means it would also look beautiful on Antoinette. I take it to the cashier and ask her to gift-wrap it.

I'm going to be the best sister ever.

5

BUNGALOW THREE, CHATEAU MARMONT, LOS ANGELES

When I get back to the Chateau with all my bags – I might have gone a little bit mad with the shopping – Antoinette is sitting on the sofa in the living area, engrossed in something on her iPad. She looks up and smiles when she sees me and my purchases.

'Ooh, show me everything,' she says and I pull various dresses out while she oohs and ahhs at them. 'Looks like you've had a good afternoon?'

'Yes,' I say, 'there's nothing like a bit of retail therapy. Look, I got you something.' I hand the carefully wrapped package to her and watch as she pulls the scarf out.

'Kitty,' she whispers. 'It's gorgeous. Thank you so much.'

I can feel myself beaming.

'You're welcome,' I say. 'What have you been up to?'

'Just bed rotting,' she says. 'And then sofa rotting. But I *did* set up a new Reddit account to find some leads on Aidan. There are a *tonne* of subs about LA and stuff.'

I'm impressed that she hasn't *just* been rotting and has been doing something proactive to find our target. Who knows, with both of us here maybe it won't take long to find Aidan Ward at all. Maybe I could be back in London in a week or so, winning Charlie back.

'Oh that's great,' I say. 'Did you find anything useful?'

'Not about Aidan,' she says and disappointment lurches in my gut. 'But I found something else you might be interested in.'

'What?' I ask, sitting next to her, my curiosity piqued.

'This.' She slides her iPad over to me. 'There's a serial killer. Right here in Hollywood.'

'Well . . . yeah,' I say.

'Not you. A different one. And he's targeting PrivatePool creators.'

'What's PrivatePool?' I ask, squinting at the screen.

'It's like OnlyFans,' Antoinette says, 'but it's Hollywood specific. Women over here basically realised they can make much more money creating adult content than waitressing or whatever.'

'That sounds horrible,' I say.

'Why?' Antoinette asks. 'I think it's great that they're taking control of their sexuality. And making money from it.'

I stare at her. 'Are you joking? OnlyFans is like dragging feminism backwards by its hair.'

'Kitty! Selling underwear pics to sleazy men is a lot more feminist than serving them their food and getting groped for minimum wage and tips.'

'It's not!' I say. 'It's really not. It's encouraging women to monetise their oppression.'

'But isn't it empowering to have the choice?'

'No! Not when that so-called empowerment is linked to

how much money you can make from sexualising yourself! And it's still patriarchy. It's for the male gaze and all these sites are owned by men, marketed to men.'

Antoinette is shaking her head. 'That's where PrivatePool is different,' she says. 'It was set up by women in LA who were sick of male-dominated business models. I've been doing my research.'

'It's still catering to the male gaze,' I grumble but Antoinette waves me off.

'*Anyway*,' she says, 'it's pissed off one man so much that he's going around *killing* women creating content on the site.' She looks at me, her face flushed with anger. Or is it excitement? 'This is perfect for us!'

'Is it?'

'Yes!' she says. 'We should find him. And kill him!'

I think for a moment. Someone out there killing women simply for the choices they make about their own lives is exactly the sort of man I wouldn't hesitate in tracking down and disposing of in London. But it feels a bit different out here. I don't have access to my family's abattoirs, for one thing. And I learned in France that getting rid of bodies without those isn't the easiest thing in the world. I haven't even worked out what I'm going to do with Aidan Ward's body once I've found and killed him. I also really want to get back to London as quickly as possible so getting involved in a hunt for a serial killer feels . . . messy.

'I don't know,' I say. 'I think the police might be better dealing with this one.' Even though I don't have any more faith in the US justice system than I do the British one. Any systems designed *by* men are essentially designed *for* men, after all.

But Antoinette is shaking her head again. 'That's the thing though,' she says. 'The police aren't even acknowledging that there's a killer!'

'What do you mean?'

'They're not admitting that there's a serial killer,' she says as she takes the iPad from me and scrolls. 'It's Redditors that have connected all the dots.'

True-crimers.

She's talking about true-crimers.

Well, that sorts that dilemma out for me.

I'm not about to start a wild goose chase looking for a serial killer that exists only in the minds of some chronically online mouth-breathers who should probably just get jobs or something.

'Redditors. Right,' I say.

'No, no! It's not like that,' Antoinette says and shoves the iPad back under my nose. 'Look, there have been at least four women found dead in the area in the last eighteen months. No one has been charged with their murders.'

I know this is by no means a shocking statistic and doesn't even begin to point to a serial killer. Almost three women are killed by an intimate partner every single day in America.

'Why do they even think it's a serial killer and not run-of-the-mill male violence?'

'This is where it gets really interesting,' Antoinette says. 'Every single one of the dead women had PrivatePool accounts. The police haven't said anything about this anywhere but everyone in this sub has been investigating.'

'Let me see,' I say, taking the iPad from her so I can take a closer look at the open Reddit page.

Potential Serial Killer in West Hollywood?
U/underdarkskies
Hey, have you guys heard about the serial killer in Hollywood? Four dead women in less than eighteen months and all of them PrivatePool creators. Too much of a coincidence atp. What do you think? Is there a WeHo Ripper?
U/pinklemonade
Haha yeah. Someone is ending those hoes.
U/edemamemama
It's like when that dude was killing homeless people on Skid Row. Prolly think he's doing society a favour or something.
U/redpillplease
He is haha.
u/showgirlbarbie
Stop it. One of the girls is my friend's cousin. Her family are super religious and asked for the PrivatePool stuff to be kept out of the news.
U/redpillplease
Sounds legit /s
u/showgirlbarbie
It's true! And you're a douche

I pass the iPad back to Antoinette. 'Just a bunch of misogynists fantasising about killing women. Disgusting but not unusual.'

Antoinette looks at me, puzzled. 'Don't you think it's something we should investigate?'

I sigh. 'There isn't enough time in ten lifetimes to investigate every red-pill limp dick, I'm afraid.'

'But if there is a killer, a killer specifically targeting women, isn't that like your MO? *Our* MO?'

I sigh. 'Antoinette, our MO is to find Aidan Ward, kill him horribly and then get back to London. That's it. Even if it is real, and I'm not convinced it is, we need to get back to our lives.'

She frowns. 'What life do *I* have to get back to? In case you'd forgotten, most of my family is dead.'

So, full disclosure. Antoinette isn't being dramatic: her father, brother and sister *are* all dead. Because I killed them. James – the man she thought was her bio dad – was actually a pervert with a predilection for girls who weren't quite legal. Yes, he was in *those* files. Hen – her sister and my former BFF – was a stalky psychopath who was threatening to reveal my little hobby, and Ben – her brother – had a secret life as a misogynistic influencer and was trying to out me for killing his dad and sister. And her mother – Laurelle, who cheated with my dad – is whacked out of her face on prescription drugs and barely notices if Antoinette is there or not.

A pang of guilt stabs me in the gut.

'Read the reports,' she says, swiping a couple of times and handing the iPad back to me.

Woman found dead in West Hollywood identified

A woman found dead by the Hollywood sign on Tuesday has been identified.

The Los Angeles Police Department has named the woman, who was discovered by tourists, as 28-year-old model Sofi Garcia.

No cause of death has yet been revealed.

Woman found dead in dumpster in West Hollywood

A woman was found dead in a dumpster behind The Viper Room on Sunday morning, authorities have said.

The remains were found by an identified person, believed to be a worker at the famous venue. Officials have yet to identify the woman but she has been named locally as 25-year-old aspiring actress Alicia Levy.

It's unclear how the woman died, but the Los Angeles Police Department has asked anyone who might have any information to contact them.

Influencer's death 'a tragic accident,' says LAPD

Police investigating the death of Instagram influencer Ellie Edwards, 24, have called her death a tragic accident but say they are not looking for anyone else in connection to her death.

A spokesperson said, 'It's with great sadness that we can confirm the body discovered by members of the public last week was that of popular influencer Ellie Edwards. Our teams have followed up leads and looked into reports of foul play but Ellie's death is exactly what is appears to have been, a tragic accident. We ask politely that people do not engage with online speculation.'

Ellie's body was found last week at the Bronson Caves by two social media content creators. It is believed that she was trying to film some footage and slipped, hitting her head, which led to her death.

The influencer community has reacted badly to Ellie's

death, with many calling out the police for not investigating the circumstances surrounding her death enough.

'There's no way this was an accident,' fellow influencer and model Kaitlyn Staines told us. 'Women are dying and the police are letting it happen.'

I read the reports twice over.

Yeah, there is something that smells both fishy and ratty about it.

'The bodies were all found at famous Hollywood landmarks?' I say and Antoinette nods.

'It's got pattern serial killer written all over it,' she says.

I turn back to look at the reports.

At the pictures of the dead women when they were very much alive. Smiling into the camera lens, life sparkling in their eyes. Life that a handful of people in a dark corner of the internet – people I don't usually take seriously – believe was snuffed out by one person.

Antoinette's right.

If there's even the *possibility* that someone is killing these women, and killing them because they're taking agency of their own bodies, then I absolutely *should* be doing something about it. Rage boils inside me and pushes my blood faster around my body.

But then an image of Tor leaps into my mind. Of *her* face, still alive but completely devoid of sparkle.

I can't start a wild goose chase for a serial killer that may not even exist. I have to find Aidan Ward and kill him. That's why I'm here. I made a promise to Tor and I can't get distracted by another project.

I hand the iPad back to my sister.

I'd almost forgotten.

I'm not doing this alone anymore, am I?

There are two of us.

That's more than enough to take on both projects.

'Look,' I say gently, 'if you can convince me that there's actually a killer out there and this isn't just some Reddit drama over absolutely nothing, then I will *think* about it.'

Antoinette smiles. 'You're the best.'

'I know that, but thank you. Now let's get changed and go and get some food. I'm starving.'

I watch as my sister skips out of the living room, placated for now.

6

THE RESTAURANT, CHATEAU MARMONT, WEST HOLLYWOOD

Antoinette stopped talking about the supposed WeHo Ripper long enough for us to decide that we're both too tired to go out for food tonight. Now we're seated at an outside table in the hotel restaurant and, in the sinking evening light, we could really be a million miles away from the hustle and bustle of LA.

Antoinette is glowing under the fairy lights that adorn the wooden beams overhead. She's twirling spaghetti around her fork and actually looks happy. She's even wearing the scarf I bought for her and I was right: it looks stunning on her. I hope she'll let me borrow it.

'Okay?' I ask. She beams at me.

'Yes,' she says. 'This is actually lovely.'

I'm not sure if she's talking about the food specifically, the restaurant in general or hanging out with me, but she's smiling and I'm taking that as a win. I knew I'd be able to convert her to loving it here. She was tired and hungry earlier. That's why she was grumpy. I get like that too. That's another thing we have in common!

'It is,' I say and clink my glass of sparkling water against hers. I'm taking a bit of a break from the booze. Something horrible happened to me in Cannes earlier this summer, something that probably could've been prevented if I hadn't been chaotic drunk. Anyway, it makes sense to keep a clear head when we've got a job to do out here. Antoinette apparently 'barely drinks anyway' because 'urgh, getting blackout drunk and ending up going viral is so cringe'. This is a little hard to believe when I saw her packing away the champagne at my mother's wedding a few weeks ago. Anyway, instead of cocktails we're going to have a nice supper and an early night, ready to properly start our search for Aidan Ward in the morning.

'Oh I almost forgot to tell you,' Antoinette says as she winds more pasta onto her fork. 'You've got an appointment tomorrow.'

'An appointment for what?'

'I found a therapist,' she beams. 'From Reddit. I arranged it all while you were out earlier. It slipped my mind with all the WeHo Ripper stuff.'

'Antoinette!' I say. 'That's amazing. Do you think it could be him?'

She gives me a humble shrug. 'I'm not sure,' she says. 'But he's definitely worth checking out. He's British and the clinic is new, according to the WeHo Local sub. It's worth a shot.'

My heart accelerates in my chest.

'For sure,' I say. 'What time?'

'Midday,' she says. 'I know you're not a morning person.'

See?

She knows me so well already.

Like only a sister could.

I'm about to ask for more details when we're interrupted by a man staggering over to our table.

'Excuse me, ladies.'

He's older, probably mid-sixties, and looks like he's been living the Hollywood lifestyle hard. His sandy-brown hair is very obviously thinning on top but he's grown the back bits long and has them tied in a ponytail. His skin is tanned and craggy in the way that skin overexposed to the sun always is, leathery. God, why won't people listen when they're screamed at about sunscreen? He's wearing a white billowy shirt that's unbuttoned almost to his navel. His torso is covered in tribal tattoos, the kind that were super fashionable in the nineties but just look faded and sad now.

Quite a bit like their owner actually.

I recognise his face in a vague sort of way but I can't think where from. He smiles down at us, one of his front teeth is gold and it glints under the fairy lights. The effect is creepy.

'Can I help you?' I say, not appreciating the intrusion.

'I couldn't help but notice you're British,' he says, or rather slurs, he's definitely one Whiskey Sour away from the ER. Then he adds in an accent I guess is supposed to be British, 'I am delighted to make your acquaintance.' He holds out his hand but, when neither Antoinette nor I make a move to shake it, runs it through his receding hairline as if that was what he'd intended all along. He leans against our table. 'What brings you girls to the Chateau?'

'I'm sorry,' I say, 'but I'm actually trying to enjoy dinner with my sister.' I catch Antoinette's eye, expecting her to back me up but she's staring at the stranger wide-eyed and open-mouthed. I'm clearly not going to get any support from her. I turn to the man again, hoping he'll pick up on my social cue to fuck the hell off.

But he does not.

He continues to stare at me.

'What are your names?'

Antoinette smiles sweetly at him. 'I'm Kate,' she says. 'And this here is my sister. Pippa.'

He smiles and that horrible gold tooth flashes like a warning light. 'I'm having a little party in my room tonight,' he says. 'Maybe the two of you would like to come along? It's the penthouse. Just a little gathering to celebrate wrapping my movie.'

Then I realise where I recognise him from.

He's Ron Wilde.

The Ron Wilde from tons of movies I watched when I was growing up. *People* magazine's Sexiest Man Alive several times in the late nineties. I peer at his face again. His fondness for alcohol and drugs has always been well documented. They should really use his current face if they want to put people off that kind of lifestyle though. With all the money in the world, he has not aged well. And, actually, I'm sure I saw an interview with him earlier this year where he was praising himself for now being sober. I surreptitiously sniff the air near him.

Sober.

What a joke.

He's practically sweating booze.

'No thank you,' I say politely. 'Now would you mind leaving us to our meals?'

He narrows his eyes at me and looks like he's about to say something. But then changes his mind and saunters back to wherever he came from, muttering 'suit yourself' and spilling his drink.

Antoinette looks at me. 'That was Ron Wilde,' she says and I'm preparing myself for a lecture on how we should have accepted his party invitation because he's one of the most famous men in the world, when she adds, 'I fucking hate him.'

'Yeah,' I say. 'He doesn't come across as the most likeable man in the world.'

She stabs angrily at her pasta. 'He's precisely the reason why we need to collectively stop telling mid white men that they're exceptional.'

I nod in agreement.

'I can't believe he's still got a career after everything he was accused of.' She glowers darkly at her plate of food. 'He should be in prison, not approaching women in hotel bars. He shouldn't even be allowed around women at all.'

Ron Wilde's name came up a *lot* when all the #MeToo stuff first started kicking off online. Three women accused him of sexual misconduct and it looked like he was cooked. The #RonWildeIsOver party was in full swing. But a year later the cases were dropped due to 'lack of evidence'. Within months he was back on set and the women had to go into hiding due to online harassment. One of them was even doxxed and had to move states. I learned all this from a gossip magazine I picked up during a keratin treatment. Now Ron Wilde is bigger than ever. A clear example that sexual assault allegations do absolutely zero harm to a man's career if he's rich and famous enough.

Antoinette is still murdering her food. 'We should kill him,' she hisses at me across the table.

'I'm sorry?'

'Ron Wilde,' she says. 'We should kill him.'

I glare at her and put my finger to my lips. 'Shhhh!'

She looks around the restaurant but no one is paying any attention to us, too engrossed in their own food, their own conversations, their own lives. 'No one's listening, Kits,' she says.

'We're *not* killing Ron Wilde,' I say.

'Why not? He's literally right here.'

'Killing an A-list actor in a super famous hotel?' I shake my head. 'It's a terrible idea, Antoinette.'

'But Kitty,' she pleads, 'those terrible things he's done. And he's just gotten away with it.' She leans across the table. 'We could do it. It's giving revenge arc.'

'It's giving reckless and irresponsible,' I say.

'But—'

'No,' I cut her off. 'It's a terrible idea.' Not that I wouldn't love to end him. Because I absolutely would. But this just isn't the time. Or place. Even the world's most famous no-tell motel wouldn't turn a blind eye to the murder of one of Hollywood's leading men. Sadly.

We finish the rest of our meal in almost silence, Antoinette throwing death glares at Ron Wilde and his entourage.

7

THERAPY 4 U, EAGLE ROCK, LOS ANGELES

I arrived early for my thirty-minute introductory consultation session with a therapist calling himself Alex Alexander, convinced it was going to be Aidan Ward. I mean, the name even sounds made up. But, after I'd filled in about a thousand forms with fake personal information and was led into the consulting room by a nervous middle-aged woman with a bubble perm, I realised that this person was absolutely *not* Aidan Ward.

Alex was about thirty years too old, for a start.

And a woman.

Which Antoinette would have known if she'd bothered looking at the Therapy 4 U website instead of just Reddit.

'I think I've made a mistake,' I'd said when I saw Alex sitting behind her desk, all huge red Hollywood waves and lipstick bleeding into her smoker's lines.

'A lot of people feel like that when they first start therapy—' she glanced at her computer screen, 'Doris?'

It was the first name that popped into my head.

'No,' I said. 'I really can't be here.'

I can't waste my time here when there's another therapist I need to track down.

'Sit down, Doris,' Alex told me. 'You've paid for the session so you might as well make the most of it. Even if you decide not to come back.'

Her voice was so nice and soothing that I guess I just sort of slipped into the cosy armchair in the office and that's how I'm still sitting here, talking about my dad.

'It's often hard to find closure when no body has been found,' Alex is saying.

And no body will ever be found.

It can't when it's been fed through the mincers at a meat-processing plant.

'But you're feeling residual guilt about the domestic violence you witnessed? Again that's a standard trauma response when a child feels like they failed to save the parent experiencing the violence.'

A mental image of my mother, Carmella, shaving parts of Ben Pemberton's corpse in preparation for feeding him to her pigs pops into my head.

She really doesn't need me to save her.

'I think you need to work on self-forgiveness, Doris,' Alex says. 'You put too much responsibility on yourself and then get cross at yourself when you can't live up to your own expectations.'

I think she might have a point.

Thirty minutes later and I'm on my way back to the Chateau, ready to give Antoinette a lesson in basic fucking research. But also with an appointment for next week at the same time.

Except, when I get back, Antoinette already has a surprise for me.

I stop in my tracks when I see her sitting casually on the sofa, iPad on her lap, resting her feet on the naked torso of a man.

The dismembered naked torso of a man.

It's not just any man.

Those ridiculous tribal tattoos . . . she's using Ron Wilde's dismembered torso as a fucking footstool.

8

BUNGALOW THREE, CHATEAU MARMONT, WEST HOLLYWOOD, LOS ANGELES

Fuck.

Fuck. Fuck. Fuck.

There is a dead A-list movie star in our hotel room.

There is a dead A-list movie star in our hotel room.

There is a dead A-list movie star in our hotel room and my sister has her feet up on his torso like this is an everyday occurrence.

'Antoinette! What the fuck?'

She looks up at me, a smile twitching at the corners of her mouth. 'Hey, sis.'

I stare at her, assuming she's going to explain what the actual fuck has gone on here, but she turns back to her iPad. I drop my bag and march over to her.

'That's Ron Wilde,' I say, pointing at the torso.

'Yeah,' she says. 'Some of him.'

I lean closer to the torso. She's done a good job actually. The cuts are clean. Really clean. Almost like . . .

'Did you use a chainsaw?'

She grins up at me. 'Yes! Aren't they great?'

'Where did you get a *chainsaw*?' I ask, panic making my voice high-pitched and squawky.

She shrugs. 'Room service.'

Fucking room service?

'What?' I say. '*What*?'

'Don't worry, Kits,' she says. 'It's the Chateau. It's *discreet*. They don't ask questions here.'

'I think they may have a few questions about this.' I take a few deep breaths to calm myself down. 'What the hell were you thinking? I told you that you couldn't kill him!'

Antoinette scowls. 'No, you told me it wouldn't be a good idea. I disagreed.'

I blink at her and take another deep breath before I speak. 'In what world did you think that this—' I gesture at the body part on the rug, 'would be a good idea?' I peer even closer.

I really can't fault her work.

It's seamless.

Almost exquisite.

I shake my head.

That's not the point here.

'What the hell are we going to do with him, Antoinette?'

'You'll figure something out,' she says. 'I've done the hard bit. The rest is just admin.'

I can't stop staring at her, my jaw hanging open like a Scream mask.

'Where's the rest of him?' I ask, dreading the answer.

'Through there,' she nods in the direction of the main bathroom, 'drying out.'

I give her a look before walking trance-like to the bathroom.

This is Not Good.

This is very, very Not Good.

9

THE MAIN BATHROOM, BUNGALOW THREE, CHATEAU MARMONT, LOS ANGELES

Sure enough, here lie the other pieces of Academy Award-winning actor Ron Wilde. His legs are hanging from the tap, draining out into the bath, and his arms have been attached to the overhead shower to do the same. His head has been plonked in the sink.

I tilt my head and take a good look at him.

'Bad luck,' I say to the head. 'I guess karma caught up with you.' There's something weird about the face though. I lean in a bit closer and then I realise that his lips are missing. Like totally gone.

Oh my God.

She's cut his lips off his face.

This is even more very, very Not Good.

Like a storm, I whirl back through to the living area.

'Where are his lips?' I say to Antoinette, who's now scrolling through her phone like she hasn't just risked our fucking freedom.

She barely looks up at me when she says, 'In the Smeg.'

'You've killed one of the most famous men in the world and put his lips in the fridge,' I say, bewildered. '*Why*?'

'So he can't shit talk in the next life, of course.' She laughs. 'It's my signature. All serial killers need a signature. Like how the WeHo Ripper dumps the bodies in famous places. I'm going to cut off the part that pissed me off.'

'This isn't funny, Antoinette.' I'm beyond furious. 'And there will be no signatures.'

'But—'

'No!' I'm pacing the room now. 'Signatures, souvenirs, that's what gets killers caught!'

What am I going to do?

What am I going to do?

The panic that has been pooling in my stomach feels like it's travelling up my throat. I slam my hands over my mouth and just about make it to the bathroom before I throw up violently into the toilet. Retching and spitting until my mouth is completely dry. 'What are you looking at?' I ask Ron Wilde's lipless face, which I swear is staring at me. 'This is your fault.'

Fuck.

We need to leave.

We have to get out of LA, out of America as fast as we can.

It's not like Antoinette has killed and carved up some random guy.

It's Ron Wilde.

One of the most photographed men in the world. People are going to notice he's missing.

Immediately.

If not sooner.

And I haven't even *found* Aidan Ward yet, let alone killed him.

I'm going to have to break my promise to Tor.

Nausea bubbles in my stomach again at the thought of letting her down.

She's going to be devastated. But what else can I do? There's a dead movie star in my bathroom and I have no idea what I'm going to do with him.

God, if he's *staying* here then the paparazzi will come at some point too.

It's not like I can slip his dismembered corpse out unnoticed.

My brain is already imagining the TMZ report.

Chaos erupted at the Chateau Marmont when two British women were caught trying to sneak the lipless remains of Oscar-winning actor Ron Wilde out of the service entrance last night. Onlookers described the scene as The Crown meets Dexter. But with better outfits.

Fuck.

This cannot be how I'm caught.

There's a gentle knock on the bathroom door. I look up as Antoinette pokes her head in, her eyes wide with concern.

'Are you okay?' she says. 'I heard retching.' She holds out a glass of water.

I should be furious with her.

I *want* to be furious with her. She completely ignored what I told her about killing this man. And because of her surprise murder I'm going to have to break my best friend's heart.

I reach out and take the glass. 'Thanks,' I say.

She tentatively strokes my hair.

I can't be angry with her. She's my sister and, however reckless she's been, her heart was in the right place.

'Are you angry?' Her voice is small.

I shake my head. 'No,' I say, 'but we're going to have to go home. Like, before people start asking questions about *him*.' I nod in the direction of Ron Wilde's head.

'What about Aidan Ward?' Antoinette asks. 'What about Tor? What about the Ripper?'

'It's too dangerous to stay here now,' I say. 'People are going to come looking for him. They probably are already.'

'I'm sorry,' she says and she actually does look it.

'It's okay,' I say even though it's not. I look at the lipless head again. 'What the hell happened? I've only been gone two hours.'

'He was at the pool earlier,' she says as she perches on the edge of the bathtub. 'Already drunk. Or still. He followed me back to the room.'

'He *followed* you?'

She nods. 'Yeah. So gross. He recognised me from the restaurant last night, which is amazing considering how messy he was then too. He sort of pushed his way in, going on about how I should come to the penthouse for a private party.' She makes a gagging noise. 'He's old enough to be my dad. My *grandad*. Anyway. I smacked him over the head with one of the bedroom lamps.'

It wasn't recklessness.

It was self-defence.

That changes everything.

I pull myself up from the floor and sit down next to her on the lip of the tub.

'Do you think he would've hurt you?'

She shrugs. 'Who knows. He was really wasted. I doubt he *could've* really done much. But, you know, he came into the room without consent, so—'

'You did the right thing,' I say.

Antoinette looks at me. 'But I've messed things up for you.'

I slip my arm around her shoulders. 'You're safe. That's more important than anything else.'

She leans into me and we sit like that for a moment before she pulls away.

'I suppose I should start packing then,' she says.

'Yeah, I'll look for flights,' I say, reaching for my phone, which I abandoned on the floor before I threw up.

Just at that moment it starts ringing.

'Kits, your phone,' Antoinette helpfully tells me.

'Yeah, thanks,' I say as I grab it.

It's Tor on FaceTime.

That's weird. It's still early in London.

'Hey,' she says as her face appears on my screen. It breaks my heart all over again when I see the bruising and swelling.

'Hey you,' I say, hoping she doesn't hear the wobble in my voice. 'How's it going?'

'I couldn't sleep,' she says. 'I thought you might be around.' She sounds so sad that my heart cracks even more.

'I'm here,' I say. 'What's going on? Is your mum there?'

Tor shakes her head, wincing again. 'She had to go off for something to do with work. She said she'd be back later.'

'You're by yourself?'

'Yes, Maisie's been brilliant but she's still struggling with really bad morning sickness.' Maisie's pregnant with twins and hasn't been having the easiest of times with it. Almost every time I speak to her she has to end the call because she needs to throw up. Either that or her face is all red and sweaty because she's just been throwing up.

'I can't believe you're by yourself,' I say. 'I wish I was there.'

'It's fine,' Tor says. 'I only really need to leave my room to use the loo. My ribs don't hurt quite as much anymore so moving around is okay. Anyway, they've given me loads of really decent painkillers.' She attempts a laugh but it comes out sounding strangled.

Something's really wrong.

'What's happened, Tor?' I say gently. 'Why can't you sleep?'

Even through the pixelated screen and the thousands of miles between us I can see her eyes fill up with tears.

'I'm scared to,' she says in a voice so quiet I can barely hear.

'Scared?' I say. 'Tor, you don't need to be scared. Aidan can't hurt you. He's over here.'

The tears fall from her eyes and she quickly raises a hand to wipe them away. 'Is he though?' she says. 'And even if he is, try telling that to my subconscious. It won't stop dreaming about him.' She gives a hollow little laugh. 'Well, they're nightmares really. Or flashbacks? I don't know the difference. But every night, I go through the attack again and again. So now I'm too scared to sleep.'

'Oh Tor,' I say, wishing I could reach through the screen and wrap my arms around her. She shouldn't be on her own.

'Promise me you'll find him, Kits,' she says, her eyes full of plea. 'I don't know how I'll have a normal life otherwise. How can I when he's out there somewhere and he could be getting ready to finish me off?' She covers her face with her hands. I can tell by the way her shoulders are shaking that she's quietly crying behind them.

'I'll find him,' I say. 'I promise you, I'll find him.'

Tor mumbles something before ending the call. She's always hated for anyone to see her cry. She always says that crying is like going to the loo, we all do it but no one should see you.

'I just can't respect someone after I've seen them ugly cry or pee,' she told me once.

She's been through so much in the last couple of years but Aidan's attack has fully broken her.

I can't bear it.

I can't break my promise to her.

I just can't.

I don't know how but we *have* to stay in LA.

We *have* to find Aidan Ward. If I have to knock on every single door in this entire city.

I can't break that woman any more.

I look up from my phone and see Antoinette staring at me. She heard the whole thing.

'I guess we're staying then,' she says.

I look again at the severed head in the sink. 'I guess we are,' I say.

I just need to figure out what I'm going to do with him.

10

BUNGALOW 3, CHATEAU MARMONT, LOS ANGELES

I decide the best thing to do with the body, for now, is to get it out of the hotel. Along with us.

This move isn't about Ron Wilde. It's about staying hidden long enough to find Aidan Ward.

I send Antoinette out to buy some hardshell suitcases. Ones that won't spill any leakage when the body gets to the soggy stage.

Although I'm hoping I'll have figured out something before then.

While she's out I get busy cleaning up the kill scene and then finding an Airbnb for us to move to. One of these tasks takes ages, the other is pretty fast. I must teach Antoinette how to put tarpaulin down on the floor before killing someone. Blood is a nightmare to get out of grouting.

There's not a great deal of choice of short-term lets with zero notice but I manage to find a Spanish villa on Orange Grove Avenue that's available immediately.

I don't bother looking at the reviews.

They're not going to be good if it's not booked up months in advance.

About an hour later, after I've scrubbed the bathroom until my fingers are cracked, I hear the door click open and Antoinette comes in wheeling two Louis Vuitton Horizon 55 suitcases behind her. They're perfect, although it does seem a shame that they're going to have to be disposed of when I've decided what to do with the body parts.

'Paid for in cash before you ask,' Antoinette says as she sees me eyeing up the luggage. 'And I kept my hat and sunglasses on so any CCTV that might have caught me will mean nothing.' She gives me a little twirl and with her cut-off short shorts, baby tee and sliders, she looks just like every other young woman in LA.

I smile at her.

See?

She's learning already.

Maybe this won't be an absolute clusterfuck disaster after all.

11

KITTY AND ANTOINETTE'S AIRBNB, WEST HOLLYWOOD, LOS ANGELES

'Before you even start,' I say to Antoinette as we walk up the drive of the three-bedroom, four-bathroom villa I've rented us for the next month. 'The selection was extremely limited at such short notice.'

'I haven't said a word,' she says, eyeing the white exterior and the palm trees bending over the pathway, like they're bowing to greet us.

'You don't need to,' I say, 'your face does a lot of your talking for you. Besides, it was the one place that has a temperature-controlled cellar.'

Antoinette looks at me, her brow furrowed. 'Why's that important?'

'We need a place to keep your friend Ron Wilde while I figure out what we're going to do with him.'

'Right, yes, of course,' she says as we reach the door and I pull my phone out, searching for the email with the door code. I tap the numbers in and the door swings open, revealing a spacious living area. I step inside and feel the air conditioning hit my skin as I look around. It's pretty much what I was expecting, basic in the way that Airbnbs are. There's a terracotta-coloured sofa, which is not living its best life, and a couple of yellow wingback armchairs around a glass coffee table. The room stretches all the way to the back of the house and I can see glass doors leading out to the garden – the yard, as it was called in the listing – where I know there's a pool and outdoor eating area.

I glance at my sister's face.

I can tell she's trying to stop it talking for her.

'It's okay,' she says. 'It's fine.'

'We'll have a proper look around in a bit,' I say. 'The first thing we need to do is get those suitcases into the cellar before your friend starts stinking.' I look behind her. 'Where are they?'

She looks puzzled. 'Where are what?'

'The LV cases,' I say. 'The ones with the human remains in them.'

'Oh! I don't know. I thought you had them?'

OhJesusfuckfuckfuckno.

I race out of the house, Antoinette on my heels, just in time to see our Uber, and what's left of Ron Wilde, disappear down the street and out of view.

12

KITTY AND ANTOINETTE'S AIRBNB, WEST HOLLYWOOD, LOS ANGELES

Several phone calls and a rather anxiety-inducing hour later, the cases are finally back in our possession.

And the Uber driver seemed none the wiser about what he'd been transporting around the city.

'Let's get you somewhere where you can't cause me any more trouble,' I say to Ron as I drag him down to the cellar.

The wine cellar is actually a lifesaver in more ways than one, not only can it keep bodies at a temperature that they won't start stinking, but it can also store an obscene amount of bottles of wine. And the owners have kindly left it fully stocked. I walk around, gently stroking the labels like I'm Belle when she finds the library in *Beauty and the Beast*. I pull out a bottle of white from its cubby hole. Burgundy, 2001. I'm about to take it upstairs and pour a glass when I remember that I'm not drinking.

I put it back in the rack.

'Later,' I promise the bottle.

* * *

We're sitting outside by the pool now. It turns out that what the villa lacks on the inside, it more than makes up for outside. Even Antoinette seems charmed by the whitewashed walls and terracotta patio, the pink and white hibiscus and hydrangeas bursting out of impossibly green shrubs. I saw her gently touching the flowers and I'm sure I heard her whisper 'pretty' before she flopped down on a lounger.

There's a large, covered area for al fresco dining with a table that could seat about twenty, a fire pit and a huge built-in barbecue. There's also an L-shaped sofa, which could also seat twenty, and a double hammock that I'm sure to fall asleep in at some point. I have my laptop and the Aidan Ward spreadsheet open and we're both stretched out on sunloungers in the shade of a lemon tree.

'So,' I say, 'I've been thinking and I reckon we need to explore options other than just therapists. We can't just visit every therapist in LA until we find him. We don't even know that he's working over here.' I'm sure it's not that easy now I've had time to think about it. Aren't there visas and things like that?

Antoinette tilts her head. 'I agree but where do we start? It's not like he's kindly posting updates on his socials, telling us where he's having brunch today.'

It's frustrating for sure. Aidan has gone completely dark on his social media accounts. His Snapchat, which is how we discovered he was in LA, has been deleted, his 'last seen' on WhatsApp was weeks ago and, although his Instagram is still technically active, there's been no activity on it for ages. How did stalkers operate before everyone was so chronically online? For a split second I feel a pang of grief for Hen, my former BFF and Antoinette's sister. She's someone I had to murder before she told everyone I was a killer.

She'd have known.

Stalking was kind of her speciality.

'I don't know,' I say with a sigh as I pick up my phone and open Instagram. I type in Aidan Ward's name and open his page. It's not locked but there aren't any new posts. There haven't been for a long time. Just the same shots of woodland vistas and arty-looking sunsets. Antoinette's right. What am I expecting? A GRWM-as-I-prepare-to-find-my-next-human-punchbag reel? A pinned fucking location with a caption saying *here I am, come and get me*? 'We need to think smart,' I say. 'Where would we go if we were Aidan Ward?'

'That's the trouble though, isn't it?' Antoinette says. 'What do we actually know about him? Apart from the fact he likes to hurt women? And I doubt there's a local meet-up group for that.'

'I bet there's several online though,' I say darkly. But she's right. We know next to nothing about this man. I rack my brain, hoping that there's a nugget of *something* that might help me. But all I can think of are those lame band T-shirts he always wore. And I doubt The Beatles or The Byrds are going to be doing any live shows in the area any time soon.

Oh. But.

'Can you do a search for like vinyl record stores in the area?' I ask Antoinette. She raises her eyebrows questioningly. 'He's a music nerd,' I explain. 'Old stuff. Older than Beyoncé.' I give her a pointed stare.

Antoinette scrolls on her phone for a bit. 'There's quite a few,' she says after a few minutes. 'What are we going to do? Just hang around outside them in the hope he comes in?'

I shake my head and grab my own phone, opening the photos app and turning it to face my sister. 'We show them this and ask if anyone has seen this man.' It's a headshot I managed to screen grab from the website of his clinic in London. Before it was taken down after he unceremoniously dumped the clinic and all his patients and fled the country.

Antoinette peers at the photo. 'He's probably changed his look,' she says. 'Bet he's got rid of that crusty beard at least.' She pulls a face.

'Gotta be worth a try though, right?' I say. It has to be. We've literally got nothing else. Antoinette swills her drink around in the glass and raises one shoulder in a half shrug. 'What?' I say. 'What is it?'

'I don't know,' she says. 'It just seems like we don't really have much of a plan here. Go to therapists and hang around record stores doesn't feel like a plan, you know.'

I sigh again. I *do* know. I just don't know what else to do.

'We need to think smart,' Antoinette is saying now like I didn't just say the same thing two seconds ago. 'Like, okay, he might not be working as a therapist but he still needs money. And groceries. Stuff like that. Does he know anyone out here? There must be a reason he came to LA of all places.'

'But how would we know that?'

Antoinette taps her phone. 'He might not be active himself on Instagram but the people he follows might be. Have you checked his tags?'

I stare at her.

His tags.

Of course.

Why haven't I thought of this?

We spend some time trawling through the bowels of Aidan Ward's Instagram tags before we find something that might be useful.

'Look,' Antoinette says, pointing to a photo of Aidan on a beach with his arms wrapped around a dark-haired woman. They're both beaming at the camera, under the shade of a palm tree. It was posted 156 weeks ago.

I click on it.

'Girlfriend?' I say.

'Definitely looks like it.'

The picture appears on the account of someone called Niamh O'Hagan. I scroll through her photos but there aren't any others with Aidan Ward in them.

'That's weird,' I say to Antoinette. 'If they were a couple, why aren't there any other photos of them together? It doesn't make sense.'

'Unless they had a bad break-up,' she says, 'and she deleted all the others. Maybe this one survived the purge.'

I stare at the photo. They definitely have that in-love energy. What happened for her to delete all other photos of him?

'I'm going to DM her,' I say to Antoinette, who nods.

I tap out a message.

'Hi Niamh, I'm really sorry to slide into your DMs out of the blue but I'm hoping you can help me. I noticed a photo of Aidan Ward on your grid. I'm trying to find him. He violently attacked my friend a few weeks ago before leaving London for LA. If you can help at all in any way, I would be grateful forever. Thank you for your time, Kitty Collins.'

I press send and look at my sister. 'And now we wait.'

Antoinette nods and looks out at the pool, squinting in the

sun. 'It's getting hot,' she says. 'I think I might have a swim. Coming in?'

I shake my head. 'I want to keep at this a bit longer,' I say, indicating the laptop. She shrugs and stands up, peeling off her cover-up, revealing a white Oséree bikini. I watch as she dips her foot into the impossibly blue water. 'Gosh, that's cold,' she mutters before arching her back and diving in, perfectly. She remerges a few seconds later, her teeth chattering. 'Gosh, that's really fucking cold!' She laughs again and swims to the other end of the pool. 'Kits. What's that building?' I follow the line of her finger and see what looks like a miniature version of the villa.

'I think it's a guesthouse,' I say. 'Funny, the listing didn't mention that.'

'Shall we go and check it out? You never know, it might be nicer than the main house!'

'It's probably just full of old furniture and pool maintenance stuff,' I say. 'I doubt it's very exciting or I'm sure the owners would've said something about it.' Antoinette's already hauling herself out of the pool though and wrapping a towel around her waist.

'I might just go and have a look anyway,' she says and sashays in the direction of the guesthouse, leaving a trail of footprints drying on the concrete behind her.

13

KITTY AND ANTOINETTE'S AIRBNB, WEST HOLLYWOOD, LOS ANGELES

After Antoinette has disappeared from view, a wave of tiredness washes over me. It can't still be jet lag, can it? I lean back on the lounger and close my eyes, stretching my legs out and letting the sun hit them. I'm almost asleep when my phone starts vibrating next to me. I reach for it, expecting it to be Tor again, but the name on the caller ID sends me spiralling.

It's Charlie.

I'm almost scared to answer it. Is him calling me a good thing? Has he realised he's missed me more than words can say? Does he want me back? Or is it a bad thing? Were there some things he forgot to say to me when he dumped me? Is he calling to tell me a few more home truths?

Only one way to find out.

'Charlie?' But there's no answer on the other end of the phone. All I can hear is some rustling and something that sounds like someone laughing underwater. 'Charlie?' I say again but there's still no reply. I guess he must've pocket-dialled me. 'Charlie!' I shout this time and I must be loud enough for him to hear because there's more rustling and then a breathless Charlie comes on the line.

'Kitty?' he says and his voice still makes me feel things no other man has ever made me feel.

'Hi,' I say, feeling suddenly shy. I can't believe we're talking.

'I'm so sorry,' he says. 'I called you by accident. I don't know how that . . . like I said, I'm sorry.'

'That's okay,' I say. 'I just wondered what you wanted.'

'Nothing.' He gives an awkward laugh. 'I should take you off my favourites really. I'm sorry.'

Take me off favourites? God, he knows how to hurt me. It's like a knife.

'How are you?' I say, not wanting him to end the call.

'I'm all right,' he says. 'You?'

'I'm not too bad,' I say, even though I'm terrible. It's not cool to let the man who obliterated your heart know that though. 'I'm in LA!'

'Oh right, that's nice.'

I'm waiting for him to ask who I'm with. Maybe he thinks I'm with a man and it'll make him so jealous he has to fly out here and beg me to get back with him. But he doesn't.

'I'm with Antoinette,' I say. Jesus, I feel sorry for myself at this point. He literally doesn't care who I'm with.

'That's great,' he says, although he doesn't sound like he really thinks that at all. 'Doing some sisterly bonding?'

'Yeah,' I say. 'Something like that. What have you been up to?'

'Not much,' he says. 'Just quite busy with work. You know.'

It's a weird thing for him to say because he knows I've never had a job in my life.

'I miss you.' It slips out before I even know it's coming.

'Kits, don't do this.'

'What? We can still be friends, can't we?' I don't know why I'm saying this. I know there's no way I could ever just be friends with this man. The thought of seeing him and not being able to touch him, not being able to kiss him, having to listen to him talk about other women . . . it just wouldn't work. It would kill me.

But.

Is it better to have him in my life as a friend than as nothing at all?

There's a long silence and then Charlie says, 'Look, Kits, I have to go. I'm sorry I called you. I'm glad you're doing okay though. Hope you have a great holiday.'

'Oh,' I say. 'Okay. Bye.'

'Bye.'

And then the call ends.

I stare at my phone screen for a minute. I'm not sure why. I guess that I'm hoping he'll call back and tell me that he misses me too. But the phone stays irritatingly silent. I'm just about to slip it back into my pocket when an iMessage notification pops up.

Charlie.

I miss you too.

He misses me too.

He misses me too!

I frantically start typing out a text to him.

Shouldn't be over here too long. Maybe we could have drinks or something when I'm back.

I press send.

He misses me!

Surely that's a good sign? Surely that means he's open to at least talking to me about what happened.

I wait for the message to deliver. But it doesn't. It must be the signal here. I try to send it again but it still doesn't go through. Then I try to send it as an SMS. That doesn't deliver either. I stare at my phone in disbelief. This can't be happening.

He's blocked me.

I can't believe he's blocked me.

I quickly open WhatsApp and scroll to the last conversation I had with him on there. Sure enough, his profile picture has disappeared, replaced with that anonymous grey silhouette, absolute proof that I've been blocked.

He really doesn't want me to contact him.

I'm about to cry when I remember that we've got location sharing switched on in the Cloud. I quickly open the app, expecting him to have removed that as well. But it's still there.

Charlie's iPhone.

He's obviously forgotten to turn it off.

I click on the little phone icon and watch as the map zooms in on London, pinpointing exactly where my ex-boyfriend is right now.

Lewisham.

What's he doing in Lewisham?

Charlie lives in Clapham and works in Brixton. Why would he be in Lewisham?

Then I remember something; Charlie might not live in Lewisham but Jenna does. Jenna is the annoyingly earnest and blonde do-gooder who works for Charlie's charity. She's not made any secret of the fact that she's got a huge crush on him. She's also the woman I accused Charlie of cheating on me with when he vanished in Cannes in the summer. When he was actually kidnapped and being drugged in an Airbnb by Antoinette's psychotic brother. Yeah, my bad. He was furious that I thought he was being unfaithful. Even crosser about that than about me being a serial killer. But it looks like he's with Jenna now. I'm sure she's only too willing to let him cry on her shoulder about our break-up. I've probably pushed him right into her arms.

The tears really do come now.

They come so hard that I wonder if they're ever going to stop.

14

KITTY AND ANTOINETTE'S AIRBNB, WEST HOLLYWOOD, LOS ANGELES

Eventually I wipe my cheeks, pick my phone back up and am about to head inside when I hear a shriek coming from the direction of the guesthouse. I jump up, grab my kaftan and pull it over my head as I quickly head in the direction of the scream.

The door is slightly ajar when I reach the little house, probably where Antoinette slipped in earlier. I push it wide open and walk into a large living area that is more tastefully decorated than the main house. The flooring is an expensive type of stone, which I wasn't expecting. There's a very luxe-looking, huge corner sofa facing a wall, which is mostly taken up by a giant screen, cinema-sized. Could it be some kind of screening room that I somehow missed in the ad? There's a dining area with a massive glass table, which looks set for some kind of dinner party. I'm confused.

'Antoinette?' I shout. 'Are you in here?'

But it's not Antoinette who answers me. Instead a small, white fluffy dog comes hurtling into the room, its lips pulled back to reveal a very unimpressive set of little teeth. It snarls and growls at me before breaking into a staccato yapping, which makes my soul want to crawl out of my body.

Urgh.

Why is there a fucking dog in the guesthouse?

'You'll need to be a bit more menacing than that if you want to scare me,' I tell it. 'I've killed people.' The dog stops barking and tilts it head to one side, regarding me with curiosity.

'Lana? Where are you? Oh!' A blonde woman has followed the dog into the room. She's tall and looks like the dictionary definition of 'SoCal Girl' in denim cut-offs and a floaty boho-style top. Her hair is shaved on one side and she looks achingly cool. The dog starts wagging its tail like it might take off and the woman scoops it in her arms like a baby. 'You must be Kitty?'

'Who are you?' I say. 'I'm looking for my sister.'

'I'm Agnes,' she says with a big wide smile. She points at the dog. 'I see you've already met my child, Lana Del Gay. Antoinette's through here. Come in, she's sampling Lauren's – she's my roommate - sangria so she might not be sober for much longer. I hope Lana didn't scare you.'

Really? I've seen scarier clouds.

The woman – Agnes – turns and walks through a doorway. She looks back over her shoulder at me. 'Coming?'

I follow her, not knowing what else to do.

Why are there people making sangria in the guesthouse?

We go through the door into a thin corridor. 'She's just through here,' Agnes says. 'Lana frightened her, so Lauren and I are plying her with booze to say sorry.' At the end of the corridor is another set of double doors that lead through to a kitchen, shiny and modern and surprisingly big. For a guesthouse, this place is huge. There's a marble island in the middle, surrounded by bar stools, one of which my sister is sitting on. On her right is another woman. She's got long, sleek dark hair and looks slightly older than Agnes. I'd put her age somewhere between Antoinette's and mine. But this is LA so who fucking knows. Really, she could be anywhere from twenty-two to sixty-two with an excellent surgeon. They're both drinking glasses of a deep red liquid. When Antoinette looks up and sees me, she's got it around her mouth. She smiles and I can see it's stained her teeth as well.

She looks like a vampire that's just fed.

'Kitty!' she says. 'I was just about to come and get you!'

'Okay,' I say. 'What's going on?'

'Sangria,' says the brunette, who I assume must be Lauren, 'it's my special recipe. Want some?'

'It's good,' Antoinette says. 'You should!' She clinks her glass together with Lauren's.

'No thanks,' I say, then I add to my sister, 'I thought you didn't drink?'

'I don't drink *much*,' she clarifies.

Lauren gives a snort of laughter and some sangria shoots out of her nose. The dog scrabbles out of Agnes's arms and races over to lick up the splashes that make it to the floor. Is alcohol safe for dogs?

'Lauren and Agnes are our neighbours,' Antoinette says.

'What do you mean "neighbours"?'

'They live in the guesthouse! Isn't that cool?'

No.

No, that is very much *not* cool.

Has Antoinette gone out of her tiny mind? Has she forgotten about the reason I found us a discreet rental? There's nothing discreet about having two strangers living in the garden. Like unwelcome gnomes.

Lauren is holding a glass of sangria out to me. I shake my head. She's wearing a frilly white apron and looks like something out of a Tradwife for Beginners Pinterest board.

'Agnes's parents own the place,' she says in a broad Texan accent. 'I was just explaining to Antoinette about how WeHo has these weird-ass rules for short lets. Pretty much they gotta keep permanent tenants living here so . . . yeah. Here we are.'

Roommates were really not part of the plan.

Now I'm going to have to find us another place to stay.

Another place with a temperature-controlled cellar.

'Lauren and Agnes are actors!' Antoinette says.

Agnes has joined my sister and Lauren at the island. 'Well, we're trying to be,' she says. 'We both study at LAAA.'

'I don't know what that means,' I say.

'It stands for the Los Angeles Academy of Arts.'

'Right,' I say. 'So you live *here*? Like all the time?'

'Mmhmm,' Lauren is nodding, 'but don't worry, we've got our own entrance and everything. You'll barely notice we're here.'

I look at her knocking back sangria and it's not even five o'clock. I somehow doubt we'll barely notice them.

'Don't guests usually mind when they find out there's two girls living in the garden?'

Agnes leans over the island and pours herself a glass.

'Honestly, no. The house doesn't get that many bookings. We try to put people off.' She gives Lauren a conspiratory wink and they both laugh. 'Didn't you read the reviews?'

Lauren has her phone in her hand and is scrolling through it. 'I'll read some out to you,' she says. 'Here we go. "Appalling standards in this villa. None of the toilets work. Had to manually 'flush' them with rubber gloves and a bucket."'

Agnes giggles.

'Here's another,' Lauren says. '"The worst rental experience of my life! Shady neighbourhood, dirty sheets, could probably recognise the people who stayed here before us by smell. One star and I would honestly mark it lower if I could."'

'Read them my favourite,' says Agnes.

'Her favourite is a one-word review. And that word is "Haunted?" with a question mark.'

'I can see why you don't get many bookings,' Antoinette says. 'But aren't your parents suspicious?'

Agnes shakes her head. 'Nah, they're too busy being Orange County rich. They forget they even have this place unless one of their friends asks to stay here and reminds them about it. It's going to be so fun being neighbours.' Agnes claps her hands together. 'You can only imagine the kind of people we get staying here. The sort of people who aren't put off by those reviews.' She gives a little shudder.

'Come over for dinner later?' Lauren says. 'I'm going to cook a chicken.'

'That's okay. And anyway, I'm vegan,' I say at the same time Antoinette says, 'Oh my God, yes please, that would be amazing!'

Lauren and Agnes both beam at us.

'We'll see you at about eight then? I'll make some more sangria.'

Antoinette smiles at them both like they're long-term friends before standing up and sliding her arm into mine. Like we haven't got the mutilated body of her impulse kill stashed in suitcases in the cellar.

'This could be so much fun, Kits,' she says to me as we get back inside the main house. I can't even dignify this with an answer. We're not here to make friends with the locals. Friends are witnesses. 'They seem really nice and can help us. They know the area much better than we do and it's not like we've had any luck so far, is it? Can we stay?'

That's true enough.

Although I'm still sceptical about two girls helping us when they have a fondness for deception and day drinking.

'We'll see,' I say and realise I sound like my mother. Well, maybe not *my* mother but definitely some generic mother figure.

Antoinette rushes over to me and squeezes me. 'You're the best, Kits.' She gives me a look I can't read and then adds, 'Don't you think Agnes is cute?'

'I mean yeah, she seems nice . . .' I start to say and then I understand what the look means. 'Oh. Like *cute* cute?'

Antoinette blushes. 'Yeah.'

'Do you even know if she's into girls?'

'Kitty,' Antoinette says. 'She's got a dog called Lana Del Gay and an undercut. Of course she's into girls.'

'Oh. Okay,' I say and she squeals again.

'This is going to be great. Wait. What's that smell?' She wrinkles her nose and her eyes land on my Chloé sliders.

Oh no. No, no, no.

I slip one off and inspect the bottom.

Yep.

Dog shit.

Perfect.

Just perfect.

15

AGNES AND LAUREN'S GUESTHOUSE, WEST HOLLYWOOD, LOS ANGELES

Just before 8pm, Antoinette and I leave the villa and walk across the garden to the guesthouse. I'm still feeling super uneasy about having two strangers in such close proximity.

Antoinette picks up on my fears.

'Just look at it this way, Kits,' she says quietly as we walk, 'isn't it better to make friends with them? Like keep your friends close and potential witnesses to murder closer?'

I sigh. She's got a point.

'Yes,' I say reluctantly, 'but that doesn't mean we can get too friendly with them. I don't want them just dropping into the main house unannounced. We've still got our friend in the cellar.'

Antoinette bumps her hip into mine. 'Okay, no house calls. But apart from that, you should loosen up a bit. You might even have a good time.'

I roll my eyes at her. 'We're not here for a good time,' I say. 'We're here to kill Aidan Ward.'

'And the WeHo Ripper. That's exactly my idea of a good

time,' she says. 'And anyway, we need to find them both first. And I don't think having two locals as our new besties is the worst thing. It's not like we've had much luck on our own.'

I sigh again. 'Don't remind me. I feel so useless.'

Antoinette squeezes my arm. 'We'll find him,' she says. 'We made a promise and we will find him.'

'I just hope we do it quickly,' I say. 'I need to be back in London putting my life back together.' Although, as I say it, I realise that it's not quite as true as it was. I was desperate to get home so I could win Charlie back. There seems very little chance of that happening now.

'We'll find him,' she says again. 'And we'll start first thing. But for now let's go and have some nice food and see what these girls can tell us about LA.' She gives me another squeeze and I feel a rush of affection for her.

We pick up our pace again and continue our walk to the guesthouse. Agnes opens the door for us and a waft of cooking meat makes my stomach churn.

'Wow,' Antoinette says. 'It smells great.'

'Lauren is a super whizz in the kitchen,' Agnes says. 'Which is just as well as I am useless and would live off DoorDash otherwise. She's made you a roast cauliflower or something, Kitty. I swear, she's a genius.'

'That's lovely,' I say, surprisingly touched by the gesture. Antoinette gives me a look that says *see*.

We walk through to the kitchen. Lauren and Agnes have gone all out for us. The table has been dressed beautifully and the chicken is sat in the middle, all golden and glowing. My stomach growls in protest.

'Ah, here are the guests of honour,' Lauren's disembodied

voice says from somewhere behind the island. She stands up and is holding a tray of perfect-looking roast potatoes. 'Right on time! And Kitty, don't worry, everything apart from the chicken has been cooked in veggie oil. And I've made you a special vegan gravy too.' She smiles and carries the potatoes over to the table. 'Almost had a heart attack that the potatoes weren't going to be ready on time and the chicken was going to dry out. But it all came together in the end.'

'She'll make someone a wonderful wife one day,' Agnes says.

'Sit down,' Lauren instructs us. 'Pour yourself some wine. I didn't know what y'all like so I just brought one of everything in.'

My heart misses a couple of beats. Has Lauren been in our wine cellar? The very wine cellar which is housing the dismembered body of an extremely famous man?

'You've been in our wine cellar?' I ask, trying to catch Antoinette's eye.

Lauren smiles. 'No, no,' she says, 'don't panic. We've got our own one here. Aggy's parents don't cut corners.'

I cast my eyes over the array of wine bottles. She's not wrong. There's quite the selection. Reds, whites, pinks, oranges.

Lauren comes over with another tray. 'So, Kitty, I've made you a harissa-roasted cauliflower. It's my go-to for my plant-based friends, but absolutely no drama from me if you don't like it.'

'No,' I say, 'that sounds incredible.'

She puts the dish down in front of me and my nose is filled with the fragrance of delicious spices.

'This is great,' Antoinette says. 'I can't remember the last time we had a home-cooked meal.'

'I just love your accents,' Agnes says. 'You both sound like the Queen. How long are you staying for?'

'I've booked a month,' I say, helping myself to potatoes. I can't remember the last time I ate carbs. 'Maybe not that long. We'll see how it goes.'

'Antoinette says you're here to soak up Los Angeles and the culture?'

'Kind of,' I say.

'Kitty's here to mend her broken heart,' Antoinette says and I glare at her. I don't want to talk or even think about Charlie right now.

Lauren and Agnes make some sounds of sympathy.

'Oh no,' Agnes says. 'That's horrible. I'm so sorry. What happened?'

But I'm saved from having to answer by a thunderous hammering coming from the corridor beyond the kitchen.

A thunderous hammering that sounds extremely FBI-esque.

16

AGNES AND LAUREN'S GUESTHOUSE, WEST HOLLYWOOD, LOS ANGELES

My heart thumps in my chest, almost as loud as the hammering at the door.

Antoinette and I look at each other, the panic in her eyes no doubt a perfect mirror image of my own. We've both seen enough TV shows and movies to know a police knock when we hear one.

No normal person knocks like that.

'Open up!' It's a man's voice that comes echoing into the kitchen.

Lauren jumps up and disappears out of the kitchen. Agnes remains at the table, picking chicken off the bones on her plate.

She looks at me and smiles. 'Wow, you've gone pale. Don't look so worried! It's just Cort. He thinks it's a super funny way to let us know he's here.' She rolls her eyes, making it clear that she doesn't think it's funny in the slightest.

'Cort?' I say. Why do Americans have such weird names? Seriously. How can an entire country think that names like Cort and fucking *Randy* are absolutely fine?

'Lauren's boyfriend,' Agnes says, and do I notice a hint of a scowl? 'They've been together *forever*.' She gives me a sly smile. 'The best advice I can give you is to dissociate when he starts speaking.'

Antoinette pulls a face. 'Really? Why?'

'You'll see,' says Agnes, that smile still dancing on her lips.

At that moment Lauren walks back in draped over a man I assume is Cort. He's tall, tanned and wearing jeans, a white T-shirt and a pink blazer. His dark hair is pulled back into a *man bun*.

I hate him on sight.

'Hey, new girls,' the man who is probably Cort says, nodding at me and Antoinette. 'Lauren told me that she's got some new roomies. Let me tell you what an absolute pleasure it is to meet you both.' He comes over to us and makes a big deal out of shaking our hands. It feels very intense.

'This is my man,' Lauren says, pride dripping from her words. 'Cortney William Goldman the Third.'

Cort laughs like she's said the funniest thing he's ever heard. 'They don't need to know all that,' he says. 'Please just call me Cort.' As if we were going to spew out that word salad name anyway. 'It really is so wonderful to meet you. Lauren says you're from England?'

Antoinette and I nod in unison.

'I love England,' he says. 'I've been lucky enough to visit several times. To do my talks.'

He stops speaking, clearly waiting for one of us to ask him about his talks.

There's an awkward silence when no one says anything.

Lauren rushes to fill the silence. 'Cort's a podcaster,' she says. 'He's pretty well known for it, aren't you, babe?'

Cort looks faux-embarrassed. 'I mean, I'm well known in the podcast industry, I suppose.'

Urgh. A podcast bro.

'It's called Man Enough to STFU,' Lauren says excitedly. 'Have you heard of it?'

Antoinette and I shake our heads.

'No, sorry,' I say, remembering that I should be polite. 'I don't really listen to podcasts.'

'Me neither,' Antoinette says and smiles apologetically.

'What's it about?' I ask, trying to arrange my face into an expression that suggests I give a fuck.

Cort chuckles and sits down at the table next to Agnes. I swear I see her flinch. 'Is there enough of this for me, babe?' he says, already helping himself to chicken.

'Go ahead,' says Agnes in a tight voice.

'What's it about?' he says. 'What isn't it about, more like. Isn't that right, Lo?'

'It's a feminist podcast for men,' Lauren says and I see Antoinette's eyes widen in horror.

'It's for men who really want to be feminist allies,' Cort says as Lauren serves him up some potatoes.

Oh.

He's a feminist.

I guess that explains the man bun.

'Oh, wow,' says Antoinette. 'Cool.' She's such a liar.

'I don't think of it as cool,' Cort says. 'I think of it as necessary.' He gives my sister a condescending smile and I know she's already mentally dismembering him. 'I consider myself a conduit between the genders.'

'He's writing a book,' Agnes tells us and from the barely there mocking tone in her voice, I can tell she gets it. I think I'm going to like this girl.

'Are you?' I say, turning to Cort, alight with fake fascination.

He gives a little humble shrug that I can imagine him practising in the mirror.

'It's less of a book and more of a *bible*,' he says without any irony at all. I see Antoinette and Agnes exchange a look. Lauren is either oblivious to the mocking or is choosing to ignore it.

'Wow, a bible,' I say. 'That's quite something.'

'He really is,' Lauren says. 'He's always being invited to places to give talks.'

Cort nods in a way that can only be described as sagely. 'It's important in these times of such rampant toxic masculinity that men have a positive role model.' He makes a hashtag sign with the two fingers of each hand and looks me directly in the eyes. 'Not all men.'

I think I see Antoinette's left eye twitch.

Lauren is gazing at him adoringly.

Agnes looks like she's trying not to laugh.

'That's really great,' I say, hoping I don't choke on my lie. 'Well done, you.'

'I'm actually doing a talk locally next week,' he says. 'You girls—' He stops, puts his hands in a prayer position and lowers his head. 'Forgive me, you *women* should come along.'

'Sure,' I say. 'Sounds great.' The lies are just sliding off my tongue.

Agnes makes a noise that I swear is a laugh, but she picks up her wine and glugs some. 'Sorry,' she says. 'Something went down the wrong way.'

'I'll find you on Insta and ping the details over,' Cort says.

'Looking forward to it.'

He turns and addresses Lauren. 'Shall we head, babe?'

'Yes, let me just grab my stuff.' She jumps up and disappears out of the kitchen to where I assume her bedroom must be. Cort stands up, ready to follow her.

'Apologies to run out. We're going to a divine feminine sound bath,' he says. 'But I really look forward to talking to you both again soon. Namaste.' He gives us a little bow and disappears after Lauren.

Antoinette and I do nothing but blink after him.

'Is he always so delightful?' I ask eventually when we hear the front door of the guesthouse close behind Lauren and Cort as they leave.

Agnes chuckles. 'Oh yes,' she says. 'You won't believe this but sometimes he can be even *more* delightful.'

My eyes widen.

I dread to think what this means.

Antoinette pulls a face packed with distaste. 'What does she see in him?'

Agnes shakes her head. 'Honestly who knows but he seems to make her happy so I've learned to tolerate him.'

'How?' Antoinette asks. 'I must learn your secrets.'

'Benzos,' Agnes says. 'Sometimes a little bit of weed. Although sometimes I think I need a full general anaesthetic to deal with him and his performative-ally shit.' She gives us a little smile and puts her fingers to her lips. 'Obviously don't tell anyone, my folks would literally murder me, but if there's anything you ever need, let me know. I can get hold of most stuff.' She grins again. 'Happy to fill your party prescriptions.'

'Maybe you should just drug Cort,' I say and Agnes smiles darkly.

'It's crossed my mind.'

I head back to the villa a little after that, leaving Antoinette and Agnes chatting about a new Netflix series they're both excited about, like they've known each other for ages. Like Antoinette hasn't just murdered a celebrity and is storing him in Agnes's parents' cellar.

Life is weird.

And I need my bed.

17

KITTY AND ANTOINETTE'S AIRBNB, WEST HOLLYWOOD, LOS ANGELES

I can't sleep.

For someone with literal bodies in my basement, I generally have a pretty clear conscience and don't suffer with insomnia.

But tonight I cannot sleep for shit.

I've tried everything.

Lying on my back.

Lying on my front.

Lying on my side with a pillow between my knees.

I've listened to two full guided meditations and I think I'm actually able to astral project but I still can't actually get to sleep.

Even though I am exhausted.

Every time I close my eyes, I see Tor's face. Her face from our call earlier, not her face how I want to remember her. I see the bruised, swollen, broken version of her. And that's usually followed up by Ron Wilde's lipless face in the sink at the Chateau, staring at me. Two really unwelcome images when I'm trying to drift into a state of rest and relaxation.

I give up and get out of bed.

Maybe I should go and ask Agnes if she's got anything that can knock me out.

When I was little and couldn't sleep, my mother used to make me warm milk – I wasn't vegan when I was a kid – and sit with me. I wish Carmella was here now to stroke my hair and tell me to think about nice things until all the horrible things go away. But she's not. I have to self-parent.

I creep out of my room and down the stone stairs.

The villa is too quiet.

I expected LA to be like London, motorbikes, cars, sirens, people shouting in the street. Proof of life even at three o'clock in the morning. Maybe this neighbourhood is one of the peaceful ones. I can't really complain about that. It's literally what I wanted.

I pad through to the kitchen, thinking I'll make myself a herbal tea and doomscroll Insta until I feel sleepy. But when I flick on the lights, I almost scream.

Antoinette is sitting cross-legged on the kitchen counter, eating a bowl of cereal. She is also very much wide awake.

'Oh,' she says when she sees me. 'Hello.'

'You scared the living shit out of me,' I say. 'Why are you up?'

She shovels a spoonful of cereal into her mouth before answering.

'Can't sleep,' she says and I watch as bits of Lucky Charms fly across the floor. 'Thought you were a burglar.'

'A burglar that turns on the lights?'

She stares at me. 'Burglars need to see things, Kitty.'

'Never mind,' I say as I fill the kettle and click it on. 'Tea?'

But Antoinette doesn't answer.

I look at her and she is staring into space like a kid from a creepy early noughties movie.

'Antoinette?'

'I can still feel it,' she says, her voice is detached, eerie.

I pull a mug from the cupboard and put it down carefully. 'Feel what?'

'Killing him.'

Ah yes.

That.

'And?' I say. Is this the moment when she crumbles? When she realises what she's done? That it's something she can't hit 'undo' on. Is there a breakdown incoming?

'I liked it,' she says. She looks at me and there's something I recognise in her eyes. A fire of purpose. 'I feel like I've done something bad but ultimately good. Was it like that for you? Your first time?'

I think back to the first man I killed – our father.

'Yes,' I say quietly. 'Yes, it was.'

She keeps looking at me, wanting me to say more.

'It felt like . . . I don't know exactly . . . like I was finally doing something worthwhile. After the adrenaline. And the excitement and the rage all went, I was still glad I did it. I've never regretted it. Not for a moment.'

She nods solemnly.

'But that time, my first kill,' I say. 'It was chaotic. It was unplanned. I needed someone else to clean up my mess for me. That's the one thing I regret. Dragging someone else into it.'

I think about Carmella's face as she watched me obliterate

my dad with that antique vase. A little bit relieved. But mostly horrified.

'It's so important to be more controlled,' I say. 'We can't bring anyone else into this.'

'But that was your mother,' Antoinette says. 'She's not just anyone. She'd clean up any mess for you.'

'Maybe,' I say. 'But she shouldn't have to. She's not like us.' Not *that* much anyway. 'I know what you did to Ron was self-defence. But we have to be careful. We have to keep this—' I gesture vaguely at the space between us, 'we have to keep this *on* the rails. It cannot get unhinged.'

Antoinette's right eyebrow shoots up. 'There's a dead A-lister in the wine cellar,' she says. 'If you don't count that as unhinged, I don't know what to say.' There's a small smile on her lips, like a secret.

I pour boiling water over the bag of miscellaneous herbs I grabbed from the caddy on the side.

'I wasn't scared of him, you know,' Antoinette says. 'Ron Wilde.'

I frown. 'You should have been. He was fucking terrifying. And twice your size. That middle-aged spread really caught up with him.'

'I just thought he looked a bit like a sad, ageing pirate,' she says. 'Like Captain Hook but in need of a midlife health check and some citalopram.'

A laugh sneaks out of me. 'That gold tooth,' I say.

'Those fucking tattoos.'

'The unbuttoned shirt! Oh my God.'

We share a tiny moment of eye contact before collapsing into waves of laughter.

‘I’m not sorry,’ Antoinette says when she sobers.

‘No one is asking you to be,’ I say.

‘And I don’t want to be some annoying kid you’re stuck with.’

I wasn’t expecting this moment of raw honesty from her. I look at her, reach for her hand.

‘You’re not,’ I say. ‘You could never be that.’

She smirks. ‘I’m not annoying?’

I laugh. ‘I’m not stuck with you,’ I say. ‘I choose you. Always. We’re sisters.’

She breathes out and it’s so heavy I feel the shudder.

And then she leans her head on my shoulder.

And I realise she’s not a liability.

Or, if she is, she’s my liability. She’s a hurricane. A force of full nature.

And I wouldn’t change her for the world.

‘Great,’ she says, ‘then you’re going to love hiking with me in the morning.’

I’m not sure my new sisterly love stretches quite that far.

18

RUNYON CANYON TRAIL, HOLLYWOOD HILLS, LOS ANGELES

Antoinette is ten years younger than I am. And it has never shown more than now. Somehow she's managed to convince me to get up early and go on a morning hike with her. It goes to show how much I want to bond with my sister because I am not a fan of either of these things usually. But there's something to be said for being up and at it this early. The searing LA heat hasn't quite kicked in yet and I feel almost *healthy* halfway up a mountain at a time I'd usually be silencing my alarm. Or I would do if I wasn't suddenly wheezing like a sixty-a-day smoker. And if my actual lungs didn't feel like they've had acid thrown at them.

Am I dying?

Is this what my death will look like?

Antoinette, however, is skipping along like a happy gazelle, swinging her water bottle and stopping every few metres to take in the scenery. And wait for me to catch her up.

'Are you having fun?' she asks me as I huff up beside her.

'Yes,' I lie. 'I actually love early mornings and exercise.' It's just a white lie really. Just a tiny one so I can bond with my sister.

'Have you had any thoughts about what we're going to do with *him*?' she says, handing me her bottle.

'Not yet,' I say when I've recovered my breath.

I look around.

Despite the early hour there are already several people out on the trail apart from us. And they're all filming content. Two girls in co-ordinating exercise outfits are laughing as they set up a tripod and yoga mats. There's a young couple with a selfie stick strolling along, their limbs wound around each other. And a man with no shirt and very precise facial hair is filming his dog doing tricks. Or at least he's trying to. The dog is much more interested in sniffing and digging.

My first – and only – idea for Ron Wilde was to cut him into even smaller parts and distribute them along a walking trail. My thought was that the coyotes and mountain lions would do the disappearing for me. But that wouldn't work with all these people and phones and dogs about. I can just imagine tossing a body part from my backpack only to have a Cavapoo immediately fetch it for me, its owner calling out, 'Excuse me, ma'am, you dropped something.'

Yeah. That totally wouldn't work.

'Can we stop for a minute?' I say to Antoinette, who's still several steps ahead of me. She turns back and gives me a puzzled look as I double over, putting my hands on my knees and taking some deep breaths. When did I get so unfit? I need to address this pretty quickly as it's kind of crucial to be in peak physical condition if I'm going to be slaying men and hefting their bodies around.

'Do you want to sit down for a minute?' Antoinette asks as she walks back over to me. 'Are you struggling a bit there?'

'I'm fine,' I say but the words come out in choked gasps.

'Sit down, Kits.'

I do.

Antoinette drops down beside me. 'Actually, there's something I wanted to show you,' she says, taking her phone out of her Lululemon belt bag and opening Reddit.

She hands it to me and I peer at the screen. It's open on a subreddit dedicated to the man in our cellar.

The dead man in our cellar.

There's a thread at the top with hundreds of comments.

r/RonWilde

Still Wilde. Ron's *allegedly* ditched his latest filming commitments and gone on a bender.

Off the wagon and MIA.

I work in the film industry and people here are going *nuts* because Ron's missed several meetings. No one is saying anything because he's made such a big thing about going sober but everyone has accepted he's disappeared off on a bender.

I skim through the comments. No one is surprised. Some people even claim to have seen him in various places from downtown dive bars to an alpaca farm in Ohio.

But most importantly, no one has suggested he's been murdered, butchered and is currently residing in a Spanish villa in WeHo.

'Good,' I say, handing Antoinette her phone back.

She nods. 'What are we going to do with him then?' she asks. I still haven't come up with a good plan. Even if it's just assumed that he's come crashing off the wagon and is currently on the mother of all benders, at some point people are going to start wondering what's happened to Ron Wilde. A-list actors can't just disappear. The trouble is, I just don't know what to do with a dead body in LA.

If we were at home in London, it would be so simple. We've already dismembered the body so all we'd need to do would be to move the body parts to one of my family's abattoirs and pop them into one of the mincers. It's an extremely efficient way of getting rid of corpses. Okay, so *some* bits might end up in the food chain but, honestly, it's probably better than some of the stuff that ends up in mass-produced sausage rolls. Having grown up with a family in the meat industry there's a very good reason why I'm vegan.

Sadly though, the family business never quite made it out to the States. So it means I've got to go back to the drawing board when it comes to body disposal. And the problem with Hollywood is that it's a living, breathing movie set; cameras are everywhere and there are always eyes on you. Where do you go to be invisible in a city obsessed with being seen?

I turn to my sister, who is still looking at me expectantly.

'I don't know,' I say. 'I really don't know.'

Antoinette's brow furrows a little. I must remember to talk to her about preventative Botox. She might only be twenty but you're never too young to start future-proofing your skin.

'Okay,' she says. 'No biggie. We just need to do some brainstorming.' She opens the Notes app on her phone.

'What are you doing?' I say.

She stares at me like I've asked her what colour the sky is.

'Making notes,' she says.

I reach across and snatch the phone from her. 'Are you insane? Why don't you just open up an email, put "Ways to Get Rid of a Dead Actor I Murdered in LA" in the subject line and send it straight to the police?'

Antoinette stares at me. 'Oh,' she says.

'Yes,' I say. 'Oh. Pen and paper only. And that's only if you can't possibly keep everything in your head. And you have to tear the paper up and burn it after.'

'Got it,' Antoinette says. 'Pen and paper only.' She pauses for a second and looks around. 'Do you have a pen and paper?'

'We're on a hike,' I say but she pulls a puzzled face again. 'No. I did not bring a pen and paper.'

'Oh. I guess we're using our heads then.'

'Yes,' I say. 'We are. So. Have you got any ideas?'

'Not really,' Antoinette says. 'I suppose Google is out of the question?' She looks longingly at her phone.

'I'm not going to dignify that with an answer,' I say. 'The best thing we can do is get rid of the body some place where it's never going to be found. So if we're caught it's much harder to prosecute for a murder if they can't actually prove that a murder hasn't taken place.'

Antoinette nods. 'No body, no crime,' she says. 'Like how we fed Ben to the pigs at your mum's farm.'

Earlier this summer Antoinette and I killed her brother Ben, who had been leading a secret double life as a misogynistic content creator, and then fed his remains to pigs my mother adopted.

'Exactly,' I say. 'So how can we get rid of a body and ensure it's never found?'

My sister frowns in concentration. 'We could get some pigs?'

'And where would we keep them? In the pool? Or maybe our new friends in the guesthouse would like them living with them?'

'There is no need to be sarcastic,' Antoinette says with a pout. She thinks for a moment, chewing her lip thoughtfully. 'How about here?'

I shake my head. 'I've already thought of that. Full of tourists.'

'In the day, yes. But not at night,' Antoinette says. 'We could bring the pieces in backpacks and scatter them in the dark. The coyotes and mountain lions would have cleared them up by the morning.'

I shake my head again. 'I'm not hiking in the dark.' I point at my feet. 'These ankles are too pretty to break.'

'Okay then.' Antoinette is thinking again. 'I read something online recently about how a family discovered another person's remains in the same grave as like their nana. Turned out it was some snitch that local gangsters had unalived and buried in the cemetery. Doesn't Hollywood have that super famous graveyard where Judy Garland is buried?'

'Hollywood Forever Cemetery,' I say. It's not actually a terrible idea. 'Although I don't think Ron Wilde deserves to be buried alongside Judy Garland. But maybe we could look into somewhere a bit more low key.'

'What about the big lake?'

'The Hollywood Reservoir,' I say but shake my head. 'Too much CCTV.'

'Could we just make it look like an accident? A drug overdose?'

I stare at her. 'Antoinette,' I say. 'You sliced his throat and cut his body up into six pieces. I think we'd struggle to pass it off as an overdose.'

Antoinette sighs. 'Well, I don't know then. But then I'm just an amateur, aren't I? What do *you* suggest, wise one?'

But I just don't have any ideas.

Other than buying an actual abattoir over here. Actually that's not a terrible idea. I should check out whatever the US equivalent of Rightmove is.

'I guess he can just stay in the cellar for now,' I say. 'It's probably safest down there.'

19

KITTY AND ANTOINETTE'S AIRBNB, WEST HOLLYWOOD, LOS ANGELES

We get back to the villa and Antoinette disappears to have a shower. I open Instagram, partly from muscle memory. I used to live on there. Back when follower count and brand collabs were the most important things to me. I still get some requests occasionally but the page is mostly dormant now.

There's a message waiting for me in my DMs. It's from Niamh, Aidan's ex-girlfriend. I feel my hands tremble as I open it.

Hi Kitty,

I'm sorry you're having to contact me in these circumstances and I'm really sorry to hear about your friend. I hope she's going to make a full recovery. Believe me when I say that the best place Aidan can be is as far away from her as possible. You were right in your message, Aidan and I dated for two years a while back, here in Ireland. There were definitely instances of violence in our relationship. He'd push me or grab me, sometimes enough to leave bruises. It was why we broke up. He left the country after my brothers paid him a visit and I haven't heard from him since. It's taken me a long time to heal from that man, as you can imagine. I'm sorry I can't help you. Please don't message me again. It was a traumatic time and I'm glad it's behind me, I don't want the wound re-opened. I hope you understand.

Love and light,

Niamh x

Antoinette comes back downstairs wearing a dress and cowboy boots. Her hair is still wet and leaving little puddles on the floor. I show her the message and she sucks in a breath as she reads it.

'I feel awful now,' I say. 'That poor woman. I've probably opened up a whole can of trauma worms.'

'At least we know he has a history of shitty behaviour,' Antoinette says as she hands me back my phone. 'And of skipping the country. What a fucking coward.'

I can't stop thinking about Niamh.

I should never have contacted her. What was I thinking? I've probably just re-traumatised her. She'll probably have to start her entire healing journey all over again. I should apologise. I begin to tap out a response.

'Kits, what are you doing?' Antoinette says, peering over at my screen.

'I'm just going to say sorry to Niamh for contacting her. I—' Antoinette reaches over and grabs my phone from me. 'What are you doing?'

'Stopping you from messaging her again,' she says. 'She's

clearly told you not to contact her. I think you should respect that.'

I sigh and close the app, throwing my phone down.

Of course she's right.

'I just don't know what else to do to find him,' I say, my jaw tensing up with frustration.

'Well, there's one thing we could try,' Antoinette says, almost shyly.

I turn and stare at her. 'What?'

'It's just something I saw on Reddit and it got me thinking.'

'What?' I ask again.

'Have you thought about hiring a private detective?'

She's a genius.

Seriously.

Why haven't I thought of this?

Antoinette is confused by my silence. 'I mean, obviously we don't have to,' she says. 'If it feels like we're cheating or something?'

'No, no,' I say. 'It's brilliant. A private detective.'

Of course.

I grab my phone. 'I'll get looking for someone.'

Antoinette flushes. 'Actually,' she says, 'I think I've already found someone.'

God.

I love having her here.

It's like having a murder-admin assistant.

20

SANTA MONICA BOULEVARD, WEST HOLLYWOOD, LOS ANGELES

'Travis Truman. He even sounds like a Hollywood PI,' Antoinette had said on the way over to the office address. 'It's like super retro and hard-boiled, isn't it?' It's the next day and we're on our way to meet a PI Antoinette found.

After promising the Uber driver that we will indeed have a good day, Antoinette and I make our way into the juice bar. This isn't going to go well. What sort of whack PI doesn't even have his own office? Inside, it's suspiciously quiet. The only customers are two women in yoga pants, chatting over mason jars filled with green liquid. And a man who looks to be in his early thirties. He's poring over a laptop when I walk in but his eyes shoot up to meet mine. He's dressed in a pair of battered-looking Levi's and a blue T-shirt with Ramones written on it in white. I can make out a pair of distressed Converse peeking out from underneath the table he's sitting at. But the thing that strikes me most about Travis Truman is how disturbingly handsome he is. He has very dark hair that looks prone to curling at the slightest threat of moisture and very dark eyes that could be black but I'm not sure that's possible. Are black eyes a thing? I must google this later. He gives me a half smile and looks at me quizzically, his eyes seeming to be asking me, *is it you I'm waiting for?*

'Travis Truman?' I ask, my voice barely more than a whisper.

'Yes, that's me,' he whispers back with a grin on his face. 'Why are we whispering?'

This makes me laugh. 'I literally have no idea. It just felt appropriate.'

'Well, it's okay to speak at a normal volume,' he says. 'It gets hard to hear over the blenders otherwise. You must be . . .' He pauses and takes a look at his laptop. 'Mary-Kate?'

'And Ashley,' I hear Antoinette's voice from behind me. She slips into a chair opposite Travis and holds her hand out. 'I emailed you yesterday.'

Travis moves his eyes to my sister and blinks at her before taking her hand and giving it a shake. 'Are you Mary-Kate? Or Ashley?'

I pull out the chair next to Antoinette and sit in it. 'I think my sister has given you fake names,' I say.

Travis raises one eyebrow. I've always found it really hot when men can do that. 'You're kidding me?' he says, completely deadpan.

'We have to be discreet,' Antoinette says by way of explanation. 'No electronic trail.'

Travis nods gravely at her. 'I understand, Ashley. Or can I call you Ash?'

I roll my eyes. 'Her name is Antoinette,' I say. 'And I'm Kitty.'

'It's a pleasure to meet you, whatever your name is,' Travis says to me with a smile. He really is almost offensively good-looking. Objectively speaking. But I suppose everyone in LA is.

'So,' I gesture around the juice bar, 'is this your office?'

Travis picks up the mason jar of green gloop on the table in front of him and takes a slurp from it, which he quickly swallows when he realises he has to answer my question. He wipes his mouth with the back of his hand.

'Not usually,' he says. 'I'm sort of between permanent bases at the moment.'

'He's homeless,' Antoinette whispers to me but she says it at the exact moment that the juice-barista – are they called that, they should be – cuts the blender and Travis Truman definitely hears her. He's a gentleman though and, after a quick couple of blinks, turns his attention back to me.

'It's temporary,' he says. 'Please don't let it put you off. I'm extremely professional. I have literally . . .' he pauses to do some quick maths on his fingers, '*tens* of satisfied clients.'

'Oh,' I say. 'Tens?' A grin spreads over Travis's face and I realise he's joking with me. 'Funny,' I say and he lets out a laugh that is so contagious I can't help but smile too.

'Sorry,' he says as he tries to arrange his face into something serious. 'I couldn't resist. My offices are being decorated at the moment. So it's either here or at a share space. Which isn't very private. I promise you, I have hundreds of testimonials who will vouch for me. Can I get you anything to drink?'

Antoinette and I both shake our heads.

'So what can I do for you?'

'We're trying to find someone,' I say.

Travis nods. 'Yeah. I am going to need a few more details than that.'

'He's a British guy. He'd have arrived here in the last week or so,' I say as Travis taps away at his laptop. His eyes don't leave mine as he writes. Who knew touch-typing could feel intimate.

'Okay,' says Travis. 'British. Recently arrived. Anything else?'

'He was working as a therapist in the UK so there's a possibility that he'll be looking for new clients over here,' I say.

'Name?'

'Aidan,' I say. 'Aidan Ward. But he could be using a fake name.'

Travis raises an eyebrow again.

'He's on the run,' Antoinette says. 'For attacking a woman.'

'My friend,' I say. 'My best friend. He left her in a coma and fled the country.'

Travis nods. 'I'm sorry to hear that,' he says. 'That must've been very difficult for you.'

'Yes, it was.'

'And do you have a photo of this man? It really helps if I know who I'm looking for.'

I pull up a couple of pictures that I have saved on my phone.

'Can you send these to me?' Travis says and I nod and Airdrop them to him. 'What about social media?'

I shake my head again. 'He's stopped posting,' I say. 'He's gone completely ghost.'

Travis purses his lips. 'Totally normal for someone who doesn't want to be found,' he says. 'Can you describe him for me? Height?'

I think for a moment. 'He's about six feet,' I say. 'Medium build. Usually wears glasses but he could have contacts now, I suppose. And he had a big beard the last time I saw him.'

'Age?'

'Old,' Antoinette says. 'Middle-aged. From the nineteen hundreds.'

'Early thirties,' I say.

'Okay, so *not* the undead,' Travis types something.

'He always wears jeans and band shirts,' I say. 'Kind of like you.'

'So, great style.' Travis adds this to his notes and I realise that I'm smiling again. Which is weird because speaking to a private detective about finding the psychopath who hurt my friend shouldn't be a smiling kind of scenario. Travis appears to notice this too and immediately makes his face settle into an appropriately serious and professional expression. He taps a few things into his laptop and then looks at us again.

'Well, I think that's all I need from you for now. Unless you can think of anything else?' We both shake our heads. 'And you've got my details in case you do so please don't hesitate to drop me a line. Anytime.' I'm pretty sure he's speaking to me when he says this. He extends his hand out towards Antoinette. 'Lovely to meet you, Ashley,' he says and she laughs. 'And you, Kitty.' He shakes my hand too and I'm sure I'm not imagining it when he lingers, just a little, instead of dropping it right away when the shake is over.

Outside Antoinette doesn't waste any time letting me know that she noticed the frisson between me and Travis too.

'Sparks,' she says, 'Absolute sparks.'

'Oh, don't be silly,' I say, even as I feel a blush creep up my neck and towards my cheeks. 'He was just being polite and professional.' Which, at this point, is exactly what we need. I've been getting more and more anxious about not really having a clue on how to find Aidan Ward. And for the first time I'm feeling relieved. Travis is going to find him and then I can get that sweet revenge for Tor.

I can't wait.

Antoinette laughs just as my phone buzzes with a text notification. I look at it. It's from Travis.

Seriously. Anytime.

I show the message to my sister, who lets out a whoop.

'Oh, Kits,' she says. 'You are so getting some of that private dick.'

21

HOLLYWOOD RESERVOIR TRAIL, HOLLYWOOD HILLS, LOS ANGELES

With Travis Truman taking the reins in the hunt for Aidan Ward for a while, I have the chance to teach Antoinette some of the basics of serial killing. She's keen and she's got a knack for it, that's for sure, but we cannot have another incident like the Ron Wilde one.

So today is a school day for Antoinette. It's another early start and another hiking trail, this time the Hollywood Reservoir. Full disclosure, even though we pretty much ruled this place out as a potential dumping ground for dead bodies, I wanted to get a better look. It's obvious right away that this is not the place for me. Or Ron Wilde. Too many cameras, too many Labradoodles and absolutely no way of getting near the actual water without ending up on some sort of watch-list. It's something of a challenge trying to find any corner of this city that isn't being filmed by either law enforcement or influencers.

I guess I'll need to keep thinking.

'The most important thing,' I say to Antoinette as we do some basic stretches to warm up, 'is that you're certain your target deserves it. This means research. And evidence if at all possible. The worst thing you could do is kill a good man. They're an endangered species as it is.'

'I did my research with *you know who*,' she says. 'It was widely documented what a POS he was.'

'I'm not entirely sure tabloid magazines and Reddit count as credible sources,' I say.

She pulls her left foot up to her bottom, stretching out her quads. 'There were legal proceedings,' she says after a moment.

'Which were dropped,' I say. 'He wasn't charged with anything. In the eyes of the law, Ron Wilde did nothing wrong.'

She changes legs and frowns at me. 'What about Believe Women?' she says. 'Isn't that proof enough for you?'

She's got me there.

'Okay,' I say. 'Ron Wilde was obviously a very bad man and deserved to die. But. Generally, it's always good to absolutely make sure your target is a terrible man. Making a mistake is the worst thing.'

I should know.

I've made two mistakes in my vigilante career. The first one was my ex-boyfriend, Adam. I loved him deeply and he betrayed me. Quite brutally. At first I thought he was cheating on me, but then I discovered that I was actually the other woman. He and his actual girlfriend were using me for my money and social media profile. While I didn't technically kill Adam, I did ruin his life. I bashed him over the head and left him with locked-in syndrome. He can only communicate with blinks now. Adam might not have been a good man, but he didn't deserve that.

Then there was Ruben Reynolds, whose only crime was looking too much like his sex-pest older brother, Rafe.

I mistook him for Rafe on a night out and Ruben played along, even taking me to his brother's home. He pretended to be Rafe until the moment I cut his throat.

Antoinette knows about both of these men, neither of them predators. She stretches her right arm across her chest now and looks at me. 'Are you still beating yourself up about Adam and Ruben Reynolds?' she asks and I nod. 'I think you should stop.'

'How can I?' I say, dropping into a forward fold. 'They were innocent.' Antoinette snorts. 'What?' I say, standing up and facing her. 'What was that for?'

'They were hardly innocent, Kits,' she says with a small shrug.

'They weren't predators,' I say.

She drops her head to one side and looks at me. 'Weren't they?'

'No . . .'

Antoinette raises her eyes. 'So, would you have slept with Adam, would you have had a whole relationship with him if you knew that he actually had a girlfriend and was using you?'

'No, of course not—'

'And Ruben. Who was pretending to be someone else, his own famous brother, to get you into bed. You don't think that's predatory?'

Oh.

I hadn't thought of it like that before.

'It's sex by deception,' Antoinette says, fixing me with a hard stare. 'Which is, legally speaking, rape.'

'It is?'

'You're not giving informed consent,' Antoinette says.

'So it's rape.' She looks at me for a moment while I digest this. 'Still think they're not predatory?'

'I loved Adam though,' I say.

'Yes, but would you ever have got involved with him in the first place if he'd been honest?'

I shake my head.

'It's back to the everyday misogyny I've been talking about,' Antoinette continues. 'Men lie all the time to get women into bed. Isn't uninformed consent as bad as no consent at all?'

'I guess,' I say, feeling shaken and angry by this revelation.

Antoinette puts an arm around my shoulders. 'I'm just saying,' she says. 'Don't feel too bad about those men. I think they deserved it.' She gives me a squeeze. 'So what's my next lesson?'

As we make our way around the trail, I tell Antoinette about the importance of having a plan for the bodies, even though my mind is still chewing on what she said about sex by deception.

'The best thing to do is try to get rid of the body completely,' I tell her. 'Obviously, in the UK we've got access to the abattoirs, so that's pretty easy to take care of over there.'

'So what happens if we can't get rid of a body?'

'In that case, you have to make it look like an accident,' I say, even though I'm thinking, *Was it sex by deception? Is Adam more of a predator than I realised? Should I have finished the job?* Anger starts to fire in the depth of my stomach.

'And what about your code?' Antoinette is saying like she didn't just detonate a bomb in my head. 'You know, Kitty's Code.' Kitty's Code is the set of rules I made for myself to make sure I only kill the very worst men, the ones who absolutely deserve it.

'Right, yes,' I say, trying to pull myself back into the present. 'So, rule one is No Women. No matter what.'

'Unless she's a psycho stalker threatening to unmask you as a serial killer,' Antoinette says. 'Like Hen.'

'Yes,' I agree. 'Maybe we should call them guidelines rather than rules.'

I *try* not to kill women. They're who I'm protecting. But Hen was an exception.

It was her or me.

I go on to explain the rest of my code to Antoinette, who nods along with a serious expression on her face.

No one innocent.

No one vulnerable.

Don't get caught.

And most importantly, the kill must serve a purpose.

We're not basic murderers. We're doing this for a reason. We're getting justice for every woman who has felt the weight of male violence hanging over her, for every woman who wasn't believed, for every woman who was too scared to speak out.

As I speak, the familiar burning in my stomach starts. The faces of all the men I've killed before flash through my mind.

One in particular.

Adam.

Adam whom I loved but who was even more predatory than I realised. The burning intensifies. Becomes a white-hot rage.

I turn to Antoinette. 'Let's go out tonight,' I say.

I think it's time for a practical lesson.

In fact, I'm itching for it.

22

BAR NEXT DOOR, WEST HOLLYWOOD, LOS ANGELES

Later that evening Antoinette and I make our way along Sunset to a cocktail bar that Antoinette saw recommended on Instagram. The strip is bustling and noisy, crowds of revellers spilling out onto the streets.

'Looking good, baby girls,' someone shouts to us as we squeeze past a group of people in cowboy boots and feather boas. 'You enjoy your night.'

'How nice is it here?' Antoinette beams. 'That would never happen in London. You'd just get a cold stare. Or some mouth-breather telling you to get your tits out.'

The bar is small and busy, but in a good way, a way that feels cosy rather than claustrophobic.

'Cute,' I say, looking around at the sepia-coloured space with its low-lit booths and dark leather seats.

'The building was once home to Marilyn Monroe's talent agency,' Antoinette tells me and I stare at her, impressed.

'I didn't think you were interested in Hollywood history?'

'I never said that,' she says. 'That old hotel was just a bit musty.'

A young woman sitting in a booth with a group of people grabs my arm.

'We're just leaving,' she says. 'Do you want our table? So hard to get a seat in here.'

I give her a grateful smile. 'Thank you so much,' I say as she and her friends slip out of the booth, allowing Antoinette and I to take their place.

'See?' Antoinette says. 'It's so friendly here.'

'Only because they're drunk on craft cocktails.'

'Drunk people in London would just try to start a fight.'

I laugh. 'That's not true. London is friendly.'

Antoinette raises an eyebrow. 'So what are we drinking?'

I look at the menu, which is really cool – designed to look like an Old Hollywood gossip paper. The cocktails look amazing. They're named after places in Hollywood like Whisky Go Go and The Roosevelt. There's even a Chateau Marmont. I shudder.

'Not alcohol,' I say. 'We need to be on our game.' I've learned the hard way that being sloppy drunk leads to being a sloppy killer. No one likes a sloppy drunk. They like a sloppy killer even less.

'Just a sparkling water then,' she says and I order the drinks on my phone.

A server brings them over a little while later. As she's placing them on our table I notice Antoinette's eyes widen in shock.

'What?' I spin round, not sure what I'm expecting, but there's nothing. Just people drinking, talking and laughing.

'That guy, the one in the grey T-shirt,' Antoinette says. 'I'm sure I just saw him slip something in that girl's drink.'

'What?' I say. 'What was it?'

'I don't know, something in a little vial. He just poured it in while she was looking away!'

I stare at the guy. He doesn't look shady. He's wearing a vintage-looking T-shirt, old-style Levi's and an earring in his right ear. There's a thin gold chain around his neck. He has that carefully curated stubble that most of the men I've seen here are sporting. He's laughing now, with the group of people he's with. They look like they're friends.

'Are you sure?' I ask Antoinette but she doesn't answer because she's jumped out of her seat and is making her way to the bar like she's on a mission. I watch as she reaches the group and leans over the bar, trying to get the attention of a server. As she moves I see her hand slip out and knock over one of the drinks lined up on the bar. It goes everywhere, all down the side of the bar, on the floor, but mostly over the guy.

'Oh my God, I am so sorry,' Antoinette squeals, grabbing a handful of napkins and dabbing at his jeans. 'I am so clumsy.'

'Hey, don't worry about it,' says the guy, appeased by having Antoinette effectively paw him. 'Accidents happen.'

'I'll replace the drink,' Antoinette says but he waves her off.

'Seriously, don't worry about it, it's fine.'

'Are you sure?'

'Of course, get back to your night.'

Antoinette gives the group a dazzling smile and shimmies back over to our booth.

'She won't be drinking that spiked drink now,' she says to me, looking triumphant.

'No,' I say. 'But you know he's probably just going to spike someone else's drink later.'

Antoinette gives me a wicked smile and holds out her fist,

it's curled around something. She unfurls her fingers and I see, in the palm of her hand, a little vial of clear liquid.

'Swiped it when I was wiping him down,' she says.

'What? How?'

'I learned how to pick pockets at boarding school,' she says with a casual little shrug. 'We used to practise when we went out on day trips. No one ever suspected a group of girls from an expensive school was going to steal from them. I'm quite good at it. My sleight of hand is unreal.'

'So I see.'

I sip my drink and turn my attention back to the guy at the bar. He really doesn't look the type to be drugging girls in bars but if I've learned anything it's that looks can be incredibly deceiving. Monsters don't always look like monsters. Sometimes they look like Jacob Elordi in a V-neck tee. He's the perfect lab rat. He must sense me looking at him as he turns and glances over at our booth, gives me a grin and then turns his attention to Antoinette. A plan quickly comes together in my mind.

'Antoinette?'

'Yes?'

'Can you quickly google the nearest rooftop bar?'

She looks at me, confused. 'Don't you like it here?'

'It's fine,' I say. 'But I'm about to give you your first practical lesson.'

Antoinette grins wickedly and reaches for her phone while I smile back at the bar guy.

'So apparently the nearest place is Ophelia's. It's a five-minute walk.'

'Great,' I say, just as bar guy approaches our booth, drink in hand.

'Hey,' he says, looking from me to Antoinette. 'Would you ladies mind if I joined you?'

'Sure,' I say. 'Sit.'

He squeezes himself in beside Antoinette.

'Hi again,' he says to her. 'Do I need to keep my drink away from you?'

He does. But he doesn't know why. Yet.

I laugh. 'She's not usually so clumsy. I'm Kitty,' I say, holding out my hand. The man takes it and shakes it.

'Very nice to meet you,' he says. 'I'm Carey.'

'You've already met Antoinette,' I say and he laughs.

'We're acquainted. I'd like to say she threw herself at me but sadly it was just a drink.' Antoinette gives an embarrassed shrug. 'Can I get you girls anything?'

'We're actually just about to leave,' I say with a sad face.

'You're not going home? The night's only just starting.'

'We're actually going to check out Ophelia's,' I say. 'Apparently the views are to die for.'

'You should come with us,' Antoinette says. 'You could be our tour guide!' She's looking at him hopefully. Carey looks over at the group he was with. I can see him wavering.

'Sounds great,' he says. 'Let me just go and tell my friends I'm bailing.' He hops out of his seat, leaving his drink on our table.

When he's out of earshot, I say, 'Now pour some of whatever you swiped into his glass.'

'How much do I put in?' Antoinette says, pulling the cap off the vial.

'All of it,' I say.

And she does it so quickly I barely even see it.

She wasn't lying about her sleight-of-hand skills.

'Told you,' she says to my impressed face.

Carey is back over. 'All cool,' he says. 'We leaving now?'

'Let's finish our drinks,' I say, sucking down the last of my water. Carey picks up his glass and downs it.

'Let's bounce,' he says.

I smile inwardly.

He won't be bouncing. That's a certainty.

23

OPHELIA'S, SUNSET STRIP, WEST HOLLYWOOD, LOS ANGELES

Carey's already wobbly on his feet by the time we've walked the five minutes east on Sunset to the hotel where Ophelia's is located. There's a security guard at the door and I hope he doesn't think Carey is already too drunk to go in. Luckily, the doorman is too busy looking at Antoinette and me so Carey glides in almost unnoticed.

'Have a great night, ladies,' the doorman says with a nod.

Did he even see him?

We take the elevator up to the rooftop. Carey is mesmerised by the strip light inside.

'I never knew elevators could be so pretty,' he murmurs, caressing the walnut wall. Antoinette and I exchange glances. He's fucked.

Ophelia's is beautiful. It's all twinkling fairy lights, antique garden furniture and vine-clad walls. There's Astroturf on the floor, which gives it a sort of English country garden vibe. The view is stunning, the Strip down below and the glittering lights of the Hollywood Hills in the distance. The best thing about it, though, is the low wall surrounding the edge, barely a barrier at all.

With all these drunk people.

It's an accident waiting to happen.

I take a sideways look at Carey as Antoinette leads us to a cast-iron table, right next to the wall. He's started to sweat. A lot. There's a thick sheen on his top lip that makes me feel queasy.

'Are you okay?' I ask him as he struggles to focus on me. Fuck, his pupils are huge. He smiles, it's slippery like he can't quite make it stay on his face.

'You're pretty,' he slurs. 'Like super pretty. I think I love you.'

'You don't,' I say as Antoinette smirks. 'That's just the drugs talking.'

Carey looks puzzled. 'I don't take drugs,' he says. 'I don't need to.'

'No? You just slip them into girls' drinks, don't you?'

He stares at me. A drop of sweat falls from the tip of his nose onto the Astroturf. He pats his jeans pockets. Can't locate his vial.

'How did you—'

'"How" doesn't matter,' I say. 'Let's get a selfie, shall we? I want one right near the ledge. With that stunning view in the background. How gorgeous will that look on Instagram, Antoinette?' I take one of Carey's arms.

'So gorgeous, sis,' Antoinette says taking the other.

Carey's legs are too liquified to do anything except let us lead him over to the wall. I look around but no one is paying us any attention. That's something I'm starting to learn and love about LA. Everyone is far too busy being their own main character to care about what anyone else is doing.

'Let's sit here,' I say and drop him on the wall. He grips the edge of it, his knuckles go white and look like they might burst through his skin.

Antoinette sits on the other side of him and leans in.

'Carey,' she says and he turns his head slowly to look at her. It's starting to loll to one side. 'Do you ever think what it's like for them? For the women? Do you ever think how scared they must be when they wake up with no memories of the night before? Have you usually left by that point? Or do you stick around and watch their confusion as they try to figure out what was put into their bodies?'

He blinks. And swallows. I'm sure I see his Adam's apple tremble.

'Wait—' he says but it's too late. I've already given him a little shove. Nothing big or dramatic. Just enough to overbalance him.

And then he's flying through the LA night.

He doesn't even scream.

There's actually not a sound at all. Until the crunch.

We look over the edge.

Carey has landed in the ornamental shrubbery outside the entrance of the hotel. One of his legs is bent backwards and his head looks like it's just sort of exploded.

'Oops,' says Antoinette.

Someone already has their phone out, filming Carey's splattered body. There's a shriek and the doorman who waved us through hurries over to where Carey has landed. He looks up just as we duck back from the edge.

We've already left by the time the police arrive.

24

KITTY AND ANTOINETTE'S AIRBNB, WEST HOLLYWOOD, LOS ANGELES

Later, back at the villa, Antoinette and I are toasting our night's work with a cup of hibiscus and rose tea.

'And that's how it's done,' I'm explaining to her. 'A simple accident.'

'Poor Carey,' she says, sticking her bottom lip out, and we both laugh.

'Just a silly, drunk reveller. And the best part is there's no mess to clean up or body to dispose of. The City of West Hollywood will literally do that for us.'

She's nodding, excited. 'That was great,' she says. 'He really was a piece of shit, wasn't he?'

'Absolutely,' I say. 'But he didn't know he was going to run into the Collins sisters.'

'The Collins sisters,' Antoinette parrots. 'Sounds good, doesn't it?'

'It really does. Cheers to us.' We clink our mugs together, grinning at each other.

Maybe this will work after all.

Maybe she is trainable and won't get us caught.

I have to admit, it was fun doing this with someone else. Someone with the same values.

Serial killing can be a lonely vocation.

'So who's next?' Antoinette asks. 'We could try to find the guy that whistled at us at the airport. Or the guy who tried to grab my—'

'Antoinette,' I cut her off. 'We can't go after every single man for the slightest little thing. We haven't got enough time, for one thing.'

She scowls at me. 'But Kitty. It's the everyday sexism, the *slightest little things*, that lead to the big things. Everyday sexism is a gateway drug. It's the literal foundations of the patriarchy.'

'I'm not saying you're wrong. I'm just saying we have to pick our battles. And I've picked our battle. It's Aidan Ward. I don't want to get distracted.'

She nods. 'And the WeHo Ripper,' she says.

'Once we're certain he actually exists outside the minds of overimaginative Redditors.'

'He does. My killer intuition is telling me that there's someone else out there.'

'Your killer intuition?'

'Yes,' she says. 'It's like my super power. And I'm telling you, Kits, we're not the only serial killers in WeHo.'

'Great,' I say, mocking. 'We could start a convention.'

Antoinette closes her eyes, like she's trying to block me and my scepticism out. 'You can be as sarcastic as you like,' she says. 'But when you know, you know.'

'Well, like I said, find me proof and then we'll talk.'

'I fully intend to.' She smiles at me. 'Agnes is nice, isn't she?' She sounds shy suddenly, like she's asking for my approval.

'She seems very nice,' I say, surprised by the sudden subject swerve.

'I think I like her.'

'Yeah, I assumed that.'

'I mean *like* her, like her.'

I laugh. 'I'd assumed that too.'

'Oh. Well, do you think she likes me?'

I sigh. 'Antoinette. I have no idea. I'm hardly the right person to be asking for romantic advice. My last boyfriend literally *fled* the country to get away from me.' She looks crestfallen and guilt jabs me in the ribs. 'Why don't you just ask her? That's the simplest thing.'

'God, no. How cringe would it be if I've read it wrong? And then she's living like two minutes away.' She shudders.

'Just do it,' I say. 'What's the absolute worst that could happen?'

Antoinette turns to me, a mischievous twinkle in her eye. 'I will,' she says. 'On the condition that you text Travis and ask him out.'

Urgh.

'But I don't want to.'

She folds her arms. 'And I don't particularly want to put myself out there either. But I'll do it if you do.'

'This feels like emotional blackmail.'

Antoinette shrugs and sips her tea. 'What's the absolute worst that could happen?'

'You're right,' I say, calling her bluff. 'Let's go and find Agnes right now.'

25

AGNES AND LAUREN'S GUESTHOUSE, WEST HOLLYWOOD, LOS ANGELES

The mood in the guesthouse is not the one I was expecting.

Lauren and Agnes are both sitting by the table. Lauren's eyes are swollen and pink-rimmed. She's nuzzling into Lana Del Gay. Agnes is staring into space, barely aware of our presence.

Something's happened.

Something bad.

'What is it?' Antoinette says, rushing over to Agnes's side. 'What's wrong?' Agnes gives her a mournful look and pushes her phone into my sister's hands. Antoinette blinks at the little screen for a couple of seconds then turns her eyes to me. They are huge with horror but, I notice, a tiny glint of something else in them.

What's going on?

Lauren rubs a hand over her eyes and turns to me.

'A woman's body's been found,' she says. 'In an alley behind the Walk of Fame.'

'Oh God, that's awful.'

She nods. 'It's even worse because we know this girl. She was in mine and Agnes's improv class.'

I look over at Agnes, who's nodding. 'Juno Blake,' she says, leaning into Antoinette's shoulder.

'And guess what,' my sister says, fixing her eyes on mine. 'She was on PrivatePool.'

She hands me the phone and I read the news report. And then the comments underneath it basically saying she was asking for it.

Antoinette's tone was loaded.

I know what she's saying.

Another murder, another woman dead at the hands of the WeHo Ripper. There's no way I can be in denial about the existence of this killer any more.

Her eyes are asking the question.

What are we going to do about it?

I give her a little nod because she's right. It would be irresponsible of me to be out here and *not* try to find out who's doing this. Especially when the police don't seem to care.

The corners of Antoinette's mouth turn up a little.

Looks like my to-do list just got a bit longer.

26

KITTY AND ANTOINETTE'S AIRBNB, WEST HOLLYWOOD, LOS ANGELES

'See!' Antoinette says to me when we get back to the villa. 'You can't possibly tell me that the WeHo Ripper isn't real now? Juno Blake is like the fourth woman from PrivatePool killed this year. And the body was dumped at a Hollywood landmark. It's got "serial killer" written all over it.'

I have to admit the evidence is pretty compelling.

It's pattern serial killer behaviour.

The exact kind of killer who is murdering these women to make a statement.

'And those comments,' she continues, her face contorts into a disgusted grimace. 'Can't even let the poor woman's body go cold before calling her a slut and basically saying she was asking for it.'

'I know,' I say.

'So we're going to find this guy then?' My sister's eyes are blazing with something I recognise, pure fury. 'I know you're focused on finding Aidan Ward but we can't just turn our backs on this, can we?'

She's right.

How would I ever be able to live with myself if I had the chance to put an end to someone's reign of terror over women?

There's no way I can just walk away from this.

There's just one problem.

'I can't even find Aidan Ward,' I say. 'And I know who he is and what he looks like. How am I supposed to find a killer who the police haven't been able to?'

Antoinette's brow puckers. '*We,*' she says. 'There are two of us. I know we can do this.'

I love her enthusiasm, even if I don't feel it myself.

I might be good at killing people but I don't seem to have a natural talent for finding them. I'm a murderer, not a detective.

'They're never going to catch him,' she's saying now. 'They won't even admit he exists. These women deserve justice, Kits.'

'I know,' I say again, but Antoinette is in full-flow rant mode.

'It's because they're adult creators,' she says as she paces the floor in the living room, looking like a caged wild creature. 'They see the word "PrivatePool" and they stop caring.' She stops pacing to look at me, her eyes big and imploring. 'Juno is the *fourth,* Kits, the fourth that we know of. How many more women have to die before the police think it's worth staying late at the office for?'

I know she's right.

If there was a serial killer targeting, I don't know, obnoxious tech bros or something, there would no doubt be a full-scale hunt for him. But because these women are selling their bodies, the police don't care. They probably think they were asking for it too.

I think of the news reports back in the UK about the systemic misogyny that's rampant in the Metropolitan Police. It's not too much of a stretch to assume that the police over here are the same. In the country where the phrase 'Your body, my choice' originated.

'Okay,' I say.

Antoinette blinks at me. 'Okay?' she says. 'As in okay, we're going to find him.'

'Well, I don't mean let's light a candle and manifest him,' I say.

She beams at me.

'Look, we can *try*,' I say. 'You're absolutely right. They haven't caught him because they're not looking for him. Because they don't care enough.'

'But we do,' she says in a voice that's barely above a whisper. 'We care about justice.'

I nod even though I'm not totally sure what I'm getting myself into here, what I'm promising. This isn't like the other men. Whoever this guy is, he's not an opportunistic date rapist. He's not an anonymous incel spewing his vile ideologies online. This man is a killer. He's someone who brutally murders women. Who plans it. Who enjoys it.

'Where do we start?' Antoinette asks.

'We start with what we know,' I say.

Antoinette slumps slightly, like some of the fight is already escaping her. 'But what *do* we know?' she says. 'The only thing we know is that he could be literally anyone.'

'That's not true,' I say. 'We know that he works in West Hollywood. We know that he targets a very specific type of woman. And we know that he likes to dump the bodies of his victims at the most famous places around here. So he's definitely got a flare for the theatrical. That's not nothing.'

'And we know that he's using PrivatePool as his hunting ground,' she says, that hard glimmer returning to her eyes.

'Exactly,' I say. 'We already know the type of woman he'll target next.'

'We can find him,' she says, buoyed up again.

'We can,' I agree. 'And when we do, we'll make sure he never hurts another woman again.'

Antoinette nods slowly, determined. 'I'm going to do some research now,' she says, picking up her iPad and swiping it on. 'Who needs sleep?'

27

KALE ME MAYBE JUICE BAR, SANTA MONICA BLVD, WEST HOLLYWOOD, LOS ANGELES

The next day, I leave Antoinette doing whatever she's doing on her iPad and I go off to meet Travis for a catch-up on how he's getting on with his hunt for Aidan Ward. I might have agreed to look for the WeHo Ripper but I can't lose sight of the reason I came here. Revenge.

Travis is sitting at the exact same table as he was the first time we met when I get to the juice bar.

He looks up when I walk in and gives me a big smile.

'Mary-Kate,' he says, his eyes twinkling in a way that should make me feel things. I don't. 'You're looking well.'

'Thank you,' I say as I pull out the chair opposite and flop down into it.

'Can I get you a drink?'

I look at the juice in front of Travis. It's green and looks like it's oozing with health. Like something I should definitely be drinking.

'I'll have one of what you're having,' I say. 'Whatever it is.'

'Kale and beetroot with added collagen,' Travis says with a megawatt smile. It sounds awful and it looks like he knows this.

'Great,' I lie.

Travis hops up and begins an easy conversation with the woman behind the bar who is so young and pretty that she probably bathes in this stuff as well as drinks it. She's the perfect advertisement for this place. Two minutes later he slides back into his seat.

'She'll bring it over,' he says.

'Can't wait.'

He gives me a look like he knows I'm lying but is amused by it.

'So,' I say, 'what have you found?'

Travis gives a quick nod and glances down at his laptop, as if he's activating business mode. 'Yes, of course, right,' he says and clears his throat with a little cough. 'A couple of things that I wanted to show you.' He reaches down and pulls a brown envelope out of the satchel at his feet. 'I've printed out a few pictures of men I thought could be potentials,' he says, handing me the envelope. I take it and slide the photos out, suddenly feeling like I'm in some old movie about a private detective. The envelope and actual tangible photos feel very retro.

'They're all British men who have arrived in LA in the past month,' Travis is saying. 'I tried to narrow it down to the, um, vague description you gave me. They're all in the right age bracket. I think. It's sort of hard to know out here.'

I run my fingers over the photos. There are about a dozen of them in total and I flip through them, poring over the images, which look like they've been taken with a long lens.

'How did you get these photos?' I ask. 'You know, without being spotted.'

Travis gives a one-shouldered shrug. 'I used to be a pap,' he says. 'You know, a paparazzi photographer. You get good at it.'

'Why did you stop?'

'Oh, you know, money. Work dried up the moment everyone had a camera and wifi connection in the palms of their hands.'

He takes a sip of his drink just as the server comes over with a glass, which she plonks unceremoniously in front of me. She gives me a cold stare but dials up warmth when she directs a smile towards Travis. I notice some of the green concoction has slopped onto the table and has made a little puddle under my glass.

'Is she always so friendly?' I ask Travis as the server slopes off.

He lowers his gaze, looks embarrassed. 'We dated for a bit,' he says.

'Ah that explains the service with a snarl,' I say. 'She thinks we've got something going on?'

'I might not have completely disclosed that you're a client,' Travis says, having the grace to look a bit sheepish. 'My bad. I'll put her straight.'

'No biggie,' I say. 'I'm not the one who has to clear up the drink she spilled. I suppose I should just be grateful it's not in my lap.'

Travis gives a nervous laugh. 'Sorry about that.'

I turn my attention back to the photographs in my hand and begin to sift through them. They're all men who look to be in their early thirties, wearing band T-shirts and glasses, that chaotic professor aesthetic thing that Aidan Ward had going on. They're in varying degrees of beardyness, all with messy, slightly too long hair. All *very* Aidan Ward coded. Yet none of them are him. My heart drops into my Saint Laurent

Tribute platforms. I wasn't really expecting Travis to have tracked him down already, not really.

But there was a tiny part of me that was hoping.

It really is the hope that kills you.

I shake my head and hand the photos back to Travis. 'No,' I say. 'None of those men are Aidan Ward.'

Travis gives a single nod. 'Sorry,' he says.

'That's okay, thank you for trying.'

He shrugs. 'No probs. It's literally my job. You want me to keep looking?'

'Of course,' I say. Travis isn't cheap but I've got very deep pockets and I'm more than prepared to keep paying until he finds him.

'Then I will.' He smiles and fiddles with a napkin on the table. 'Actually, there was something else I wanted to ask you.'

'Okay,' I say, intrigued. 'Go ahead.'

'Right, yes.' He clears his throat again. 'So, first of all I don't want you to get the idea that I do this kind of thing a lot. Because, obviously, you're a client and it's a bit creepy now I'm saying it out loud.'

This doesn't sound good.

Has Travis found out something?

Something about me?

Something I would really quite like to keep hidden?

Something like the number of dead men in my past?

But no, it couldn't be that, could it?

Surely he's not *that* good a detective. He'd have found Aidan Ward by now if he was.

And we wouldn't be sitting here making jokes over gross green juice if he *knew*.

Would he?

'Anyway,' he's saying now, 'I know it's unprofessional. But I looked on your socials and I saw that you're single. And, um, I was wondering if you'd like to go for a drink. With me. Obviously.'

Oh.

Well.

I suppose Antoinette did call this one.

'Oh,' I say.

His face falls and he gives an awkward laugh. 'I'll be honest, Kitty,' he says. 'That wasn't the response I was hoping for.'

I don't know what to say.

I mean, Travis is objectively hot and everything. I just don't want to go on a date with him.

I don't want to go on a date with anyone.

I only want Charlie.

'Sorry,' I say. 'I'm not really dating at the moment.'

He looks crestfallen. 'That's disappointing,' he says. 'Are you sure I can't persuade you?'

I shake my head. 'Sorry,' I say again, although it doesn't actually make any sense that I am apologising for saying no to a date I don't want to go on.

Why are women conditioned to be sorry for everything all the time?

'I've only recently broken up with someone and I'm just not looking for anything right now. It's nothing personal. Promise.'

Although it is quite personal.

He's not Charlie.

'Sorry to hear that,' he says. 'And sorry to put you in an awkward position.'

'It's fine,' I say. 'Don't worry about it. Gotta shoot your shot.'

He smiles and looks so handsome I almost change my mind. Almost. 'And you don't think I'm horribly unprofessional and creepy? I feel a bit creepy. Please don't put it on Yelp.'

I laugh.

He's cute and funny.

It's such a shame that I seem to have died inside.

'I promise,' I say as I gather up my things. 'Let me know when you've found anything about Aidan Ward.'

I swing my bag over my shoulder but as I do, it hits the glass of swamp-water, sending it flying. Travis yelps as the majority of it lands in his lap. I stare in horror as a puddle of green appears on the crotch of his cream chino shorts.

He jumps up.

'Oh my God, I'm so sorry,' I say, grabbing a handful of napkins and thrusting them at him.

'First you reject me and then you throw a drink at me,' Travis says, but he sounds more amused than annoyed. 'I think I get the message at this point.'

He takes the napkins from me.

'Sorry,' I murmur again. 'Do you need any help?'

He looks up at me. 'I think I've got this.'

The waitress is on her way over too with another wad of napkins. She gives me a glare, which I take as my cue to leave.

Outside, I look back in through the window. The waitress is dabbing at the stain on Travis's trousers and they're both laughing.

Any guilt about saying no to the date dissipates.

I think he'll be just fine.

28

KITTY AND ANTOINETTE'S AIRBNB, WEST HOLLYWOOD, LOS ANGELES

'Any wins?' Antoinette asks when I get back to the villa.

'No,' I say. 'Well, actually that's not strictly true. Travis asked me out.'

She gives me a smug little smile. 'I knew I was picking up on a vibe between you two! My instinct never lets me down. So? Spill.'

'Nothing to spill really,' I say. 'Unless you count the green juice that the waitress slammed in front of me.'

'I noticed her last time too,' Antoinette says. 'She was as green as the juice with envy.'

'Anyway, I said no.'

'Whyyyyyyyyy?' Antoinette asks me, somehow making the word have four syllables. 'Travis is cute. And funny and he's clearly super into you.'

I shift in my seat and shrug. 'I just don't feel like I'm in the right mindset to be dating anyone,' I say. 'And if he is "super into me" I'd be leading him on. It doesn't seem fair.'

Antoinette fixes me with one of her stares. One of the

ones that I've learned means some hard truths are about to follow.

I mentally brace myself.

'It's just a date, Kits, no one's suggesting you have to spend the rest of your life with the guy.' Her expression softens. 'Is this because of Charlie?'

I nod. 'It's too soon. I'm not even slightly near beginning to be over him.'

Antoinette gives me a sympathy face and sidles over to me. She touches my arm. 'That's why you want to get back to London so quickly, isn't it? You want to get him back.'

I nod again, suddenly mute.

My sister sighs heavily. 'Kits,' she says. 'This is going to be hard to hear, but know that I say this with love. Let him go. You have to let him go.'

'I can't.' The words come out thick and desperate. 'I just can't. I love him. And I know he loves me. That doesn't just disappear, Antoinette.'

She presses her lips together. 'Maybe not. But he's made it clear that he doesn't want any contact with you, Kits. You have to respect that. I know it's hard.'

How could she possibly know the depths of my heartbreak?

She's only twenty.

But she isn't much younger than I was when I met Adam.

And he totally fucked me up.

Maybe she's got a story of her own.

'Think about the date, Kits,' Antoinette is saying now. 'You might have fun,' she says. 'I know it's hard to believe. But you might. And it could even take your mind off Charlie. Even just for a night.'

'He's really not on my mind that much,' I lie.

Antoinette rolls her eyes. 'Kits,' she says sternly. 'How thick do you think these walls are? As if I don't hear you crying every night.'

Damn.

I thought I was doing that silently.

She tilts her head and considers me for a moment. 'Between Charlie and Aidan Ward, you are really letting men live rent free in your head.'

'And you're suggesting I add another one? Make it some sort of mental *ménage à trois*?'

She smiles. 'No, I'm suggesting you do something that takes your mind off the other two. Before you drive yourself insane.' She squeezes my arm again. 'Look at you. You're smart, beautiful and still quite young—'

'I'm thirty, Antoinette.'

'Exactly. You've still got a lot of your life ahead of you. You shouldn't be spending your nights crying over old text messages from your ex.'

How does she know that's what I've been doing?

'That's not—'

She waves my excuses away. Then her eyes light up and she claps her hands together.

I don't like this.

It means she's had an idea.

'Oh my God, Kitty,' she says, her voice rising several octaves. 'I've just had the best idea.'

Knew it.

'Why don't we go on a double date? You and Travis. Me and Agnes? It would be perfect. You can have a date without it feeling too date-y. And, if things go well, we can slip off and . . . you know . . . do our own thing. What do you think?'

What do I think?

I think it sounds nightmarish.

I think I'd rather spend an evening peeling off my hangnails and dipping my fingers in salt.

But Antoinette's face is pink with excitement. It's the only thing I've seen her excited about that doesn't involve doing unspeakably violent things to mildly offensive men. And she's clasping her hands together, almost begging me.

How can I say no?

'Fine,' I say. 'I'll do it. But on the condition that if it starts to feel awful at any point, we can leave.'

She gives a little squeal and throws her arms around me.

It's the most physical contact I've had with another human in weeks.

It actually feels nice.

'I'm going to go and tell Agnes right now,' she says. 'You text Travis and tell him you've changed your mind. Ask him if he's free tonight.' She squeals again. 'This is going to be so much fun! You're the best.'

And then she skips out of the door like Christmas is waiting for her outside.

I stare after her.

I don't remember the last time I was that excited about anything.

Anything apart from killing Aidan Ward.

What has my life become?

I pick up my phone and stare at it for a few seconds before I tap out a text to Travis.

Been thinking about what you said. Maybe a date would be fun. If you're happy to share it with Antoinette and her current love interest? Free tonight?

I sigh and open the message thread with Charlie. The thread I've protected like a newborn. I stare at the messages for a moment. They become blurry and I can taste the salt of my tears when I lick my lips. Before I can change my mind, I swipe and hit the little red bin icon that appears.

Gone.

Just like that.

The archive of our relationship.

Of course, I could always just restore them and I'm not feeling brave enough to delete them permanently.

But it's a step forward.

A positive one.

Because Antoinette is right.

I have to let him go.

It might kill me, but it's something I have to do.

'Set it free to get it back,' I whisper at my phone.

And, as if it's heard me, it lights up with a notification.

A text.

From Travis.

I am unbelievably glad you changed your mind, Kitty. Tonight is perfect. Message me the deets.

I stare at the words for a bit, my stomach in knots of anxiety and anticipation.

It's just a date.

What's the worst that could happen?

29

LAUREL HARDWARE, WEST HOLLYWOOD, LOS ANGELES

So the venue for the double date that I've been looking forward to as much as a root canal is actually a renovated hardware store. I thought this was quite fitting considering my penchant for duct tape and zip ties. It's actually pretty cool. The lighting is dim enough to hide my anxiety but golden enough to make me look like I'm glowing. It makes everyone look like they're glowing, actually. I don't think I've ever been anywhere with this amount of beautiful people. And that's really saying something considering the amount of time I've spent in places like Cannes, Mykonos and Marbella. The only complaint I have is that the chairs were clearly designed by someone who hates backs. I'm not going to voice this, however, as Antoinette would just use it as another opportunity to mention my ancient age. There's nothing quite like spending time with a twenty-year-old to make you feel like Methuselah's maiden aunt.

We're seated in a back patio area, which is shrouded with evergreen trees dressed in fairy lights. One thing about LA is it *loves* fairy lights. There's a slight warm breeze, which carries the smells of cooking food and a heady mix of different perfumes to our table in regular wafts.

Travis is looking almost outrageously handsome. He's wearing a khaki Henley shirt with black Levi's and smells of something expensive. I look at him, urging myself to feel something other than a general appreciation for his aesthetic pleasantry.

But there's nothing.

Not even the ghost of a fanny flutter.

What is wrong with me?

Am I broken?

What if I can never get it up for anyone apart from Charlie for the rest of my life?

I must look panicked because Antoinette kicks me under the table and mouths *be cool* at me.

I realise I've made a mistake.

Not the evening, because I'm actually having an okay time and Travis is good company. But by agreeing to be here with Antoinette and Agnes who are supposed to be keeping things chill.

They are not keeping things chill.

Not at all.

Antoinette has not stopped squealing at the décor. It's literally like she's never seen a fairy light before. Meanwhile, Agnes has taken her jacket off to reveal a top that would stop traffic on the King's Road.

Travis is being very good humoured about our date companions though. Even though Agnes keeps staring at him like he's something she's studying.

'I definitely recognise you,' she's saying for about the fifth time. 'Do you go to Beach Yoga SoCal?'

Travis shakes his head. 'I just have one of those faces,' he says. For the fifth time.

She points a finger at him. 'I'll figure it out,' she says. 'I never forget a face.'

'Kitty tells me you're studying at LAAA?' Travis says in a bid to change the subject from his recognisable face. I suppose it's not a great selling point for a PI. Agnes is drinking cocktails and has become a little bit full on.

'I am!' she says, delighted to talk about herself. 'Do you want to see my fake crying? I've been practising.'

'No,' I say at the same time that Antoinette says, 'Yes!'

Agnes beams at her and then immediately bursts into tears like she's auditioning for *Euphoria*. Like actual real tears.

I'm more impressed than I should be.

'Wow,' Antoinette says. 'That is amazing.' She's gushing. But it's cute. I like seeing her like this. Happy, not spikey.

'Thank you,' Agnes says. 'Actually. I've got some quite exciting news.'

'What?' Antoinette is all ears. And eyes.

'My agent called me earlier to say that Richard Stone has asked to see me for a casting!' She claps her hands together and Antoinette does the same.

'Richard Stone as in *the* Richard Stone?' Travis asks.

I look at all of them.

I am clearly the only one here who doesn't know who Richard Stone is or the significance of this agent call.

'He's a super-producer,' Travis explains to me under his breath. 'You'll have seen at least twenty of his movies, guaranteed.' He reels off a list of movies and, yes, I have indeed seen most of them.

'Wow, Agnes,' I say. 'That's amazing. Congratulations.'

'Thank you,' she beams. 'I'm really excited.'

'When is the meeting?' Antoinette asks.

'The day after tomorrow.'

'He's keen!' says Travis.

Agnes nods as she takes a sip of her margarita. 'My agent thinks it's a good sign.'

'Well, here's to you, Agnes,' Travis says and we all clink our glasses together.

After we've eaten, Agnes and Antoinette decide they're not ready for their night to end.

'We should go to The Abbey,' Agnes says. 'You can't say you've experienced WeHo nightlife without going there.'

Antoinette nods and looks over to me.

I can tell by the look in her eyes that she'd rather I *didn't* tag along for stage two of this date night.

'You go,' I say. 'I'm actually feeling quite tired. I'm going to call it a night.' I pat my stomach, which is full of pasta and broccolini. 'I think I should probably walk some of this food off anyway.'

'Can I walk you home?' Travis asks and I say yes because it's never a good idea to walk alone at night as a woman.

Even when you kill predatory men for fun.

Plus I'm way too full to have to activate vigilante mode.

'You two be careful,' I say to Antoinette and Agnes as they leave.

Antoinette rolls her eyes. 'We'll be fine,' she says. 'We don't have PrivatePool.'

And then they're gone, into the WeHo night.

Travis, gentleman that he is, helps me slip my cardigan on.

'Antoinette and Agnes are cute together,' he says. 'How long have they been dating?'

I laugh. 'Oh God,' I say. 'They've literally just met. Like a week ago.'

He raises his eyebrows, surprised. 'Wow. They're like they've known each other for ages.'

'I know,' I say. 'I'm surprised. Antoinette is usually much pricklier. Agnes brings out her softer side. It's nice.'

We're outside on the street now and Travis smiles at me. It's the sort of smile that should make me melt, but I still don't feel anything.

It's not fair.

Travis is gorgeous and sweet and funny.

I should be wanting to drag him home and rip his clothes off.

But all I can think about is Charlie.

How on my first date with him he gave me a Hello Kitty keyring that I still carry around with me.

How I'd thought it was super-tier cheesy, but it had charmed me anyway.

How we'd walked and walked and somehow ended up in a proper London boozer that was completely not the kind of place I would usually go to. But we'd ended up having the best time.

'Are you okay?' Travis says. 'You look melancholic all of a sudden.'

'Melancholic?' I say, teasing, trying to lighten my mood. 'Did you swallow a thesaurus before you came out?'

He thinks for a moment. 'Pretty sure it was just a plain old dictionary.'

This makes me laugh.

I need to stop thinking about Charlie.

We fall into a steady pace, but the silence is loud.

'What would you like to talk about, Mr Dictionary?' I say, hoping that easing Travis into conversation might stop me feeling so sad. He's lovely. I wish I could just enjoy his company.

'Tell me about London,' he says. 'What's it like living there?'

'That's a big question,' I say. 'Um . . . I've never lived anywhere else so it's just normal for me. But I love it.'

Outside it's still balmy but not so much that I don't need the cardigan I've brought. I wrap my arms around myself to keep warm.

'I'm glad you came tonight,' Travis says as we start walking towards the villa.

'Me too. I've enjoyed myself.' It's not a total lie.

'So, how long do you think you'll be sticking around for? Just, you know, a ball park.'

'As long as it takes,' I say and catch his questioning glance. 'To find that guy.'

'Not long then?'

I smile and shake my head. 'Probably not.'

'Well, in that case, I don't want to miss a moment.' He stops walking and turns to face me. 'May I kiss you?'

He's paused right under a streetlight and the beam is catching on his hair, making him look otherworldly handsome. Maybe him kissing me wouldn't be the worst thing in the world. Maybe his lips can somehow wash away the last parts of Charlie that are still lingering on my own. Maybe, like a fairytale prince, this man can help heal the parts of me that Charlie left broken.

I look up at him.

'You may.'

His lips touch mine and I wait for the miracle to happen. The romance-novel moment where my knees weaken and my pulse quickens and my memories of Charlie melt into nothing.

But that's not what happens.

That's not what happens at all.

Travis has me in his arms. They're not letting me go anywhere. They're gym-toned and strong.

My heart is beginning to quicken.

An alarm starts going off in my brain. No, not an alarm, a siren. The relentless screaming of an emergency phone alert. Danger to life.

Danger to life.

Those arms.

They're not letting me go anywhere.

They're not letting me go anywhere.

I pull away and Travis is smiling down at me. But it's not Travis's face anymore. It's a face that haunts my dreams, my nightmares.

A buzzcut and a sneer.

The man from the beach in Cannes.

Connor.

But I killed him.

How is he here?

Travis is still holding me tightly and I struggle in his arms. Those arms that aren't letting me go. That could hold me down and keep me there. The hands that could easily slip around my neck and squeeze my last breaths out of me. I'm breathing hard now and I need to escape. That's the only thing my brain can focus on. It knows I'm in danger and I need to run. My legs are buzzing with the need. I barely realise I'm doing it but my knee is rising and then it hits its target. He falls to the ground, holding his groin, looking up at me in confusion. But I don't have time to think about the man on the floor because *flight* has taken hold and I'm running and running and running.

30

KITTY AND ANTOINETTE'S AIRBNB, WEST HOLLYWOOD, LOS ANGELES

'You did *what?*' Antoinette and Agnes are staring at me like I've just confessed to drowning baby hamsters and enjoying it. They crashed through the door about half an hour ago, kissing and grabbing at each other, only stopping when they saw me, sitting on the sofa in the dark, a picture of abject mortification.

Now they've made me rose tea and I'm sitting, wrapped up in a blanket while I try to explain the terrible turn my date took after they left. Antoinette's eyes are as wide as saucers and Agnes has been pressing her lips together in an attempt not to laugh. She may be able to cry on demand but her serious-face acting needs some fucking work.

'I just don't understand,' Agnes is saying. 'He seemed such a sweetheart.'

Antoinette turns to her. 'He *is*,' she says. 'Kitty has PTSD that she's refusing to acknowledge. Even when it leads her to hoof some poor man in the baby makers for having the audacity to ask before he kisses her.'

'PTSD?' Agnes says. 'Why?'

Antoinette begins to explain to her what happened with Connor when I was drunk and heartbroken on that Cote d'Azur beach in the summer. How he forced himself on me when I decided I didn't want to be alone on a beach with him after all. When I sobered up enough to realise I'd only gone down there with him to stop the intrusive thoughts about Charlie, who I'd convinced myself was cheating on me. When I couldn't fight him off and thought he was going to rape me and then kill me.

She leaves out the part where I throttled him with a string bikini and dragged his body into the Med.

Thankfully.

I like Agnes but I don't think she could handle the full, unadulterated truth.

Not yet, anyway.

'Oh God,' Agnes says, clamping a hand to her mouth. 'Kitty, I am so sorry. How horrible for you. So it was what, like a flashback or something?'

Antoinette is nodding.

I guess that's exactly what it was.

'Have you thought about seeing someone?' Agnes asks. 'Like a therapist?'

Antoinette and I lock eyes.

'Yeah,' I say. 'I've tried out a few. None of them have been quite what I'm looking for.'

Agnes nods empathetically. 'It can take some time to find the right therapist.'

She's not fucking wrong.

'Poor Travis,' Antoinette says.

'Poor Travis,' I echo.

I've tried calling him and have sent him about a bazillion

texts apologising and trying to explain myself. But, so far, crickets. He could still be lying on the sidewalk, nursing his love stones for all I know.

'Jesus, what if I've damaged him for life?' I wail. 'What if he has to have a conversation with a future girlfriend about the possibility of them having kids being ruined by some unhinged British woman who kissed him then dealt him a death-blow to his danglies?'

Agnes is no longer able to hold her laughter in. She erupts in giggles, doubled-over, holding her chest. After a couple of moments she rises again, only to catch Antoinette's eye. And then the pair of them are at it, cackling away like a couple of junior witches in an unruly coven.

'It's not funny,' I say, but a laugh is already sneaking out of me. 'I assaulted him. For literally nothing. I'm so embarrassed.'

'He'll get over it,' Antoinette says. Then she adds darkly. 'Women have to.'

Agnes nods in solidarity.

Then she looks at her Apple Watch. 'Oh it's late,' she says. 'I'd better get home. I need to spend tomorrow preparing for my meeting with Richard Stone. I don't even know what I'm going to wear.'

'I could come over and help you choose?' Antoinette says and Agnes kisses her on the mouth.

'That would be great. I'll text you.' She looks at me. 'You'd both better go to bed too,' she says. 'Antoinette's got a surprise for you in the morning.'

My sister bats her lashes angelically.

I narrow my eyes at her.

I hate surprises.

How doesn't she know this about me?

31

THE SOLSTICE STUDIO ROOFTOP, WEST HOLLYWOOD, LOS ANGELES

Why are all Antoinette's surprises early mornings and exercise?

Why did I tell her that I enjoy them?

This is why you should never lie. Even a white one will come back and bite you on the arse.

Before the sun is even up.

I am not designed for early mornings. I am designed for waking up late morning, having a leisurely brunch and several vats of coffee before my day starts.

Mornings that begin at 5.45am have never been part of my life, so when Antoinette barged into my room at that god-forsaken hour earlier, demanding I get up, I may have thrown a few expletives her way. When I pulled the covers over my head, she pulled them back down and threw a few expletives of her own at me.

I do want to bond with her though.

So I pretend that I actually *do* like surprises. Love them. Nothing better, to me, than being dragged somewhere and you have absolutely no idea what or where it is.

That's why I'm here now, on the rooftop of some hyper-trendy wellness centre, trying to hold a plank.

And I say 'trying' because I am struggling.

My head is swimming and my abs are screaming at me like they're auditioning for *Real Housewives of Beverly Hills*. Once again, I'm confused as to how I'm so unfit. I suppose I've let thing slip a little this year. I had a personal trainer four times a week in London so I suppose it's not that crazy that I can now barely hold a plank without feeling bone-aching fatigue.

I don't want to look at all the lithe young things who are doubtless planking without breaking even a bead of sweat but I can't help myself. They all look like they eat kale for every meal.

The instructor is called Sage – because of course she is – and has been throwing side-eyes at me that land like knives.

'Just flow with your breath,' she says, placing a hand on my back that threatens to destabilise me completely.

My breath is currently *not* flowing.

In fact it's doing the exact opposite and coming out in short, staccato bursts.

I'd tell her exactly what she can do with her namaste if I could speak.

I catch Antoinette's eye and she looks like she's trying not to laugh.

'And now, glide into downward dog,' Sage says, and I contort rather than glide, my arms and legs shaking. 'Trust your inner strength.'

My inner strength is still in bed at the villa.

I sneak another glance at my sister, who is in a perfectly inverted V and barely breaking a sweat.

For the tiniest flicker of a moment, I despise her.

It feels like months before Sage guides us into corpse pose and I am free to lie on the ground and pant.

But at least I can see the sun rising over the LA skyline, turning everything in its path into the most delicious shades of apricot.

'That was awesome,' Antoinette says when Sage finally releases us from her rooftop jail. She is glowing. Literally glowing. I feel like a recently released prisoner of war.

'I think I may have died,' I say. 'It's possible you're speaking to my ghost.'

Antoinette laughs. 'You need to exercise more,' she says. 'Don't women your age start getting like osteoporosis or something?'

I glare at her. 'I'm not *menopausal*, Antoinette. I'm just a bit out of shape. That's all.'

'Sure, sis,' she says.

'I'm only thirty, for God's sake!'

'You're from last *century*,' she says.

'I'm going to join a gym,' I say.

She snorts. 'You need a repair café.'

I scowl all the way home.

Antoinette doesn't stop mocking me until she disappears into the shower. 'Maybe we should have found a place with one of those alarms,' she says as a parting shot. 'Just in case you have a fall when I'm out.'

I throw a cushion at her, having to disguise the wince as the movement sends a shooting pain through my protesting muscles.

I need to do something about this.

I pick up my phone and type 'West Hollywood gyms' into Google.

The screen is instantly filled with gym suggestions. Every type of gym you can imagine from yoga studios to bounce classes. There are boxing gyms with neon lights and outdoor Pilates sessions.

Then I notice an ad.

It's for a brand-new gym called Flexual Healing.

I chuckle at the name as I click on the link, which takes me through to the gym's Instagram page.

They've only posted a handful of photos so far but it looks like exactly the kind of torture chamber that Antoinette would drag me to.

I scroll through the pictures.

And then one catches my eye.

It's a group shot, a mix of people caught mid-class through a mirror, all solid abs and high-on-endorphins smiles, posted yesterday.

It's one of the people that makes me pinch the screen and zoom in. Dirty-blond hair, a patchy beard, a band T-shirt that stands out because everyone else is in designer sportswear.

The image is grainy, his head is turned slightly away and the lighting is terrible.

But.

Could it be?

I zoom in even more.

And then I'm certain who I'm looking at.

It's him.

It's Aidan Ward.

32

KITTY AND ANTOINETTE'S AIRBNB, WEST HOLLYWOOD, LOS ANGELES

'Antoinette,' I yell as I run up the stairs, clutching my phone like it's the most precious thing to me in the world. Which, I suppose, at this moment, it is. 'Antoinette!' I pound on her bathroom door. 'ANTOINETTE!'

Two minutes later she emerges, water from her hair dripping on the floor.

'What?' she says. 'What's happened? Is it your hip?'

I ignore her comment and thrust my phone into her hands.

'Look,' I say.

She squints at the screen. 'I thought there was a fire or something,' she says. 'What am I looking at? Gym selfies? CrossFit bros?'

'It's him,' I say and point at the figure. 'It's Aidan Ward.'

Her eyes widen and her lips twist into a smile. 'Are you sure?'

I nod. 'One hundred per cent.'

'Well,' she says, 'it looks like we're going to Flexual Healing.'

'We are,' I say. 'We absolutely fucking are.'

33

KITTY'S HIRE CAR, OUTSIDE FLEXUAL HEALING CROSSFIT GYM, LA BREA, LOS ANGELES

First of all we *had* to hire a car.

Apparently an on-foot observation mission is out of the question.

'I've seen the movies,' Antoinette said. 'Cars are the best cover for a stake-out.'

So we headed into town and I am now the proud temporary driver of a black SUV with blacked-out windows.

It looks like something we could be running a meth lab from.

Oddly, it's quite inconspicuous in LA.

Antoinette has somehow managed to procure a pair of binoculars too.

I don't ask for details.

For all I know, she's had them on her this whole time, just waiting for this moment.

We've been waiting in the car for hours. Well, it's actually been about forty-five minutes but it feels like hours. Antoinette's getting restless, clicking her nails on the dashboard, sighing loudly, fidgeting. I can feel my jaw tightening with every second that passes. The hire car is hot. It smells like the previous occupants, who were clearly weed smokers. The AC is running but all it's really doing is blowing the smell around the car.

'What if there's another exit?' Antoinette asks for the fiftieth time. 'I wish we'd brought snacks.' I'm glad we didn't because I don't think I could handle the sound of her chewing on top of all her relentless complaining.

This girl can bring on misophonia in anyone.

'There isn't,' I say. 'I told you that I checked. Several times.' The gym, which is actually just a sort of windowless concrete box with a chain-link fence around it, is in the middle of an asphalt parking lot where we are currently situated. It looks more like a serial killer's storage unit than a gym.

I'd imagine.

There's one way in and one way out for anyone who isn't staff and we are perfectly located to spot Aidan Ward if he comes.

'Be patient,' I tell my sister. 'We need to give it more time.'

People have been drifting in and out the whole time we've been waiting here. Mostly men whom I'd describe as soft-core gym bros in washed-out muscle tanks and Nike trainers. They all look exactly the same. Like the gym is actually some sort of factory that is pumping them out. I feel my eyes beginning to glaze over and they all merge into one.

Fuck, I'm tired.

I blame the early-morning yoga session.

I'm tempted to close my eyes and take a power nap when Antoinette starts urgently tapping my arm and pointing.

‘Kitty, over there!’ I squint at what she’s looking at. A man is walking out of the door of the gym. He’s in conversation with one of the few women I’ve seen since we arrived. He holds the door open for her and then says something that makes her laugh. We’re not super close but I can tell right away it’s him. The mannerisms, the slight stoop – you’d think he’d find himself a decent chiropractor out here to sort that out – and his signature shitty band T-shirt, which sticks out like a screamingly sore thumb among the muscle-vests.

It’s him.

There’s no question.

The man who broke my best friend. Who made her believe he loved her, then beat her half to death.

It’s him.

And he’s rebuilding and rebranding himself over here in LA with an all-access pass to a fresh crop of vulnerable young women.

I feel a wave of anger and hatred bubble up from my core. It’s so intense I almost choke on it.

He’s tanned now and his hair is longer than I remember. He looks for all the world like he belongs here. Like he doesn’t belong in a fucking shallow grave. I watch as he says something to the girl. She laughs again and he puts his hand on her shoulder. It makes me shudder. Over-familiar. Creepy. My jaw clenches even tighter.

‘That’s him, isn’t it?’ Antoinette whispers.

‘Oh yes,’ I say. ‘That’s him all right.’

He turns now, faces us. The sunlight catches his face and there is no doubt. I’d recognise those eyes anywhere.

Cold as steel.

He's staring directly at us and I worry for a minute that he can see me. But then I remember the blacked-out windows, which every car in LA has because of the blazing sun.

He can't see me.

But I can see him.

I can see him right through to his bones.

I can feel how fast I'm breathing, how quickly my heart has started beating.

I don't think I've ever looked forward to killing someone as much as I have this man.

We watch as he gets into a car, a battered VW, parked not too far from us.

'What now?' Antoinette asks, watching through her binoculars as he drives away.

'Now,' I say. 'You're about to become the newest member of Flexual Healing CrossFit Gym.'

34

FLEXUAL HEALING CROSSFIT GYM, LA BREA, LOS ANGELES

'I've never belonged to a gym before,' Antoinette tells me as we walk from the car into the building. 'I've always had personal trainers. Mummy insisted on it. It's actually quite exciting.' But her face falls when we get inside and she realises it's not the kind of high-end health club she was expecting. It's not a 'juice bar and spa' kind of place, more like a fight club. 'It's giving dungeon,' Antoinette mutters as we approach the brushed-steel reception desk. There's a flickering neon sign behind it, saying, 'Now get flexed.'

'Welcome to Flexual Healing,' the guy at the desk says, barely looking up from his phone. Even though his face stays at a forty-five-degree angle I can make out at least three piercings and a face tattoo. 'Help you?' He looks up now and takes us in, not bothering to hide his disdain. I suppose we don't really look the part in our brightly coloured Live the Process bodysuits.

I nudge Antoinette towards the desk.

'We're looking to sign up!' she says in a voice as bright as our out-of-place gym wear.

The desk gremlin scowls. He's like the antithesis of LA wellness and good vibes.

'CrossFit?' he asks, the words coming out long and slow. 'Have you done it before? Because this isn't really a beginner's place.'

'Of course,' I say brightly. 'We do it all the time back home. Every day.' An image of me panting as I struggle to hold a plank for more than three seconds in this morning's yoga class pings into my head. I shake it away.

His eyebrow shoots up. It's pierced and possibly a little bit septic. 'Every day?'

We nod enthusiastically.

'Sometimes twice,' Antoinette says and I nudge her again because she's laying it on a bit *too* thick.

The desk goblin presses something in his ear. An earpiece. 'Zane. I've got two British girls at front desk who want to join. They're wearing pink. But they CrossFit every day back home.' There's a ghost of a smirk on his face. 'Zane will be with you in a minute.'

We stand awkwardly and the desk monkey turns his attention back to his phone without even another look in our direction. We have simply ceased to exist to him.

'Kitty,' Antoinette says quietly as we wait for Zane. 'You don't have to do this class, you know.'

I glare at her. 'Um. What do you mean?'

'It's just,' she fiddles with her fingers, avoiding my eyes, 'you were sort of struggling a bit with yoga this morning.'

'I was not!' I say. 'It was fine. It was just very, very early.'

'No shame,' Antoinette says. 'I'm just saying that maybe you could sit this one out. If you felt like it.'

'I do not feel like it,' I snap. 'I can cope with an exercise class.'

'Okay then. If you're sure . . .'

I don't like the way she tails off. 'I am.'

'Hi, ladies, I hear you'd like to join us here at Flexual Healing,' a voice suddenly booms, echoing around the reception area. It's followed by the appearance of a man who I assume must be Zane. He's wearing a sweat-stained T-shirt with the words 'WOD Warrior' on it, shorts that are so short they're borderline obscene and a beard that looks like it takes longer to style than my actual hair. His arms are tattooed and *big*. 'Indigo here tells me that you're CrossFit pros from the UK?' The desk troll gives us a sardonic smile.

Of *course* he's called Indigo.

I'm beginning to wonder if overplaying our CrossFit prowess may have been a mistake.

But Antoinette is not backing down.

'Yes,' she's saying, giving me a barely noticeable side-eye, 'we absolutely love it. We love it so much that we just had to find somewhere out here.'

Zane is nodding. 'That's great,' he says. 'In fact, I'm just about to start a session. Why don't you come and join in? I can see you're dressed for it.' He turns and walks through a door that I fear will lead to this 'session'. Antoinette gamely trots along behind him. It seems there's nothing for me to do apart from follow too. It feels like I'm heading to the gallows.

I swear I hear *Indigo* on reception laugh.

One hour later and I think I'm about to die. It hurts to breathe. It hurts to stand. It hurts to exist. I think my bones have all turned to liquid and I have no idea how I'm going to drive home. There don't seem to be any messages being relayed from my brain to my legs.

'That was great!' Antoinette is saying, unaware of my imminent death. 'What a buzz. I feel so strong.' How nice it must be to be twenty years old and have muscles that don't scream at you when you try to utilise them.

'Great class, Antoinette,' Zane is saying, visibly impressed with my sister. He looks at me. 'And Kitty. Well, that was . . . something.'

It was.

Something awful.

He walks – well, *he* walks, I sort of waddle – us back through to the reception, where Indigo gives Antoinette a look of respect and me one of pity.

'Are you going to sign up?' Indigo asks my sister with more animation in his voice than I've heard.

'Yes!' she says. 'I loved it. Best feeling ever.'

Indigo passes an iPad to her and points out the sections she needs to click on to be a fully signed-up member of this cult.

'I don't think I'm going to,' I say.

Indigo gives me a hard look. 'I didn't ask you.'

Ouch.

I think I've just been rejected from Flexual Healing.

35

KITTY AND ANTOINETTE'S AIRBNB, WEST HOLLYWOOD, LOS ANGELES

'Are you sure you're going to be okay?' I ask Antoinette the next morning. She's getting ready to head back to Flexual Healing, where she's going to hang out until Aidan Ward turns up again. Which won't be long, judging by his new physique. And when he does, she's going to use her feminine wiles to lure him back here. And . . . well . . . that's when I get to have my turn with him. The only thing is I'm starting to worry that using her as bait is stupid and dangerous. This is a man who attacked a woman so viciously that we almost didn't think Tor would pull through. Am I a monster for asking my sister to put herself in a potentially dangerous position?

'I'm fine,' she says as she pulls her hair up into a ponytail and checks her make-up in the mirror in her room. I'm sitting on her bed watching her, anxiety doing backflips in my gut.

'Because I could just come and wait in the car, just in case anything goes wrong.'

Antoinette meets my gaze in the mirror. 'Kitty, I'll be

fine,' she says. 'He's not going to do anything to me in broad daylight, surrounded by witnesses. CrossFit bro witnesses.'

'I know, but he's a monster.'

'Besides, you need to get everything ready here, don't you? So we can end that monster once and for all.'

She's right, of course. There's a *lot* of preparation to be done here. I need to turn the wine cellar into the perfect torture and murder den. I have to go and source tarpaulin, cable ties, duct tape, bin bags, lye, scented candles. I'm not planning on letting Aidan Ward off the hook with a quick and easy death either. I want to make sure he suffers to the absolute max. Like how he made Tor suffer. I want the last moments of his life to be filled with fear and pain. I want to see the look in his eyes when he knows he's going to suffer horribly. I also need to do some research on torture. It's not really been something I've dabbled in too much before, usually preferring a quick kill. I'm making a special exception for Aidan Ward.

'Just make sure you stay in touch with me at all times,' I say. 'I couldn't bear it if anything happened to you.'

'I'd be in more danger if he knew I was anything to do with you,' Antoinette says. 'Imagine if he saw you in the parking lot or something. You'd be putting us both in danger.'

I sigh. She's got a point. I'm just so nervous.

'How do I look?' She's finished with her hair and make-up and has turned around to face me. She looks perfect. She's wearing a gym onesie in a pastel blue that makes her eyes pop and her skin glow. It hugs her figure in all the right places. There's no way Aidan will be able to resist. There's a steeliness in her gaze and I feel my anxiety ebb away. Antoinette is not a lamb to the slaughter. She's the one holding the taser and axe.

'You look amazing,' I say.

'I second that,' says another voice. It's Agnes, who has just poked her head around the door. We really need to start locking that back door. We've still got Ron Wilde in a suitcase in the cellar, for God's sake. 'I still think it's hilarious that everyone in LA treats the gym like a catwalk,' she's saying. 'Are you going to film some content?'

Antoinette gives a noncommittal shrug as Agnes walks fully into the room. She also looks absolutely stunning. She's wearing a long white boho skirt with dark brown cowboy boots and a black baby tee. Her blonde hair is falling in loose waves almost down to her waist.

'Aggy!' Antoinette squeals. 'That fit is such a slay. You look amazing.'

Agnes beams.

Of course, it's her big brunch meeting with Richard Stone today.

'Thank you,' she says with a blush.

'How are you feeling?' I ask her.

'So nervous, but you know, nerves are a good thing. They're good for focus.'

I internalise this, ready to repeat it back to my anxiety if it makes another appearance today.

'You'll absolutely smash it,' Antoinette is saying. 'How could you not? I bet he offers you a part in his new superhero movie on the spot.'

Agnes laughs. 'Well, that would be nice. But honestly, just having the chance to meet him and grill him for tips and advice is such a great opportunity.' She glances at her Apple Watch. 'Anyway, I'd better get going. Lauren's going to give me a lift into the Hills. I'll see you guys later. Have fun at the gym!'

'Oh I will,' Antoinette says. 'And good luck. Come over when you're back.'

I glare at her.

I'm hoping to have Aidan Ward here later today. We can't have Agnes dropping in unannounced. She just rolls her eyes at me.

'Antoinette,' I say when Agnes has left. 'Do you want us to get caught?'

She frowns at me. 'Don't be silly,' she says. 'Agnes is cool.'

'Not sure how cool she'd be knowing we're murdering a man in her parents' rental,' I grumble.

Antoinette laughs. 'You're so serious, Kits,' she says. 'It's such a shame things didn't work out with Travis. You're really becoming quite uptight. I think you could do with some sex.' I'm about to snap back at her but her phone buzzes. 'That's my Lyft,' she says. 'Wish me luck.'

'Good luck,' I say. 'And please, please, please make sure you keep in contact. And let me know right away if anything creepy happens. I need to know you're safe.'

'I'll be fine,' she says. 'Don't worry. Soon we'll have dealt with Aidan Ward and we can focus on the WeHo Ripper.'

'But—'

I don't get to finish my sentence though because Antoinette breezes past me and down the stairs.

Please let her be okay.

36

NAILED IT HARDWARE STORE, WEST HOLLYWOOD, LOS ANGELES

While Antoinette is off at Flexual Healing, I've come to a local hardware store to get some supplies for our new guest's imminent arrival.

I'd be a really terrible host if I didn't get some special things in for his stay with us.

Now, really, what I should be doing is splitting these purchases up over a number of different stores because it looks extremely shady and very serial killer coded buying duct tape, zip ties and tarpaulin all in one place. But this is Hollywood, if anyone raises a suspicious eyebrow at me, I can just say I'm working on a movie and the producer has sent me to buy some props.

I've filled my basket with all the essentials and am just deciding whether to buy extra duct tape – you can never have too much of the stuff – when I feel a tap on my shoulder.

I turn around and am greeted by a face I kind of recognise but I'm not sure where from.

I'm trying to place it when the face speaks to me.

'Kitty,' it says. 'I thought it was you.'

I stare at the man in front of me for a full minute before I recognise him.

'Cort!' I say. 'I'm so sorry, I'm in another world today.' This isn't entirely true. I couldn't place him because he isn't sporting his man-bun. Instead his dark tresses are swooshing around his shoulders like something out of a prestige shampoo commercial.

I'm actually very envious of the shine on his hair.

It looks almost laminated.

I wonder if he glosses.

Would it be rude to ask which one he uses?

'What are you doing here?' he asks, peering into my basket. 'It's not the kind of place tourists usually come to.' He looks into my basket again. 'Is there something wrong over at the villa? You just need to speak to Agnes about that. She'll call her parents to sort it. You don't need to do it yourself.' His tone very much suggests that he wants to add, 'silly girl' at the end but can't. Because feminist man.

I look into my basket as well.

It *does* look very Serial Killer Starter Kit and I can't use the movie assistant line on Cort. He knows full well I'm not working on a movie.

'No,' I say. 'It's um . . . art. It's for my art.'

Cort's brow puckers slightly. 'Art?' he says. 'I didn't know you were an artist, Kitty.'

'Oh, I'm not, not really,' I say. 'Well, not seriously, I should say. It's just something I like to do in my spare time.'

He looks at my haul yet again.

Jesus Christ, does the man have no concept of privacy?

Then again, I can tell he's the sort of man who would stop me in a drugstore buying tampons and have a full conversation with me about my flow.

'Art,' he says again. 'I'd love to see some of it sometime. I'm intrigued as to what sort of art you do with . . . duct tape and . . . are those zip ties?'

I smile and try to flutter my eyelashes at him. 'It's very modern stuff,' I say. 'Sculpture. Like installation art.' I have no actual idea what the words I'm saying mean. I'm just hoping Cort isn't secretly an avant garde art buff who'll easily catch me out in my lies. 'I'm very amateur,' I add, just in case.

'Right,' he says, nodding. 'I don't know much about that sort of thing. Bananas taped to walls and exploding paintings. To my shame. I can just about identify a Banksy and that's it.' He says 'Banksy' in a faux British accent that makes me cringe into myself.

'What are you doing here?' I ask, desperate to change the subject before he starts grilling me more about my 'art'. One thing that can always be counted on with men is that they love the opportunity to talk about themselves.

They can't resist.

Even the 'feminist' ones.

I peer into the basket Cort is carrying but it's completely empty.

'Oh,' he says, looking at the nothing he is carrying too. 'I'm just running a few errands for Lauren. There's some stuff over at the guesthouse that she needs fixing. Think it's a leaky pipe. Agnes's parents don't tend to extend their hosting responsibilities to the girls so I end up doing a lot of their DIY for them.' He points at the wall of duct tape we're standing in front of.

'That seems unfair,' I say but Cort just shrugs.

'I mean, I don't believe in gender roles, but if it makes Lauren feel supported then I'm more than happy to pick up a drill. Or a roll of Gorilla Grip.'

I meant it didn't seem fair that Agnes's parents only fix up problems in the main house but I don't correct him. I actually want to get out of this conversation – and store – as quickly as possible now.

'That's great,' I say.

I try to step away from him to get to the till, but Cort steps the same way. Then I step the other way and he does too. And now we're doing some weird no-contact waltz in the duct tape aisle.

'You know,' he says, not reading the social cues and trying to carry on the conversation. 'Lauren's always saying that we should do more cultural stuff. Maybe we should all go to an exhibition together sometime?'

'Sure,' I say noncommittally. How did I get from staying at the most discreet hotel in Hollywood to ending up somewhere where my roommate's *boyfriend* is trying to bond with me?

This was very much not the plan.

His gaze lands on my basket *again* and sweat is starting to prickle my underarms. I need to get out of here. 'It's cool you make things,' he says, putting his hands over his heart. 'I think it's so important to have a creative outlet for our emotions. I find working with my hands very grounding.'

'Yes,' I say in agreement.

It will be very grounding, what I'm planning to do to Aidan Ward with my hands later.

I really *do* enjoy my creative emotional outlet.

'I actually make my own jewellery sometimes,' he says. Of *course* he does. 'I find the use of crystals and the physicality of threading beads very meditative.'

I take a pointed look at his empty basket. 'I suppose you should be getting on then.'

'Yes,' he says, casting a glance at the different brands of tape. 'I suppose I should.' He looks around. 'Actually, I think I might leave it for now,' he says and puts his basket down on the floor. 'I've just remembered that I need to plan a sound bath immersion experience for later tonight.' He does that funny little pray-bow thing and gives me a smile. 'Good to see you,' he says. 'I'll catch you later.'

And then he disappears down the aisle and out of the store.

Well.

That was bizarre.

I stare after him but then I hear someone clear their throat behind me.

'Help you with anything?'

I turn around and it's a store assistant with a badge saying 'happy to help' pinned to his chest. And he actually *does* look happy to help, not like he'd rather be vaping and texting round the back of the shop like retail staff in the UK.

'No thanks,' I say. 'I'm good.'

'Cool,' he says. 'We've got heavy-duty tarps on sale if you want them. Buy one get one free?'

That sounds like a good idea.

I let him lead me to the tarps and pick up two.

Because you just never know.

37

KITTY AND ANTOINETTE'S AIRBNB, WEST HOLLYWOOD, LOS ANGELES

Where is she?

Where is she? *Where is she?*

I check my phone again but there's still nothing from Antoinette. I try to call her and it goes straight to voicemail. Again. I open Find My Friends but it tells me she's still offline. I check the time. It's half past five. She should be back by now.

I don't know what to do.

I'm about to head to the guesthouse and ask Agnes if she's heard anything when I hear a key in the door. And Antoinette's voice rings out through the downstairs.

'This is where I'm staying, Aidan,' she says loudly. 'I think we have the place all to ourselves.'

Aidan.

She's done it.

She's only fucking done it.

I'll have a word with her later about her terrible interpretation of 'make sure you keep in touch' but right now I could kiss her.

Aidan Ward is here.

In our house.

And then he's in our kitchen and we are face to face.

Finally.

The moment I've been waiting for.

My heart quickens and a thrill skates down my spine.

LA suits him, that much is clear. He's lightly tanned and looks relaxed. Well, in the split second before he realises who he's looking at.

'What the—?' The colour drains from his face. Every drop of it.

'Hi, Aidan,' I say. 'Fancy seeing you here.'

He spins around to Antoinette, who is standing behind him, blocking his escape.

'This is my sister Kitty,' she says with a too-sweet smile. 'Kitty, look, I made a new friend.'

Aidan spins back around and stares at me again. His eyes narrow.

'I've been looking for you,' I say. 'We've got some unfinished business, haven't we?'

'I don't know what the fuck you're playing at but no, no, we don't.' He turns again and tries to walk past Antoinette but she sidesteps him and blocks his path.

'I don't think so,' she says.

Aidan lets out a roar of anger and grabs my sister, trying to shove her out of the way. She stumbles and he almost gets past her.

But I'm quicker and, before he can make it out of the kitchen, I slam the coffee machine against his head and he falls to the ground at Antoinette's feet. We both watch as a trickle of blood snakes across the floor.

'Is he dead?' Antoinette asks. 'Already?'

I shake my head. 'I doubt it.' But I drop down next to him and put my fingers to the pulse point in his neck just in case. I feel a throb against my flesh. 'Not dead,' I confirm. 'Just out cold.'

She beams at me. 'Yay.'

'No, Antoinette,' I say. 'Not yay. What the fuck?'

She looks at me puzzled. 'Aren't you happy?'

'I'm happy that you've found him,' I say. 'Less so that you've been completely radio silent for the past two hours. I've been worried.'

'Oh yeah, that,' she says. 'Sorry, my battery died. I forgot to leave it in to charge last night and then I was just waiting around at the gym so I was playing games on it and it died.' She gives a little shrug like it's no big deal, like I haven't been here picturing the worst things in the world happening to her.

'For God's sake, Antoinette,' I start to say but am interrupted by a groan from Aidan. He can't be coming to already, surely? I grab some cable ties from where I left them on the table and hand some to Antoinette. 'You do his wrists,' I say. 'Use a few and make sure they're tight.' She nods and I loop two ties around his ankles, pulling them so tight they cut into his skin. That will hurt when he comes round fully.

Good.

I slap some duct tape over his mouth because he'll probably scream when he regains consciousness and, although the sound would be like the sweetest music to my ears, the walls here aren't the thickest. Then we stand up and admire our work when the back door rattles.

'Antoinette? Kitty?'

It's Agnes.

Antoinette and I stare at each other and then at Aidan hogtied on our kitchen floor.

Thank fuck I remembered to lock that door.

'Shhh,' I say to Antoinette. 'She might think we're out and go away.'

I can tell Antoinette doesn't approve of this plan and she's about to say something when Agnes wails through the door. 'Please answer the door, please.' She's crying. She sounds really distressed.

'Something's wrong,' Antoinette says. 'I have to let her in.'

Urgh.

Not now.

This is the moment I've been waiting for.

'Help me get Aidan into the cellar first,' I hiss.

'Two seconds,' Antoinette calls through to Agnes. 'I'm just coming.'

We grab his feet and heave him through the door before dragging him backwards down the steps, his head making a pleasing little cracking sound as it hits each one. Then, before I can say anything, Antoinette is racing back into the kitchen to let Agnes in.

'I guess you can't get into any trouble down here,' I say to Aidan's prone body before I follow Antoinette back up the steps.

When I get into the kitchen, Antoinette has already let Agnes in and she's sitting at the table, her head in her hands. My sister is sitting next to her, her arms wrapped around Agnes, who is sobbing.

Antoinette looks up at me, her eyes wide.

'Something's happened,' she says. 'Something bad.'

38

KITTY AND ANTOINETTE'S AIRBNB, WEST HOLLYWOOD, LOS ANGELES

'What is it?' I say as Antoinette pulls Agnes in closer to her. 'Agnes?'

Agnes looks up at me. She looks wretched. Her eyes are all red and swollen and I notice she's trembling. 'Agnes?'

She lets out a whimper. 'I don't want to say. It's humiliating.'

I pull up a chair on the other side of her. 'Agnes, please tell us. Let us help you.'

Agnes wipes her nose. 'It's too horrible,' she says.

'What is?'

She takes a deep, shaky breath. 'I thought we'd moved on from this sort of thing. As like, an industry and as a place,' she says eventually.

Oh no.

No.

It was her audition today.

Please no.

'The producer?' I say and Agnes nods. 'What did he do?'

She looks at me, eyes full of shame.

'I really thought he was interested in my tape. In me,' she says sadly. 'But they're still doing it. They're still getting away with it.'

'Tell us,' Antoinette says, so quietly I can barely hear her.

'It was just us,' Agnes says. 'At his house. At the brunch. No other actors. And I shouldn't have been so stupid. I should've known something wasn't right because who even does that? Who willingly goes into a house with a man, alone?' She looks at me again. 'What was the fucking point of #MeToo if it's still happening?'

'It's not your fault,' I say. 'Whatever he did, Agnes, it's not your fault.'

'It is,' she sniffs. 'I was stupid and naive.'

'No,' says Antoinette. 'Did he—?'

Agnes shakes her head vehemently. 'No, but he touched me. He groped my boobs. Put his hand up my top and tried to kiss me, tried to touch me under my skirt. It was horrible, his hands were everywhere and I didn't think he was going to stop.' She lets out an anguished wail. 'And he made it clear that if I sucked his dick he'd give me a role in a movie. And that if I didn't, he'd make sure I never ever got a role. He said he would make sure I ended back at home with my parents and that he'd get me kicked out of school.' She takes another deep and shuddering breath. 'I tried to run out but he'd locked the door and I just started crying and crying. He just laughed at me. Told me not to be such a pathetic baby. Then he unlocked the door. He didn't say another word to me. Didn't even look at me.' She sniffs and wipes her nose with the back of her hand. 'He'll tell my agent some fucked-up version of events and that will be that. No one will touch me.'

'Oh, Agnes!' Antoinette pulls her closer into her chest and lets her cry it out.

That piece of shit.

That fucking piece of shit.

Antoinette locks eyes with me. Her expression is cold as steel. I know exactly what she's thinking. And I'm thinking it too.

There's no way we're going to let Richard Stone get away with this.

We walk Agnes back over to the guesthouse after she's calmed down a bit. She's told us that she doesn't want to go to the police, that she doesn't see the point.

'It's his word against mine,' she'd said miserably. 'And who's going to believe me, a nobody, over one of the biggest producers in Hollywood? He's obviously got away with it before.'

And she's right.

But there's another type of justice heading Richard Stone's way.

'Thanks, you two,' she says to me and Antoinette. 'I think I just want to go to sleep now. I want to forget about today.'

'I'll stay with you?' Antoinette says but Agnes just gives a little shake of her head.

'I just want to sleep.'

She disappears down the hallway, an exhausted and slightly forlorn figure, leaving Antoinette and me in the kitchen with Lauren and Cort.

'Did she tell you what happened?' Lauren asks.

I nod. 'Yeah. What a piece of shit.'

Lauren makes a noise of agreement and Cort lets out a

loud performative sigh. Like he wants us to know that he is Very Deeply Concerned.

Lauren puts her hand on his arm. 'What is it, baby?' she says.

'It's just . . .' he says, tucking a stray lock of hair that escaped from his bun behind his ear. 'Women should never be put in that position. I just hate living in a society that commodifies female bodies. It's disgusting.'

Antoinette gives me a look and presses her lips together until they go white. She reminds me of a cobra right before it pounces.

'Right,' I say.

Cort holds his hands over his heart. 'But also, and I say this with love, so much love, we've got to talk about boundaries.'

Antoinette narrows her eyes at him. 'Go on,' she says but it sounds almost like a threat.

'Agnes shouldn't have gone alone,' he says. 'Men like that thrive on blurred lines. I tell Lauren all the time to protect her energy, don't I, Lo?' Lauren nods. 'Don't give men access they haven't earned.'

'It was literally an audition,' Antoinette hisses. 'You're not meant to need an intimacy coordinator at a fucking job interview.'

Cort nods hard. 'Totally,' he says. 'I hear you. I'm just saying that we need to coach our women to navigate these systems safely.'

'Coach our women?' Antoinette echoes in disbelief.

Cort ignores her and keeps going. I get the feeling that this is the sort of thing he always does. For someone who is apparently so here for the women, he talks over them a lot.

'If Agnes ever wants to talk to a man about healthy masculinity, I'm here,' he's saying now, his hands still over his heart. 'I've done the work.' He looks around at the three of us as if he's expecting us to applaud or something. We don't. And he keeps talking. 'Shadow work, mirror work. I've done rage circles with my men's group.'

'Jerk circles more like,' I hear Antoinette mutter.

'I've cried with so many brothers this year alone,' Cort continues. 'And I want to bring that healing and energy into my everyday life, you know. I want all men to be able to tap into those parts of themselves.' He leans back now, stretching but somehow making it smug. 'Predators like Richard Stone give all men a bad name. It's embarrassing for those of us who are doing the work.'

I stare at him.

I know all of the words he's just said but somehow they mean absolutely nothing.

Lauren closes her eyes. 'Cort,' she says. 'Please stop talking.'

'What? I'm just trying to bring some consciousness to the space.'

I see Lauren take a deep breath. She looks like a harassed mother of a toddler.

'Come on, Kits,' Antoinette says. 'Let's go.'

'Oh stay,' Lauren says. 'Ignore him. He may be a self-proclaimed feminist ally but he just likes the sound of his own voice sometimes.'

Cort shrugs. 'I can't help it if I'm self-aware,' he says.

Antoinette looks like she's about to uncoil and strike.

I grab her arm.

'Come on,' I say. 'We need to go.'

And we do.

There's a producer we need to kill.

Now.

39

KITTY AND ANTOINETTE'S AIRBNB, WEST HOLLYWOOD, LOS ANGELES

'If we're going to do this, we need to do it now,' I tell Antoinette the moment the kitchen door closes behind us and I've double-locked it.

'This minute?' Antoinette says with surprise. 'What about all that stuff you told me before about planning and blah blah blah?'

'It needs to be now,' I say, 'because we know where he is. We might not get this opportunity again. He assaulted Agnes, plus God knows who else, and he deserves to pay for it.'

Antoinette beams at me. 'Glad to hear it. It's hard to know with you at the moment. You seem to have lost your edge since we've been out here.'

'Lost my *edge*?' Now I'm seething. 'What are you talking about?'

'It's like you've gone soft,' she says. 'You weren't happy at all about Ron Wilde.'

'Because you weren't careful,' I say.

I need a massage.

I thought LA was supposed to be all chill and relaxed but I have honestly never felt so stressed in my whole life. 'You just killed him with no thought of the consequences and knew I'd clear up your mess.'

'That's not fair,' Antoinette says and I'm sure she sticks her lower lip out a bit. 'He deserved it.'

I let out a huge sigh of exasperation. 'Antoinette,' I say. 'We've been through this, it wasn't a smart kill. Which reminds me. We still need to figure out what we're going to do with that body. Now, come on. Get in the car.'

Antoinette looks at the door to the cellar.

'What about Aidan Ward?' she says.

'He's not going anywhere. We'll deal with him when we've sorted out Richard Stone. Come on. We need to go now.'

In the car, Antoinette does some Richard Stone research. 'Originally from London,' she tells me. 'God, we really produce some pieces of work, but has been working over here for the past thirty years.'

'Family? Who'd miss him?'

'Can't find any evidence of a wife or kids on his socials. He seems to prefer hanging out with women who look like models in Malibu and Miami.'

Urgh, an ageing bachelor who can't take no for an answer. The worst.

'What's Reddit and X saying?' I ask. 'Any chat about him on those about him being inappropriate?'

Antoinette shakes her head. 'Nothing concrete but there are some mutterings about a well-known male producer who hasn't learned anything from the Weinstein situation. That could be referring to him.' Or any of the infinite number of producers out here.

It really *is* like #MeToo never happened.

'Okay and we know where we're going?'

'I got his address from Agnes's phone,' she says, tapping something into the car's sat-nav.

He lives in The Hills. Specifically in The Bird Streets where the houses are huge and, for some reason, the roads are like goat paths.

And it's dark.

Like really fucking dark.

I am not enjoying this drive.

Not one bit.

But dark is good.

No witnesses.

And that's exactly what we want.

As I drive, I tell Antoinette the plan. It's a bit off the cuff, but it should work as long as everyone sticks to her role.

By everyone I mean Antoinette.

I hope Richard Stone is still awake.

He's about to take his own life.

So sad.

40

RICHARD STONE'S MANSION, THE BIRD STREETS, HOLLYWOOD HILLS, LOS ANGELES

Richard Stone's house is exactly what you'd imagine the house of a successful Hollywood producer to be. Garish and unsubtle. He wants the world to know that he's made it. That he's not just a man, but The Man. It's gated, of course. Not very easy to escape from on foot. Probably deliberately so when you take into account what goes on behind the big, reinforced steel doors.

It's dark when we arrive, which will work to our advantage when we spot the CCTV camera pointed directly at the gate.

I press the button on the security gate. It rings a few times and then a gruff voice answers.

'Yes?'

'Oh hi,' Antoinette says. 'My name's Glinda. I'm here to see Richard Stone.' I look at Antoinette and mouth *Glinda?* at her. She lifts a shoulder in response.

'Glinda?' says the disembodied voice. 'I'm not expecting anyone.'

Antoinette looks directly into the camera and bats her

eyelashes. 'That can't be right. He told us to come to his house for a private meeting. I'm here with my sister, Elphaba.'

Oh for fuck's sake, Antoinette.

'Sister?' The gruff voice suddenly sounds a bit more engaged. 'Is she there with you now?'

'Yes,' I say, squeezing my face next to hers so we're both in view of the camera. I bat my lashes as well. 'I'm Elphaba.' I give her a look and she shrugs back at me. 'You know they're not sisters, right?' I hiss at her.

'Yes they are,' she hisses back.

'They're not!' I say. 'They're friends!'

'I'll think you'll find they were sisters, Kitty.'

'One of them was *green*.'

Antoinette shrugs. 'Whatever.'

Elphaba and Glinda.

He's never going to buy this.

Except he does.

Because sometimes men believe what they want to believe.

And right now Richard Stone wants to believe that two beautiful young sisters are standing at his gate, begging to be let inside.

'You may as well come in then, seeing as you're here,' he says.

And then the gate opens, revealing a long driveway leading to the steel door and those huge glass windows.

'Remember we have to wipe the footage,' I tell Antoinette as we make our way up to the house, sprinklers on the manicured lawns misting us with drops of water. Normally I'd be pissed off and worry about my hair frizzing, but it's actually quite a nice relief after the heat of the day.

'Wipe the footage. Got it,' Antoinette replies. I sneak a look at her. Her eyes are focused on the door and I can see her chest rising and falling as she breathes. There's an almost electric charge bouncing off her and I wonder if I'm the same. There's something so perfect, so almost sensual about this moment. The moment leading up to killing a man. Knowing we're about to make the world a safer place for women. Knowing we're about to serve a justice that would go unpunished otherwise.

'You good?'

Antoinette looks at me and smiles. 'So good. I can't wait to make him pay for what he did to Agnes.'

It's Richard Stone himself who answers the door, which I'm slightly surprised by. I'd have imagined a man of his standing to have an army of staff to do the grunt work like answering the door. I really should've thought about that before rushing out here. But then again, I suppose he doesn't want any witnesses if he's spent the day groping young actresses.

'Hello,' he says as the door opens. He's not a large man but it's apparent that he takes care of himself. He's wearing a T-shirt, which shows off relatively toned biceps, and a pair of grey joggers. Objectively, he's not a bad-looking man for someone his age, which I would say is around mid-fifties. He has a full head of hair but I suppose anyone with money can buy themselves a hairline. 'I'm so sorry but I didn't have this meeting in my diary. I can only offer my full and wholehearted apologies.'

'No problem,' I say with a little giggle. 'We really appreciate you seeing us anyway.'

'Yes,' Antoinette echoes. 'We really appreciate it.'

'Well, let's get you inside,' Richard Stone says. 'Can't have two lovely young things like you standing on the doorstep all night.'

Things?

I can't wait to kill this guy.

So the plan Antoinette and I hurriedly put together is that we'll overpower Stone, strangle him and stage it to look like a suicide. We're hoping to get access to his phone so we can send out a confessional email to some news outlets saying how he couldn't live with himself after everything he's done to young women. It's a great plan because not only do we get to kill him, but his reputation and legacy also get ruined. Perfect. His eyes are all over both of us and I just know he's thinking it won't be long until it's his hands doing the roaming of our bodies.

'Come in, come in.' He stands back to let us inside the house and into an entrance hall the size of a classroom. It smells like wealth, which is a really hard scent to describe. It's a sort of combination of expensive room fragrances, leather and fucking money.

'Wow,' I say and make my eyes go huge as I pretend to take in the vastness of the entryway. 'Your house is amazing.' It's too showy, too gauche but I think I'm doing a good job of appearing impressed by it.

Antoinette catches on. 'Yes, oh my God, it's *so* big.'

Richard Stone pulls a face that is meant to say 'what? This old thing?'

'Are those *Oscars*?' Antoinette manages to make her voice crack so convincingly on the words 'Oscars' that I think she should be awarded her own for this performance.

Richard Stone gives a small laugh, the laugh of a humble man who barely notices the two Academy Awards sitting on a console table in his fucking massive hallway. 'Well, yes, I didn't really know where else to put them,' he says in a voice that was born in East London but has been toned and honed after three decades in LA. 'No one really talks about the best place to keep your Oscars.' He laughs again and I'm going to enjoy killing him oh so much.

'Come through,' he's saying now, walking ahead of us. 'I'll get you both settled and sort you some drinks.'

'Do we need to take our shoes off?' Antoinette asks, her face a picture of innocence. Richard Stone stares at her blankly for a moment.

'What?'

'Shoes.' Antoinette points at her feet. 'I don't want to be walking muck all on your nice clean floors.' She's gone full Eliza Doolittle now and I have to give her a little nudge.

'Tone it down,' I whisper. 'We're not in a George Bernard Shaw play.'

'Oh right, no don't worry about shoes,' Richard Stone is saying. 'Someone will clean it tomorrow anyway.' I bristle as I think about how this man is the kind of man who does whatever he likes, safe in the knowledge that someone will be along at some point to clean it all up.

Not this time, motherfucker.

He leads us through the house, which is honestly enough to get my entire step quota in for the day, to an open-plan living room that is no doubt one of many reception rooms. The floors are a walnut-coloured wood and Stone guides us to a sitting area consisting of gigantic sectional cream sofas in butter-soft leather.

'Please, take a seat,' he says, indicating the couches and

we obediently sit down. 'I'll get us some drinks. What's your poison?'

'Just water, please,' I say. No drinking on the job. Antoinette nods.

'Oh come on, that's not a party,' Stone says as he makes his way over to the full-sized bar at one end of the room. 'I've got everything here. Vodka, gin, champagne. I'm even a bit of a whizz with cocktails if you fancy something a bit special?'

As if we're dumb enough to drink anything he makes us.

'Really,' I say, 'water is fine. We're into taking care of ourselves.' Wellness trends must have really fucked with predators like Stone who like to ply their targets with drink and drugs before pouncing on them.

'Can I not twist your arms at all?'

'Sorry,' I say. 'We need to look our best.'

He gives me an approving once-over. 'Well, you're doing a really good job of that so who am I to interfere.' He pauses. 'But do let me know if you change your minds.' He smiles and busies himself pouring some bottled water into two glasses and adding ice before slicing up a lemon and dropping a couple of slices into the drinks. He fixes himself a vodka martini, pops it all on a tray and brings it over to the coffee table in the middle of the sofa arrangement. Such a gracious host.

'So, you girls are from London?' he says. 'I can tell from your accents. Whereabouts?' He takes a seat next to me, his knee gently touching mine.

'Islington,' I say and he nods sagely. 'It was just us and our mum.'

'I was born near Whitechapel,' he says, leaning in closer. 'I grew up with a single mum too. So I know how you've had to work harder than most people to get here.' He holds his hands out but I'm unsure if he's indicating LA in general or just his house. 'You want to act, right?' We both nod enthusiastically. 'I'm only too happy to give my fellow countrymen, *women*, a helping hand. If they're hungry enough. If they want it enough.' His voice dips a key. 'Do you girls want it enough? That's the question. How hungry for it are you?'

Antoinette and I look at each other.

'We're absolutely starving for it,' she says. 'Like, more than you can even imagine.'

Richard Stone smiles at us and it's all impossibly white teeth and leer. 'I'm so pleased to hear that,' he says. 'Now that we're friends. But it's a two-way street, you know.'

I look at him full-beam wide-eye innocence. 'What do you mean?'

He leans back in his seat now, spreading his legs wide. I feel Antoinette bristle next to me. 'I mean, if I do something for you, I expect you to return the favour. That's all. That's what friends do, isn't it?'

'But we haven't got anything!' Antoinette says, fake dismay.

'I'm sure we can think of something,' Richard Stone says, running his tongue over his lips. 'I mean, surely you both know what you look like? You must know the effect you have on men?'

He really doesn't waste any time getting to the point.

'Oh,' I say. 'I think I understand what you're saying.'

He looks at me. 'Clever girl. Elphaba, isn't it? Or are you Glinda?' He raises an eyebrow as he says our pretend names.

'Elphaba,' I say, hoping I'm right.

'Well, Elphie, why don't you come sit on my lap and we can show Glinda what I mean.'

I smile and stand up. He pulls me down onto his lap. Then his hands are on my thighs and his face is in my neck. I grit my teeth hard.

'My God, you smell good.' He breathes his words into my skin, which is now crawling, a million spiders all over my body. I feel his hands squeeze the flesh of my thighs and now is the point where I should be reaching into my pocket and pulling out the knife I planned to scare him with. But my fingers are barely grazing the handle when I feel something wet splash across my face. Richard Stone makes a wet grunt and I feel him slump beneath me. Antoinette is now standing in front of us, breathing hard and brandishing an ice pick that now has a bloody red tip. I wipe my hand across the wetness on my face, not even flinching when I see that it's blood.

'What the fuck?' I say to my sister. 'This wasn't the plan.'

Nowhere near the plan.

Because who kills themselves by jabbing an ice pick into their own neck? I blink at the blood, which is now pooling on the cream leather.

Fuck my life, this will take some ferocious cleaning.

'I'm sorry,' Antoinette says, sounding anything but. 'I couldn't stand it. Just sitting here while he was pawing you.'

I slide out from underneath the weight of a collapsed Richard Stone. He makes an agonised groan, part dying animal, part sexually frustrated male.

'Antoinette! I literally have a knife in my pocket. I wasn't in danger!'

'I'm sorry! I'm sorry!' She has the decency to sound

remorseful now at least. 'I couldn't help it! It was like instinct or something. I like fully dissociated!'

We stare at Richard Stone, who is clawing at the ice pick sticking out of his neck.

'You don't want to pull it out,' I tell him. 'It's literally keeping you alive at the moment.'

He howls again, which makes another jet of blood spurt out of the hole in his throat.

For fuck's sake.

41

RICHARD STONE'S MANSION, THE BIRD STREETS, HOLLYWOOD HILLS, LOS ANGELES

He's staring at us, his stupid brain unable to properly fathom what's happening to him.

That he's bleeding out over his own Poltrona Frau sofa.

That he's not the predator.

We are.

He's unable to say anything apart from wet gurgles but his eyes are asking that all-important question, *why?*

I'm more than happy to fill him in on that.

'Did you think you were going to get away with it forever?' I ask him as he weakly clutches at his neck. 'We know exactly what you've been doing. Why you get young women to your home. So I'll ask you again. Did you think you were going to get away with it forever?'

He still doesn't answer, mostly because he can't, but I'm not accepting that. I kick him in the groin and he slides off the couch and onto the floor.

'That's becoming like your signature move, Kits,' Antoinette says as she delivers her own blow to his most sensitive parts.

I suppose it is.

I crouch down so my eyes are level with Richard Stone's and I slowly and excruciatingly pull the ice pick out of his neck. It glides through his jugular like it's butter. And then the damn bursts. Blood spurts hard and fast from the now-open wound, gushing out like it's escaping. The redness of the blood still fascinates me even after all this time and . . . hmm, not quite sure how many kills it is now. The brightness surprises me, almost like I expect something else to run through his veins. Something black and toxic, like oil.

It's actually a shame that I can't take my time with this one. The thought of torturing him and making him suffer. The idea of killing him slowly, more of a death-by-a-thousand-cuts kind of approach. I wish I could savour this kill and make him fully regret every single one of his crimes.

But time is something we don't have on our side right now.

He gurgles something but it's too late for final words.

He had his chance.

When Richard Stone is dead, I look around at the blood-soaked living area.

Fuck.

How are we going to clean this up?

Usually the post-murder clean-up is one of the things I like most of all. There's something almost meditative about it, about the mental checklist where I can mark off everything I need to do. The cleaning, the disposal of anything I've touched, the routine to it is comforting. But it soon becomes clear that it's cleaning up *alone* that has always made it so meditative. It's not the same almost spiritual experience with a twenty-year-old who was raised by YouTube.

'Get ready with us as we clean up a murder scene,' Antoinette chirps into her phone. She sees me watching her and winks.

'Are you fucking kidding me?' I say, lunging for the phone.

She rolls her eyes and holds it out of my reach. 'Chill Bill. I'm *obviously* not really recording, am I?'

'You're twisted,' I say.

'Yes,' she says. 'I take after my big sister.'

I can't argue with her on that one.

'Seriously though,' I say. 'How are we going to clean this mess up? There's no way we're going to be able to get all that blood off. There's not enough bicarbonate of soda in the world.'

We stare at the pool of blood that has spread like an angry oil slick over the couch and walnut floor.

'Cleaning's not really my thing,' Antoinette muses.

No.

She prefers to leave that part to me.

'Well, we can't stage a suicide, for obvious reasons.'

We stare at the gaping hole in Richard Stone's neck.

'We're going to have to make it look like an accident,' Antoinette says.

'What? He *accidentally* skewered himself through the throat? With an ice pick?'

She shrugs. 'He could have *fallen* on it,' she says. 'Everyone knows the home is the most dangerous place in the world.'

'Hmm. A freak accident in the home.' It could work.

I just need to think with the creative part of my brain.

I walk over to the bar area and am impressed by the size of it. It's got everything. Including a dishwasher.

A story I read online recently pops into my head. A news feature about a man who'd fallen in his kitchen and accidentally impaled himself on a knife that was blade up in the cutlery bit of the dishwasher. I look around the bar. There are knives here, ones he obviously used to cut up the lemon earlier. A plan forms in my brain.

'Antoinette,' I say, 'bring the ice pick over here.'

She does as she's told and I use my shirt to wipe it clean. No blood, no fingerprints. Then I open the dishwasher, which is full of dirty glasses and cutlery, and pop the ice pick in, sharp side facing up. I add the knife he used as well.

'Okay,' I say, 'now we need to drag his body over here.'

He's not the lightest man in the world but we are able to drag him across the smooth flooring without too much trouble.

'Right,' I say, 'now we need to flip him over and get the ice pick in his neck hole.'

Trying to manoeuvre the body of a grown man onto such a precise point isn't the easiest thing but after some 'to me, to you'-style back-and-forthing we manage it.

'There we go,' I say to Antoinette.

'Ooh, wait,' she says and, covering her hand, knocks a bottle of vodka over so all the liquid trickles onto the floor.

'What are you doing?' I ask her.

'Making the floor slippery,' she says. 'So dangerous in here.'

Not bad.

I stand back and admire our handiwork.

'So he was in the bar fixing himself a drink, slipped and impaled himself on the ice pick that was perilously placed in the dishwasher.'

'Perfect,' Antoinette says. 'Now all we need to do is clean up the blood on the sofa?'

I'd forgotten about that.

It takes us another hour or so to scrub the living area clean. Then we have to wipe our prints off everything we touched.

'We need to do something about the security footage as well,' I say. Fuck's sake. It feels never-ending.

'Say less,' Antoinette chirps and disappears off.

I look at our crime scene again.

It's actually not bad.

I go and take another look at Richard Stone's dead body.

Yep. It looks pretty convincing.

I feel my stomach churn and something wet and slick rises up my throat.

Oh God, no.

I can't be sick here.

Far too much DNA.

I crouch down and put my head between my knees, taking some deep breaths.

Thankfully the urge to purge passes just as Antoinette comes back in.

'I've wiped all the footage,' she says. 'No one will know we've been here.'

'Are you sure? How did you do that?'

'I'm Gen Z,' she says by way of explanation. I'm not going to argue with that.

I take one last look around to make sure we haven't missed anything before we let ourselves out.

'The home is such a dangerous place,' I say as we leave.

42

KITTY AND ANTOINETTE'S AIRBNB, WEST HOLLYWOOD, LOS ANGELES

We barely speak on the way home but as soon as the door shuts behind us I can't stop the words from flying out of my mouth.

'We had a plan, Antoinette,' I hiss at her and she shrinks away from me, surprised by my wrath. 'We had a plan and, yet again, you going off script nearly ruined it for us. It still could. We need to hope and fucking pray that whoever finds Richard Stone believes that staged accident was real.' I slump into the couch, all of my energy seeping out of my body. 'What the hell were you thinking?' I stand up and stride through to the kitchen, where I wash my hands, scrubbing the last bits of blood and dirt from under my nails.

'I'm sorry,' she says, following me. 'But he was touching you. He had his hands all over you.'

'And I was *handling* it,' I say. 'Jesus Christ, Antoinette, this is hardly my first fucking rodeo. I've dealt with creepier creeps than that.'

Much creepier.

'And look how it's affected you!'

What?

'What?' I say. 'It hasn't *affected* me. Not at all.'

Antoinette gives me a look. 'Oh, really?'

'What do you mean?'

'Do you think it's normal behaviour to kick a man in the balls when he kisses you?'

Oh. She's talking about Travis.

'Well, no,' I say, 'obviously not.'

'No, Kitty. It's a trauma response. You had a horrible, traumatic experience and your body reacted to it. And when I saw Richard Stone touching you like that *my* body reacted. Because I wanted to protect you. Because I didn't want you having another panic attack like you did with Travis.'

Protect me? Like I'm some fucking damsel in distress.

'Well, that was very gallant,' I say, anger bubbling up inside me. 'But I really don't need you jumping in to defend me!'

'But Kitty—'

'No,' I say. 'I don't want to hear it. Your recklessness is going to get us caught. I've already spoken to you about this but it doesn't seem to be getting through, does it?'

'I was just—'

I hold up my hand. 'Stop. I'm starting to think it was a mistake bringing you out here. I've been doing this on my own and it's been fine. Now you're involved and there's a dead movie star and a woman beater in the basement. And now there's a dead producer and some *Final Destination* fucking accident that we have to hope people believe.' I let out an exasperated sigh. 'I should've done this alone. I could be home by now.'

Antoinette swallows hard. She looks like she might be about to cry. 'Well, let's just finish Aidan Ward off now and you *can* go home,' she says. 'We can both get on with our lives.'

I stare at her. 'Oh no,' I say. 'You're not having anything to do with killing that man.' I jerk my chin towards the cellar door. 'He's the reason we're here and I'm not having you mess that up.'

'What? But I—'

'No,' I say. 'I'm killing Aidan Ward *by myself*. You're a liability, Antoinette, and I'm not going to risk you fucking this up.'

She stares back at me and I wonder if she *is* actually going to cry. But then her eyes narrow and she says in a voice cold as steel, 'Fine. I'll just get out of your hair then.' She turns away from me and walks out of the room. A few seconds later I hear the front door slam shut.

Great.

A tantrum.

Just what I need.

I don't go after her. She'll cool off.

Besides, I meant what I said. I want to kill Aidan Ward alone. And what better time than now? The sooner it's done, the sooner I can get on a plane and get home. I can't wait to tell Tor it's done and she can finally rest, knowing the man who hurt her will never be able to do it again. The look on her face when she knows it's over will be worth all this. Also, it means I can get back to Charlie. I'm sure if I plead my case to him properly he'll understand. I'm still me. And he loved me once. You can't just turn those feelings off. I miss him so much. I'd do anything to have him here right now, to be able to poke my finger into that adorable dimple he has in his cheek. Urgh. I need to stop thinking about Charlie.

I need to focus on Aidan Ward for now.

First I grab some duct tape – I can't risk anyone hearing his screams as I murder him – and then I pull a knife out of the knife block and examine it. It's a MAC Professional chef's knife. Not my knife of choice but sharp and lightweight. I swoosh it about a bit and make some stabbing motions.

It will do.

The basement is dark and Aidan Ward blinks a few times when I switch the light on. He's huddled into a corner, as far away from the LV cases as he can get. I'm not surprised. It's starting to smell a bit down here. My stomach does a roll of protest.

'I thought you were going to leave me to die down here,' he says. His voice is little more than a croak. He must be really thirsty. Good. He can stay that way.

'And miss out on all the fun of killing you myself?' I hold the knife up and his eyes widen. 'Don't be silly.'

'Can I have some water?'

'No.'

'You don't have to do this, Kitty,' he says quietly. He's using his therapist voice. I've heard it before. And I trusted it last time. When he told me that he was in love with Tor. That he would never hurt her. That I should give him a chance, even though I *knew* he was targeting her because she was his patient and vulnerable. I will never ignore what my gut is screaming at me again.

'That's where you're wrong,' I say. 'I absolutely do have to do this. Because I promised Tor I would. You remember Tor, don't you? The woman you battered and left for dead because she wouldn't have sex with you?'

'You haven't got it in you to kill, Kitty,' he says.

This makes me laugh.

'Really?' I say. 'Well actually, you won't even be the first man I've killed. You're not even the first man I've killed today.' Okay, so technically Antoinette killed Richard Stone, but Aidan Ward doesn't need to know that.

He stares at me and I see it, a tiny glimmer of fear sparking in his eyes.

I love it when men realise they've underestimated me.

It's better than sex.

'What do you mean?' he asks.

'Your voice is annoying me,' I say as I reach for a roll of duct tape and slap some across his mouth, slicing it off with the knife. 'And I mean I've already murdered someone today. A producer who got handsy with a friend. Stabbed him through the neck with an ice pick.' I move closer towards him and feel a little rush of endorphins as he tries to scuttle away from me. Not an easy move when your ankles are cable-tied together. I squat down so I'm on my haunches at the same level as him. My thigh muscles protest. Loudly. They still haven't recovered from that impromptu CrossFit session.

I look him directly in the eyes. 'And over there,' I nod towards the LV cases, 'are the remains of Ron Wilde. The movie star? I'm sure you've heard of him. He had to go too.' Yes, Antoinette killed Ron Wilde as well, but the actual details don't matter. The spark of fear in Aidan's eyes has turned into a full flame. 'So I really *do* think that I have it in me to kill, Aidan.' I hold the tip of the knife to his throat. 'And I think I'm going to enjoy you the most.'

He gulps and then a horrible stench hits my nostrils.

It's acrid and bleachy, ammonia.

Almost like really potent . . .

I glance at Aidan Ward's crotch. A dark, damp stain has spread around the groin area of his jeans.

That's disgusting.

The smell fills my nose again and I can feel my stomach clench.

I just about make it out of the cellar and into the kitchen before I throw my guts up into the sink.

What the hell is wrong with me?

Maybe I do need Antoinette to help me with this after all.

I'll wait until the morning and we can do it together.

43

KITTY AND ANTOINETTE'S AIRBNB, WEST HOLLYWOOD, LOS ANGELES

I still feel a bit queasy when I wake up the next morning. I'm going to have to swing past a pharmacy and get something to settle my stomach if this continues. I can't put it down to jet lag now. I must've picked up something on the plane. All that recycled air. Flying germ boxes. I check my phone and am surprised to see it's almost eleven in the morning. I really must've been tired.

I stagger down to the kitchen, desperate for a coffee, and am surprised to find no sign of Antoinette yet either. No rogue coffee cups or glasses with the remnants of a green juice. No tell-tale toast crumbs on the counter and – I look around the kitchen – no sign of the milk being left out.

She must still be in bed. If she was up early for a yoga class or something, there would definitely be proof of life in here.

She must've come back late last night.

I was a bit hard on her actually. To make amends I decide to make her a nice breakfast for when she comes down. Antoinette isn't vegan like me so we've got all sorts of gross things in the fridge like butter and eggs. I pop a couple of slices of sourdough into the toaster and crack two eggs to scramble for her. My poor stomach turns over on itself as I watch the snotty things plop into the pan. She'd better appreciate the sacrifice I'm making here.

I scramble the eggs, butter the toast, slice up some avocado and make a cafetière of coffee. But when I'm done there's still no sign of my sister. It's almost half past eleven now. I have a quick root around in the kitchen cupboards and find a tray. I'll take her breakfast in bed. That – along with the news that I've decided I do need her help to kill Aidan Ward – should cheer her up. And maybe an apology. I was a bit harsh on her last night. She was only trying to help me. If I'd seen that horrible sleaze-weasel pawing at her, I'd probably have stabbed him in the neck too.

I arrange all the things on the tray and then, on a whim, go into the garden and pluck one of the hibiscus flowers and lay it down next to the cutlery. Yes, this is definitely a good way to apologise. I carry the tray up to Antoinette's room and balance it on my knee as I knock the door.

'Antoinette?' I call. 'Are you awake?'

There's no answer.

'Antoinette?' I say her name a bit louder this time. 'I've made you breakfast.'

Still nothing.

She's either dead to the world or she's still furious at me.

'Please, talk to me.' I'm pleading now. 'I'm really sorry about last night. I shouldn't have shouted at you. And I'd really like your help with Aidan today. Please, Antoinette.'

She still doesn't answer.

I hope she's okay. Maybe she's coming down with whatever I have.

I put the tray on the floor and knock once more. 'I'm coming in.'

I turn the knob and open the door but there's no one here.

No sign of Antoinette at all.

The bed is made. It doesn't even look like it's been slept in.

'Antoinette?' I call out again before pushing open the door to her en suite. If she's in the shower she might not have heard me. But the bathroom is completely empty. And it doesn't look like it's been used this morning. The air is completely dry, no lingering steam from the shower, no residual smell from deodorant or perfume.

It's like she hasn't been here all night.

Did I even hear her come in?

I don't think I did.

After I left Aidan in the cellar to puke in the sink I'd come straight up to bed, passing out the moment my head hit the pillow.

Maybe she didn't come home.

But where would she have gone?

I hurry back down to the kitchen and pick my phone up from the table. I call Antoinette but it goes straight through to voicemail. Urgh. She probably forgot to charge it again.

I jam my feet into a pair of trainers by the back door and half-walk, half-run past the pool and to the guesthouse.

The door is open when I get there but I call through anyway.

'Agnes? Lauren?'

'In the kitchen,' Agnes's voice bounces back. She's perched on a bar stool at the island, eating a bowl of cereal and scrolling through her phone. She looks a lot brighter than when I last saw her. 'Hey, Kitty,' she says when she sees me. 'Are you okay? You look ghost-pale.'

'Is Antoinette here?' I ask but Agnes shakes her head.

'No, I haven't seen her. I've been trying to get hold of her. Have you seen the news?'

I shake my head this time. 'No. What's happened?'

Agnes passes me her phone. 'Richard Stone,' she says. 'He was found dead in his kitchen this morning. Fell on a bunch of knives in the dishwasher. How fucked up is that?'

I stare at the news story on the gossip site on the phone. 'Oh,' I say. 'Wow. That's grim.'

Agnes raises both shoulders. 'Couldn't have happened to a nicer guy. Imagine dying like that. He must've been in agony.' A mischievous little smile spreads across her lips. 'Queen Karma serves again.'

I scan the article but it doesn't say anything other than that the LAPD think it's a tragic accident and they're not looking for anyone else in connection with the incident.

Thank God.

One less thing to worry about.

I hand her phone back. 'But you haven't heard from Antoinette at all?'

'No. What's wrong?'

I sigh. 'We had an argument last night and she stormed out. I don't think she came home.'

Agnes's blue eyes go wide. 'But where would she go? She doesn't know anyone else. Does she?'

'Maybe Lauren's seen her?' I ask but Agnes shakes her head again.

'Lauren was at Cort's last night. She hasn't been back yet.'

Just then we hear the front entrance of the guesthouse slam shut and Lauren walks into the kitchen.

'Did I hear ya'll taking my name in vain?' she asks before seeing our worried faces. 'Oh God, what's happened now? Agnes? Are you okay?'

'It's not me,' Agnes says. 'Kitty says Antoinette didn't come home last night.'

'Have you heard from her at all?' I ask Lauren a bit desperately because I know it's a long shot. It's Agnes she's close to, not Lauren. I don't even know if Lauren has her number.

'No, I haven't,' says Lauren. 'Are you sure she didn't come back? Maybe she's just gone to an early-morning yoga session or something?'

'We had an argument,' I say, 'and I'm pretty sure her bed hasn't been slept in. Fuck, where is she?'

'I'll try calling her again,' Agnes says but the call goes straight to voicemail again.

'Do you think she might have stayed at a hotel or something?' Lauren says. 'You know, to cool off if y'all were quarrelling?'

'I don't know,' I say, 'she didn't have anything with her when she stormed out. She might have done, but . . . shit.'

Agnes touches my arm gently. 'Okay, don't panic. She'll be fine. She's probably just cooling off somewhere. Let's go and have a look for her, Lauren?'

Lauren nods. 'Yes, of course.'

'We'll take Lana Del Gay. Kitty, you should go back to the villa in case she comes home. She's probably on her way back now and doesn't even realise we're all panicking about her.' Agnes gives me a smile but I can see she's worried. 'Let me know if she turns up,' she says to me.

I don't want to go back to the villa.

I want to go and look for her too but Agnes is right. Someone should be there if she comes back. And it should be me. So I can yell at her for being irresponsible. And then hug her and tell her to never, ever worry me like this ever again.

Who fucking pulls a vanishing act when there's a serial killer on the loose?

I'll kill her myself.

Agnes promises me that they'll call if they find anything. 'I bet she's back before we are,' she says as we all leave the guesthouse.

I don't know what to do with myself in the villa though. Anxiety ties itself in knots in my stomach and the only thing that calms it seems to be relentless pacing. I just can't believe that Antoinette would deliberately leave me to spiral like this. Not with one man to kill and the pieces of another that we still need to get rid of. She just wouldn't do that.

But where could she be? She doesn't know anyone here apart from me and Agnes and Lauren.

Does she?

Am I sure about that?

She's been spending a lot of time on Reddit since we got here.

Maybe she's been chatting with someone on there.

Maybe there will be some clues on her iPad.

I hurry up to her room.

It's gone noon now, she's been gone for almost fifteen hours.

I try to swallow down the panic I'm feeling as I find her iPad plugged into a charger next to her bed. Why can't she ever remember to charge her phone? She hasn't bothered putting any security on the iPad so I can click right into her web browser. Reddit loads immediately and I can see she's been scrolling through local subs, especially those focusing on the WeHo Ripper. But it doesn't look like she's commented or been chatting to anyone. I click open her iMessage app but there's nothing in there apart from texts from me and Agnes.

There must be something here.

I open up the browser again and click on the search bar to see her search history. There might be some clues in there if she *has* gone to a hotel. I know she wanted to go to The Edition. But there's no sign of the hotel in the history.

There is something though.

Something that chills me to my marrow.

A PrivatePool URL.

I click on it and immediately wish I hadn't as it takes me to a creator page.

My heart skips several beats when I see the username.

Naughty Netty.

And then I see the pictures and I'm almost sick.

There are about half a dozen photos taken in this very room.

Photos of my sister in her underwear.

'Oh Antoinette,' I say out loud. 'What have you done?'

44

KITTY AND ANTOINETTE'S AIRBNB, WEST HOLLYWOOD, LOS ANGELES

I can't stop staring at the screen. At the moody black-and-white aesthetic. Like she's aiming for high-end content, but it's very clearly been shot in this very room. Her grid is a series of carefully posed, self-shot images. There's one of her stretched out in her underwear on the unmade bed. Another where her hair is wet, like she's just stepped out of the shower. One of her leaning against the window in a tiny slip dress. The captions are minimal – *new set, what do you think?, Felt cute, might delete later* – but the comments are thirsty.

I like you wet.
What would you let me do to you?
I bet you're a very good girl.

Why would she do this?
Why?
She doesn't need money.
I don't understand.

‘Kitty? Are you upstairs?’ It’s Agnes.

‘I’m in Antoinette’s room,’ I call back and moments later her blonde head appears around the door.

‘What’s happened?’ she asks me, coming into the room. ‘You look like you’re going to pass out.’

‘I found something,’ I say, ‘on Antoinette’s iPad.’

I hold the tablet out to Agnes, who takes it. Her eyes widen.

‘What the—’

We both stare at the page for a moment before either of us says anything.

‘But *why*?’ Agnes says eventually, echoing my thoughts. ‘Antoinette doesn’t need the money.’ She looks at me, her brows knitted together in confusion. ‘Does she?’

I shake my head. ‘No. I don’t understand—’

But then I do.

And it’s so obvious that when it hits me it’s like a fist.

‘The WeHo Ripper,’ I say and Agnes gives me a puzzled look. ‘Antoinette thought we could find him.’

I sink down onto my sister’s bed as the enormity of what I’ve found hits me. ‘She’s made an account to lure him,’ I say to a horrified Agnes. ‘She’s used herself as bait.’

And right after I made her bait herself to get Aidan here.

This is all my fault.

‘I really don’t think she’s holed up in a hotel, Agnes. I think she’s gone after the Ripper. Or he’s gone after her.’

‘Oh God,’ Agnes says. ‘This is bad.’ She sits down next to me. ‘I found something too. Outside.’ She looks at me and bites her lip, like she has something to tell me that she doesn’t want to.

‘What?’ I say, frantic. ‘What is it?’

'We found something,' she says. 'Well, Lana did. Just a few yards from the house.'

Oh God.

'What? What did you find?' I almost don't want to know because, judging by the look on Agnes's face, it's not good.

She reaches into the pocket of her cut-offs and pulls out something that makes me cry out in horror.

It's a phone.

In a pink glittery case.

Antoinette's phone.

'I'm sorry,' Agnes whispers as she hands the phone over to me.

I turn it over and over again in my fingers.

There's no doubt that this is Antoinette's phone.

It's covered in mud and the screen is smashed.

But the worst thing is a dark red smudge staining the pink case, seeping into the glitter.

I've seen enough blood to know that's what I'm looking at.

Wherever Antoinette is, she didn't go there willingly.

45

KITTY AND ANTOINETTE'S AIRBNB, WEST HOLLYWOOD, LOS ANGELES

Lauren has come over and is making tea for us in the kitchen. I can barely think straight. All I can do is stare at Antoinette's phone.

I have no idea what to do.

I'm completely out of my depth.

'It's my fault,' I say for probably the hundredth time.

'It's not, Kitty,' Agnes says but I'm convinced she doesn't believe it.

'It is!' I insist. 'We argued. I said some really mean stuff to her.'

'You're sisters,' Lauren says as she places a mug of something hot in front of me. I'm loathe to call it tea because it looks more like gravy. Americans really have no idea about tea. But I give her a grateful smile anyway. 'I fight with my sister so much, you wouldn't believe it.'

'You can't blame yourself, Kitty,' Agnes adds and puts a comforting hand on my arm. 'Look, we need to focus on what we're going to do. How we're going to find her.'

Lauren slips into a chair at the table. She reaches across and places a hand on top of mine. I'm not totally comfortable with all this touching, to be honest. 'We're here. We're going to help you. It's going to be okay.'

'Thank you,' I say. 'I really appreciate it.'

Agnes is fiddling with her hands now, picking the skin on the side of one of her nails.

'What do you think about calling the police?' she says.

What do I think?

I think I've got a man and the corpse of a missing star in the wine cellar.

I think if the police start looking into me, they'll find a long trail of dead or missing men that I won't be able to talk my way out of with a giggle and a smile.

I think that I'll be spending the rest of my life in prison.

The police can absolutely not come here.

'I don't know,' I say, hoping neither of them notices the wobble in my voice. 'I'm worried that they won't take it seriously. Especially when they see the PrivatePool account.'

'You know, they probably wouldn't do anything anyway,' Lauren says with a little shake of her head. 'Antoinette's not even been missing for twenty-four hours yet. They'd just come over and take some notes. She's an adult. She's not vulnerable. And yeah, the PrivatePool thing might make them a bit . . . you know . . . judgy.'

I think of all the comments I've seen online.

Those awful misogynistic comments under the reports of the dead girls.

How they deserved what happened to them.

That they were sluts.

Agnes turns and looks at her. 'Even with all the other girls off that site that are dead?'

Lauren snorts. 'You know they're not even linking that. Not publicly anyway.'

Agnes grits her teeth and lets out a sigh of frustration. 'No, you're right. It's probably not a great idea to have the cops crawling over the place anyway.'

She's talking about her pharmaceutical sideline, of course.

I guess calling the cops will be the absolute last resort.

46

AGNES AND LAUREN'S GUESTHOUSE, WEST HOLLYWOOD, LOS ANGELES

'Maybe you shouldn't panic yet,' Cort says. 'There could be another explanation.' It's late afternoon now and I've moved Find Antoinette HQ over to the guesthouse. I can't have a house full of people when I've still got Aidan Ward alive in the wine cellar.

I must do something about that.

Cort has come over to help. Although so far he's done nothing apart from annoy me.

'Like what?' I say. 'All her stuff is here. And she doesn't know anyone apart from the people in this room. Please tell me, Cort, what could be another explanation?' I know I sound snippy but I don't care.

'I think you need to centre yourself, Kitty,' he says. 'I understand that you're worried but snapping at the people who are trying to help you isn't going to find her.'

'Give her a break,' Agnes says. 'She's fucking worried about her sister. We all are.'

Cort remains unperturbed. 'All I'm saying is that there

might be, and probably is, a more likely scenario than she's been snatched by a serial killer. It's a bit farfetched. Reddit would have you believing there's a serial killer around every corner.' He turns back to me. 'Have you tried calling friends or family back home? Maybe they've heard from her. You said you'd argued? Maybe she's just lying low for a night or two?'

'Without her phone?' Lauren says but presses her lips together when Cort gives her a look.

'She might have dropped it.'

'There's *blood* on it,' I hiss and Agnes puts a hand on my arm.

'It might be worth having a look on some of her socials,' she says gently.

'How would she post when her phone and iPad are here?'

'I know, but there might be some other clues on there. Maybe in her DMs?'

I pick up Antoinette's iPad and open the Instagram app. 'I'll have a look through here,' I say, 'there might be something that helps.'

Agnes nods. 'I'm going to call the local hospitals,' she says in small voice. I must look completely horrified because she quickly adds, 'just to check.' She puts a reassuring hand on my arm. Although maybe it would actually be better if Antoinette was in hospital. At least she'd be in a safe place. It certainly beats the alternative.

'Thanks, Agnes,' I say. 'I really appreciate it.'

'You're not on your own. We'll find her.'

I don't have any doubt that we'll find her.

It's *where* we'll find her that worries me.

And what state we'll find her in.

'Let's meet back here later,' Agnes says. 'I'll let you know if we find anything.'

She gives my arm a reassuring little squeeze and I head back over to the main house, opening Antoinette's iPad again, heading straight to Instagram.

The first thing that strikes me is that, for a twenty-year-old woman, Antoinette is pretty off-grid when it comes to social media. She only has a few hundred followers on Instagram and just a handful of posts; the most recent being a photo of the two of us at my mother – Carmella – and Gabriel's wedding earlier this year.

She's tagged it *#FoundFamily*.

Oh, Antoinette.

I click into her DMs, hoping I'll see something that might be of use. Even just a message to a friend ranting and slagging me off would be amazing. Especially if it says something along the lines of 'going to teach Kitty a lesson by staying out all night and throwing my phone away'.

But of course it doesn't.

I do find something though.

A handful of messages from someone whose username is just a string of numbers.

I click on them.

It's a one-way conversation. Antoinette has read them but hasn't replied.

I've seen your photos
On PrivatePool
I'm going to find out where you live
Slut

You deserve to die.

You're just like the others.

The words send chills through me. Could this be the killer? Why didn't Antoinette say anything to me about this?

I click on the profile but there's nothing to help me identify the sender. It's a new account, no posts yet and that ambiguous grey silhouette as the profile picture. No followers and not following anyone. There's nothing I can do with this. I sigh and report it anyway, just to feel like I'm doing *something*.

Where are you, Antoinette?

47

KITTY AND ANTOINETTE'S AIRBNB, WEST HOLLYWOOD, LOS ANGELES

I don't sleep.

How can I? Knowing Antoinette is out there somewhere. With someone who either means her harm. Or has already caused her harm.

Why else would there be blood on her phone?

Why else would it be in a bush with the screen smashed unless it was lost in a struggle?

I'm almost tempted to take Agnes up on her offer for something to help me sleep. But that would be worse. What if something happens? What if there's news and I miss it because I'm out of it in an artificial sleep? I can almost hear Charlie or my mother reprimanding me.

'You're no use to Antoinette if you're exhausted.'

And they'd be right.

But I'm even less use to her whacked out on benzos or whatever Agnes has in her stash.

So instead I do the only thing that I can think of to do.

I research.

Knowledge is power, after all.

Although I feel the complete opposite of powerful right now.

I'm sitting in bed with my laptop open on a Reddit sub about the WeHo Ripper. This is a different one, one where users speculate about things like motive and patterns.

The villa feels so wrong without my sister, like her absence is a living, breathing thing. It's too cold and too quiet.

Just me.

And the brutal absence.

The Ripper sub seems like it's grown since the last time I looked at it. There are so many new threads. None of them are exactly comforting bedtime reading.

I click one titled *He Strikes After Dark* and scan through the replies, hungry for information but also aware of the sickness it's causing, the cold bile biting into my stomach.

The post is full of people speculating about when the Ripper likes to hunt. I scroll until my eyes hurt. The one thing they all agree on is that his favourite time is after midnight. And that he stalks his intended victims until they're walking alone in the dark.

It's got to be someone that no one notices, one poster helpfully points out. *Someone who blends into the background. Like Kevin Spacey in that old movie.*

Get that name off of this sub.

Bro, this is LA, no one blends into the background here. No one wants to.

Background artists do. That's literally their entire point.

Honestly? Its more likely that he's an influencer or YouTuber. They're everywhere all at once. They're like streetlamps. No one pays them any attention.

I reckon he's a rejected actor with an axe to grind.

Nah. It's someone who hates women. Who hates women?

Everyone.

There's a link that I click on that takes me through to a colour-coded spreadsheet.

Jesus, someone has really put *time* into making this thing.

The women I know about are on there: Alicia, Sofi, Ellie and Juno. Their last known movements tracked. The places where their bodies were dumped. Links to their PrivatePool accounts. But I'm shocked to see more names. Names of women who are missing in Hollywood. Could there be even more victims than the ones we know about?

Marissa Hale – yoga instructor. Last seen New Year's Day, early hours, left a house party in The Hills to walk home. Had a PrivatePool.

Talia Shah – model. Reported missing by her boyfriend when she failed to arrive at his house in Fairfax. She'd texted him to say she was five minutes away and was never heard from again. Had recently set up a PrivatePool.

Brooke Chandler – actor. Missing for two years. She was last seen saying goodbye to friends on Sunset. Was very active on PrivatePool and had a large following.

There are half a dozen similar stories and no one can agree if they're victims of the Ripper or not. The conversation about them is predictably misogynistic.

Nah. The Ripper dumps the bodies at landmarks. He wants us to know he's killed them. These hoes are probably just junkies.

Or they've run off with a sugar daddy.

Or they've been trafficked to Dubai and are living that porta potty lifestyle.

Do you think he fucks them before he kills them?

Nah. These skanks are too dirty. He just eliminates them.

None of them are ugly though? I'd stick it in before I choked them.

LMAO. Right?

I wonder if he's looking for a Robin to his Batman.

The amount of men who want to hurt women never fails to horrify me. After everything I've seen. Everything I've done. It still chills me to my core. And now one of them has my sister.

I slam the laptop shut, unable to bear reading any more of the vitriol. How are men applauding someone who murders women? And just because the women make content for men exactly like them? It's so fucking backwards that it makes my head spin.

I suddenly feel very scared and alone.

I pick up my phone and check the time. Just after 11pm. I do some quick maths. It's seven o'clock in the morning in the UK. Would Charlie be awake? I know he would. He was always a lark and I think I've established that I very much am not. But it was never something that clashed for us. It meant that he'd make a lavish breakfast before I woke up. Or he'd clear up any mess we'd made the night before. Mess we didn't tidy because we were too busy pulling each other's clothes off.

I miss him so much.

I want to talk to him so badly.

I want to tell him about Antoinette and how scared I am for her. How scared I am for myself.

I scroll to his contact but, just as I'm about to hit the call button, I remember.

I remember that he's blocked me.

That he wants nothing to do with me.

I blink the tears away. I can't let myself crumble. Not now.

But I need to speak to someone.

Not Tor. I can't burden her with this. Not with everything she's dealing with.

Not Maisie. She's probably got her head in a toilet bowl. And she's growing actual people. I can't stress her out.

I scroll to my mother's number instead. There's very little chance of her being awake but I try anyway.

The phone rings and rings until her voicemail kicks in.

I don't leave a message. I want to talk to her, not her answering service.

I end the call and stare at the phone in my hand.

The loneliness is a punch when it hits me.

I have no one.

Absolutely no one.

48

THE WINE CELLAR, KITTY AND ANTOINETTE'S AIRBNB, WEST HOLLYWOOD

So it's not technically true that I have absolutely no one. There's one person I can talk to right now. And there's the added bonus that he can't walk away from me. He can't even answer me back if I leave the duct tape on his mouth.

I pull a robe over my pyjamas and head down the stairs, quietly, like I don't want to be caught.

Aidan Ward is asleep when I creep into the cellar. He startles like I've fired a gun when I flick the light on. His eyes are saucer-wide and confused. Then the confusion morphs into fear. He looks frantically at my hands, trying to figure out if I've brought a weapon down this time to finish him off.

'Don't worry,' I say. 'I'm not here to kill you. I'm just here to talk.'

His eyes get wider.

'That's what you do, isn't it? Talk. Listen. Aren't you a therapist? Somehow?'

He nods.

'Will you behave if I take the tape off?'

He nods again so I go over and rip it off. He presses his lips together, licks them. It's actually funny that my emergency contact is a man I've got tied up in my basement.

One I'm still planning on killing.

'How are you?' I say, backing away and sitting on the bottom step.

Aidan gives me a look that answers the question. His beard is getting bigger, but unevenly. There's a yellowing bruise on the left side of his face from where I knocked him out. A crust has formed in the corners of his mouth. I can smell his breath from here.

'Couldn't sleep?' he asks. The words come out in a croak.

'Well, it's obvious your education hasn't been wasted.'

He squints at me a little, his eyes still adjusting to the light from the single naked bulb. 'You don't look great, Kitty,' he says.

'You're not going to endear yourself to me with comments like that.'

He thinks about this for a moment. 'I'm not going to lie to you. I don't lie to people I work with.'

'I think Tor might disagree with that,' I say. This was a bad idea. What was I thinking? I stand up and get ready to leave but Aidan calls out to me.

'Wait,' he says. 'You've been crying.'

I turn back around and stare at him. 'I haven't,' I say.

He frowns slightly. 'The honesty thing has to work both ways, Kitty. Why have you come to talk to me? Your hostage?'

I sit back down on my step.

'What's happened? Is it your sister? Have you found her?'

I stare at him. 'How do you know about that?'

He tilts his head and stares back at me. 'This place isn't soundproof.'

I look at my hands clasped together in my lap and nod. 'Yes,' I say. 'She's still missing. And I made the mistake of going online. I think, I *know*, she's been taken by someone. Someone who wants to hurt her.'

The crease between his eyebrows deepens. 'You must be very worried.'

'I am.'

'And you can't call the police because . . .' He does a funny little jig with his head indicating himself, his predicament.

'Obviously not,' I say.

'So you think she's been taken? By someone who wants to hurt her. That must feel bad?'

'It does,' I admit. 'Because it's my fault.'

He nods. 'It's very common to blame oneself when something bad happens to someone we care about.' He frowns at me for a moment, like he's trying to work something about me out. 'I think it's a pattern with you.'

'Excuse me?'

'You blamed yourself for Tor as well, didn't you? After the attack. You felt like it was your fault because you didn't protect her.'

I stare at him, my mouth open. 'That *was* my fault too. I should've protected her from you. I knew you were bad news. I *felt* it. And I ignored that feeling. I'll never forgive myself for that.'

He spends a moment or two just looking at me, still assessing me.

'You have a saviour complex, Kitty,' he says finally. 'Has anyone said that to you before?'

I shrug.

'You have to realise that you're not responsible for every woman. How can you be when there's only one of you? How can you expect to save them all?'

'I don't,' I say. 'But I should be able to help those close to me. The women I love.'

He stares at me again, like he's still figuring me out. 'This is because of what happened to your mother, what you saw when you were young.'

Aidan knows a bit about my childhood. When I was checking him out on Tor's behalf I pretended to be a patient. I told him about how my father had been violent towards my mother for most of my childhood. And how I blamed myself for never stepping in to help her. I should've made up a cover story. I should've known that would come back to bite me.

'That need to protect, Kitty, it comes from fear. Not from strength. You're scared that if you lose control, even for one minute, everything will fall apart. You're scared that it will mean you've failed.'

He watches my face in silence for a moment or two.

Is he right?

'We're all scared though, aren't we?' I say. 'Of losing something.'

'But you haven't failed, Kitty. You've attached yourself to a responsibility that was never yours to carry. You've made it your whole existence.'

'No,' I say. 'You're wrong. I *was* supposed to protect them. These are the women who mean more to me than anything. My mother, my best friend, my sister. I've let them all down.'

Aidan tilts his head. 'That's just not true. You were a child.

Then you were a friend. And then you were a sister. You're human. You're not a shield.'

I don't say anything. I just continue looking at my hands.

'Kitty, you inherited guilt. Guilt that doesn't belong to you. And you've built your entire personality around it.' He pauses for a moment, still looking at me, still trying to get me to make eye contact with him. 'Kitty, you're not trying to save people because you care or because you're selfless or because you've got this warped idea that it's your calling. You're trying to save them because you're scared of what it says about you if you don't.'

Is he right?

Am I?

He can't be right.

'You're wrong,' I say, finally lifting my head and looking him in the eyes. 'I do this because I care. Because I see justice screwing women over again and again. Because men go around saying things like 'your body my choice'. Because they think they're entitled to women's bodies. Because the law *lets* them do that. Because patriarchy lets them do that. Because everywhere, all over the world, men hurt women without consequence. They get away with it. Over and over.'

He smiles sadly at me. It's patronising. And it makes the hot rage in my chest begin to bubble and spit. 'You're not a god, Kitty. If Antoinette's in trouble, it's because bad stuff happens in this city. In this world. Stop trying to take responsibility for the universe. It's not a battle you can ever win.'

'You're wrong,' I say. 'And I've heard enough from you.'

I slap some fresh duct tape over his mouth.

'You're wrong,' I say again before flicking the light off and leaving him alone in the darkness.

49

AGNES AND LAUREN'S GUESTHOUSE, WEST HOLLYWOOD, LOS ANGELES

'We're going to have to call the police,' Agnes says. We're sitting at the kitchen table the next morning, drinking the rose and hibiscus tea that Antoinette liked so much, as if it could somehow help in manifesting her back. I've told Agnes about the messages I found on Instagram.

Neither of us knows what our next move should be.

Well, Agnes does, but it's not one I can go along with.

'I know you don't want to, Kitty, but there's really nothing else we can do. We don't know where she is and all we have to go on is a stupid smashed phone with *blood* on it. The police will be able to go through Antoinette's tech with a fine-tooth comb. They'll be able to trace things like IP addresses. They'll help us. Even if they don't think there's really a killer out there, Antoinette is still missing. That's just a fact.'

I sigh. I know she's right. But the police.

I can't call the police.

I just can't.

It's not just the corpse and the chatty hostage in the wine

cellar, it's everything. I can't have them raking over our lives. Once they find a thread and start pulling, who knows where it will end.

And it's not just me it implicates; Carmella and Gabriel helped us get rid of Ben Pemberton's body, they'd be pulled into this whole mess too.

I can't let that happen.

Not until I've exhausted every other avenue.

'Everyone knows the first forty-eight hours are crucial,' Agnes is saying now. 'After that . . . well, the chances of finding her alive . . . they aren't good, Kitty.'

I look at her, those ice-blue eyes are filled with concern.

'It's barely been twenty-four hours' I say. 'They won't even take it seriously yet. That's what Lauren said.'

Agnes purses her lips. I can tell she's getting angry with me. 'Kitty, respectfully, do you know everything about US cops from watching *Law and Order*? It doesn't work like that.'

I sigh again.

I know we're going to have to call the police.

It's inevitable unless we have a breakthrough ourselves. And right now we're closer to breakdown than breakthrough.

But I need time to clear the cellar out.

'Twenty-four hours,' I say. 'Give me twenty-four hours. And then we'll call them.'

Agnes's brow puckers. 'We're wasting time—'

'Twenty-four hours,' I say, more firmly this time. 'I'm sure you need some time to clear out the guesthouse.' She blinks at me. 'Do you think they won't be all over your place as well?'

Agnes's eyes widen and I feel a stab of guilt.

'I'd never hurt her!' Her voice is high-pitched with outrage.

'Agnes,' I say carefully, '*I* know that. Of course I know that. But the police don't, do they? They know that most women are harmed by someone known to them. A romantic partner.' I know the stats are typically *male* intimate partners but I let the insinuation sit there for a moment.

'I've got nothing to hide,' she says, jutting her chin out defiantly. 'But okay. Let's leave it twenty-four hours.'

Inspiration hits me suddenly.

'Hey,' I say, 'so maybe we can't call the police right now but we could call someone police adjacent.'

Agnes gives me a puzzled look. 'What's police adjacent?'

'A private investigator. Travis.'

'Travis who you kneed in the nuts and haven't spoken to since?' She looks sceptical. 'Do you think he'll help?'

I think about this.

I really have no idea. I wouldn't want to help me after what I did. But he *did* like me. And what's more attractive to a man than a damsel in distress? Doesn't it make their protector instinct kick in or something?

'There's only one way to find out,' I say to Agnes as I pick my phone off the table and scroll through until I find Travis's name.

I press it and wait as it rings and rings.

I'm expecting it to go through to voicemail but then I hear his voice.

'Kitty,' he says. I try to decipher his tone. He doesn't sound thrilled to hear from me, not by any stretch of the imagination.

But he answered. That's got to count for something, right?

'Hey, Travis,' I say. 'How are you?'

'Not bad,' he says. 'I mean, no one has physically assaulted me after what I thought was a good date for a few days.'

I cringe.

'I really can't tell you how sorry I am about what happened,' I say.

'I know how sorry you are. I got your texts.'

'Oh. Good,' I say. 'I wasn't sure because you didn't reply.'

I hear him sigh. 'I've just been busy. I'm sorry. I wasn't deliberately ignoring you.' He sounds kinder now, his voice doesn't have the edge to it that it did when he answered. 'What are you up to?'

'Actually,' I say, 'this isn't a social call. I need your help with something.'

'Okay. What?'

I don't want to go through it all over the phone. 'It's complicated,' I say. 'Can you come over?'

There's a pause. 'I'm out on a job at the moment,' he says. 'But I can stop by this evening. Is that okay?'

It'll have to be.

'That's great,' I say.

I hang up and turn to Agnes, who's looking at me with expectation.

'He's out of the area at the moment, but he's going to come over later.'

She closes her eyes with relief. 'Do you think he'll be able to help us?'

'I'm sure he will.'

I think about Travis and his not-that-brilliant attempt at finding Aidan Ward and suddenly I'm not so sure at all.

But it's not like we have any other options.

50

THE WINE CELLAR, KITTY AND ANTOINETTE'S AIRBNB, WEST HOLLYWOOD, LOS ANGELES

I head back to the villa after I've spoken to Travis.

There's something in the wine cellar I need to deal with.

I've grabbed a knife from the kitchen.

Something small and mass-produced.

It's not ideal.

I wanted to take my time with this kill. I wanted to really make him suffer.

But now, it just needs to be quick.

He's still curled up in the corner when I turn the cellar lights on. He doesn't even turn to look at me this time.

Is he dead already?

No, I can see him breathing.

'Aidan,' I say but he doesn't respond. 'Aidan. I've got some water for you.'

That gets a response.

A grunt.

It's not easy for him to move with his wrists and ankles cable-tied but he tries to shuffle himself into a sitting position.

He doesn't manage it the first time and rolls back onto his side. He's persistent though and tries again, using the wall to lever himself up. It's painful to watch. So painful that I almost offer to help him. But then I remember that he left Tor unable to help herself after he attacked her. How he didn't even call an ambulance, just fled the country instead. I go from wanting to help him to wanting to kick him.

So I do.

But he doesn't even give me the satisfaction of a wail of pain. He just gives me a look like he's some injured pet and I've hoofed him for lols.

Surely I can't have broken him down this easily.

'You said you had water?' he croaks, eyeing the knife in my hand.

He sounds so pathetic that I sigh, tuck the knife into the waistband of my shorts and trudge back up the stairs into the kitchen and fill a Stanley with water from the tap.

He can think of it as a kind of last supper.

I take it back down to the cellar and crouch down, near enough that I can hold the straw to his lips but far enough that he can't head-butt me should he get any ideas. He doesn't make any attempt to lash out though. He just gulps the water through the straw like a dying man. Which is quite fitting really.

'Thank you,' he says when he's finished.

'That's okay.' I stand up and slide the knife out again.

'Wait,' he says and I look at him through narrowed eyes. 'What are you going to do with me?' There's a tremor in his voice and it's real fear.

Good.

'Why?' I say. 'Are you scared?'

'Look at me, Kitty,' he says in a pitiful voice. 'Of course I'm scared.'

'It's what you deserve.'

'I'm sorry for what I did to Tor. I really am.'

This is the first time he's admitted it. That he hurt her. I'm not sure I believe the remorse though.

'Why did you do it? Why did you hurt her like that?'

He looks down at his bound ankles, like he can't bear to hold eye contact with me any longer.

It looks like shame.

A fresh pang of pity pricks at me.

I shake it off.

I need to remember that Aidan Ward is a manipulator and a liar. Not only that but he's literally *trained* in psychology. He *wants* me to feel sorry for him. He thinks that if he calls me by my name and reminds me that he's human then I won't be able to kill him.

Well, he's wrong.

And he's not human.

He's a monster.

I walk over towards him, the knife glinting under the single lightbulb.

51

KITTY AND ANTOINETTE'S AIRBNB, WEST HOLLYWOOD, LOS ANGELES

Just as I touch the tip of the blade against the soft part of his throat that's fluttering like a butterfly's wings, there's a knock at the door.

Oh come on, not now.

Not on murder attempt number four. Or is it five? I've lost count.

I ignore it and concentrate on the knife. But the door thumps again. Harder this time.

For fuck's sake.

Can I not kill a man in peace?

My phone lights up with a text notification.

Finished up earlier than I expected. Am outside.

Travis.

Of all the times for him to be early.

'Do you need to get that?' Aidan says.

I glare at him. 'I'll be back for you. Don't think you're off the hook.' I rip off a new strip of duct tape and slap it across his mouth. 'Don't go anywhere.'

Then I go up the steps and lock the cellar door behind me.

There's another knock at the door.

'Coming,' I say.

I open the door and he's standing there, leaning against the frame in that louche way of his, his hair curling slightly into his eyes.

'Hey,' I say and he smiles.

'Hey, yourself,' he says. 'Hope I'm not interrupting anything?'

Just a casual spot of mid-afternoon murder.

'Nothing that can't wait,' I say. 'Come in.' I stand to the side and let Travis step in. 'Thanks so much for coming. I wasn't sure if you would.'

He gives a little shrug. 'Of course. But you should know that I've got a can of Mace in my pocket so don't try anything.'

I stare at him in horror.

'Kitty, I'm kidding,' he says. 'It's fine. Now what's going on? You sounded panicked on the phone.'

I lead him through to the kitchen and tell him to take a seat.

Travis pulls out a chair and I sit opposite him.

'So what's going on?' Travis asks again, opening his big hands and laying them palm up on the table.

'Antoinette is missing.'

'Missing? What do you mean?'

'She's gone,' I say. What else could *missing* mean? 'We argued two nights ago and I haven't seen her since.'

Travis's face rearranges itself into concern. 'And you haven't heard from her?'

I take her battered phone out of my pocket, where I've been keeping it like some sort of talisman, and lay it on the table between us. Travis reaches for the phone and inspects it, his eyes widening when he sees the dark red stain.

'Is this—'

'Blood,' I say. 'Yes, it is.'

He sucks in a deep breath. 'And you haven't called the police?'

I sigh. 'It's complicated,' I say. 'So, no.'

His eyebrow twitches slightly but his face remains neutral. Private investigators must meet people all the time who don't want to involve the police. That's pretty much their bread and butter, isn't it? Helping people who have been let down by law enforcement.

We're actually quite similar when you think about it.

He reaches into the pocket of his jeans and takes out a small notebook and the stub of a pencil.

'Let's keep this simple then,' he says, scribbling something down. 'So it's Antoinette Collins?'

'Pemberton, actually,' I say and he writes this down. 'She's my half-sister.'

'And her date of birth?'

I tell him.

'So you say you last saw her two nights ago? Walk me through it. What happened? What was she wearing?'

I describe Antoinette's outfit to Travis, her slip dress, her vintage Chanel flats. 'And a scarf,' I say, remembering the pale pink silk fabric looped around her neck. She's barely taken it off since I gave it to her that first day.

'A scarf?' Travis repeats, his brow troubled. 'In LA?'

'Not like a *winter* scarf,' I say. Urgh. Men. 'You know, like a delicate one. An accessory.'

'Right, yes.' He nods and scribbles something down. 'And how was she? When you last saw her? Was she distressed? Did she seem worried about anything? Anything on her mind?'

Anything other than the producer she'd just stabbed in the neck?

I take a deep breath in. 'We'd had a bit of a disagreement.'

Travis holds my gaze. 'So you argued?' he asks and sweat begins to bead on my upper lip. God, I can never get questioned by the police, without being nervous about giving away that we were arguing about her sloppy attitude to murder.

I'd fold like a deckchair.

'A bit,' I admit.

'What about?'

'I honestly can't even remember,' I lie and hope I'm doing a good job of it. 'Just something silly.' I give a little laugh that sounds fake even to my ears. 'Sister stuff.'

Travis narrows his eyes at me. 'Kitty,' he says, 'if you want me to help you then I need you to be honest with me.'

I sigh. 'We just argued about some of her behaviour,' I say.

'Okay. In what way?'

'Just like, well, we're here looking for someone, as you know, and she's just been getting distracted.' It's not exactly a lie.

More scribbling. 'Distracted with what?'

Oh God.

This was a terrible idea.

'By Agnes!' I say. He saw them at dinner after all. He thought they were cute.

He purses his lips. 'Interesting,' he says. 'I think I need to speak to Agnes.'

'Really? Why? She's as baffled by Antoinette's disappearance as I am.'

Travis nods slowly. 'Maybe. Or maybe she knows something.'

I shake my head. 'There's no way. Agnes is the sweetest. She's got a little dog.'

His eyes narrow. 'Do you know who else had a dog, Kitty?' I shake my head. 'Jeffrey Dahmer.'

'Oh.'

'Yes.'

'So, I'm thinking we call Agnes in. See what she knows.'

'Who's name-dropping me?' Agnes pokes her head around the back door. 'Knock knock.'

'Come in,' I say to her. 'Travis is here.'

She wafts in, Lana Del Gay in her arms, and Travis considers her for a moment.

'Cute dog,' he says eventually and Agnes gives him a smile. She puts Lana on the floor before pulling out a chair and sitting next to me. The dog immediately snarls at Travis.

'Oh be quiet,' Agnes tells her in a baby voice. She looks back at Travis. 'Sorry about that. She doesn't really like men.'

Travis's eyebrow twitches again.

'No problem,' he says and then clears his throat. 'So Kitty and I are talking about Antoinette's disappearance.'

Agnes nods solemnly.

'Where were you the night she went missing?'

'Excuse me?' Agnes is taken aback.

Travis leans across the table. 'Here's the thing,' he says. 'Antoinette hasn't been seen since the night before last. And she doesn't know many people in this town. So I need to speak with the people she *does* know.'

'I was at home,' Agnes says. 'All night. In my room.'

'Is that so? Can anyone confirm that?'

Agnes's eyes widen. Two nights ago was the day she was assaulted by Richard Stone.

'Travis,' I say. 'You're oiling the wrong hinge. Agnes doesn't know what happened to Antoinette. She's as worried as I am.'

'Thank you, Kitty,' Agnes says with a hard stare at Travis, which Lana Del Gay backs up with a low growl. She turns to me. 'Have you told him? About the WeHo Ripper?'

Travis flicks his gaze over to me. 'The what?'

'The WeHo Ripper,' I say. Surely a private investigator would know about the theories circulating online. His face is blank though. I sigh and take Antoinette's iPad from the counter. I slide it over to him, open on her PrivatePool page. His eyes widen and I notice a flush creep across his face when he sees the photos she's uploaded. 'There's speculation on Reddit that WeHo has a serial killer who's targeting women from this site.'

Travis takes the tablet from me and frowns at the screen. 'You think she's been targeted?' he says after a moment or two, and Agnes and I nod.

'Not just targeted,' I say. 'I'm pretty sure she set this account up as a trap. She wanted to try to catch the killer.'

'But her trap was used against her,' Travis says almost to himself, running his hand over the scruff on his jaw. 'A classic story of cat and mouse. But the hunter becomes the hunted.' He stares at the iPad for a few moments, deep in thought.

Then he looks up at me. 'And you haven't called the police? Is that right? Even though you think she might have been taken by a murderer?'

I shrug helplessly.

'Show him the messages as well,' Agnes says. 'The Instagram ones.'

I take the iPad back from Travis and swipe through to the DMs.

'She'd been getting these messages,' I say. 'They sound like they could be from the killer.'

He holds out his hand for the iPad and I pass it back to him. He regards it for a minute, a serious look on his face.

'Okay,' he says. 'Leave this with me. I'm going to see what I can find out from this.' He stands up to leave. With the iPad.

'Is that it?' I say. 'Are you going?'

'Yes,' he says. 'If you're right and she has been taken by this WeHo Ripper then we have no time to waste.' He taps the iPad. 'I'll mine this for data. Sit tight. I'll be in touch. I'll see myself out.'

And with that he disappears out of the kitchen.

A moment later the front door slams.

Agnes stares at the space where Travis had been sitting.

'Well, that was weird,' she says and I nod. 'Do you trust him?'

'I have to,' I say.

But the truth is, I really have no idea who to trust.

52

KITTY AND ANTOINETTE'S AIRBNB, WEST HOLLYWOOD, LOS ANGELES

Agnes leaves soon after and I realise that Travis is right about one thing.

We don't have any time to waste.

And that means I need to get rid of the men in the cellar.

It's time to kill Aidan Ward.

Like, actually this time.

Without any interruptions.

I'm not sure what I did with the knife I had earlier. Did I put it in the dishwasher? Maybe. Anyway, I haven't got time to think about that now. What else can I use to kill him quickly? I do a quick recce of the kitchen and my eyes land on a collection of kettlebells in the corner. Who wouldn't want the option of a kettelbell workout while they're away?

I select a 10kg one and take it down to the cellar.

Aidan is scrunched up in the corner now. He hasn't eaten since I locked him down here two nights ago so he's probably feeling very weak and faint. It won't be a challenge to finish him off but at least it will be quick and easy.

He sits up when he hears me.

I notice the moment he sees the kettlebell and registers what it means for him. His eyes grow from slits into saucers and the flicker of fear I see in them gives me a little thrill.

He groans when I rip the duct tape off his mouth. I like to hear the sounds they make when they die.

'You've come to finish the job then?' he says.

'Of course I have,' I say. 'I need you gone.'

'I can hear everything down here by the way,' he says. 'I know you still haven't found your sister.'

I don't say anything. He clearly thinks I'm stupid and that his psycho-babble mind games will work with me.

'And I heard you talking about a serial killer. That must be very scary for you, Kitty. I can't imagine how you must feel.'

'Do you want me to put the duct tape back?' I say. He shakes his head. 'Then shut up. The only thing I want to hear coming out of your mouth is screams.' He shuffles back further into the corner.

I peer at him and wonder, not for the first time, what it was that Tor saw in him. He's so pathetic. But I guess that's what grooming does, isn't it? She didn't see anything in *him,* just in the person he pretended to be.

'Do you remember when you came to see me,' he's saying now. 'You said you were there to check me out when Tor told you we were together. But that wasn't the real reason, was it? You wanted to know how to stop killing. You pretended you were talking about social media, but really you were talking about murder.'

'Be quiet, Aidan,' I say. 'You're making me angry and this will be a whole lot nastier for you if you put me in a bad mood.'

'You don't want to kill me, Kitty,' he says. 'You want to stop. You want to be normal. I can help you with that. I can help you deal with your rage. Let me go and we can work together.'

Is this man clinically allergic to reality or something?

'Aidan, killing you is literally the only thing I want to do at the moment,' I say as I drop down to my knees so I'm right in front of him. '*You* are the sole cause of my rage right now. Not only did you hurt my friend, but you then skipped the country, which meant I had to come after you. If it wasn't for you, I wouldn't be here and my sister would be safe at home.'

'That's another reason you shouldn't do this, not now.' He looks pointedly at the kettlebell on the floor next to me. 'You're not thinking clearly,' he says. 'You're reacting with your lizard brain, Kitty.'

I hate my name on his lips.

It sounds like the worst word in the world.

I want to rip it out of his mouth.

'Stop saying my name,' I say. 'And stop insinuating that I'm stupid. I do not have a lizard brain.'

'No!' he says quickly. 'That's not what lizard brain means. It just means the bit of your brain that is in survival mode. It means you're not able to think logically right now.'

I frown at him and pull myself back onto my feet. 'You're wrong,' I say. 'I'm thinking very logically right now.'

I reach down and pick the kettlebell up with both hands and raise it high above my head like I'm about to do a swing.

Aidan cowers as much as a man can cower when his hands and feet are bound.

I'm about to bring the weight crashing down onto his skull when a sound stops me in my tracks.

An urgent hammering.

Fuck.

It's the door.

Again?

Why am I suddenly the most popular person in West Hollywood today? Does no one know I'm busy?

Aidan risks me a look while I decide what to do.

I have to answer it. No one hammering that loudly is going to leave in a hurry.

Am I *ever* going to be able to murder this man without someone interrupting me?

'I'll be right back,' I tell Aidan as I put a fresh strip of duct tape over his mouth. 'Don't go anywhere.'

I take the kettlebell up into the kitchen with me and lock the cellar. Whoever is at the door is still hammering and my heart joins in.

I take a deep breath, count to five and pad across the floor.

53

KITTY AND ANTOINETTE'S AIRBNB, WEST HOLLYWOOD, LOS ANGELES

It's probably the police.

And they're here to tell me they've found Antoinette.

Or what's left of her.

There's a weird mix of fear and fury fighting for dominance in my blood.

Fear seems to be winning.

I don't want to open the door.

I don't want to know what's behind it.

'Kitty. Open up!'

It's a man's voice and I wonder for a second if I'm still asleep because I must be dreaming. Surely this isn't real because that voice sounded just like . . .

'It's me. Charlie.'

Charlie.

I'm racing to the door now.

I yank it open, half expecting there to be no one there at all. Some sort of aural hallucination brought on by my stress and lack of sleep.

But it's not.

He's here.

He's really here.

He's standing there, staring at me – a bit dishevelled – a battered leather holdall I recognise at his feet.

I want to pinch him just to make sure, but I think that might be a bit weird. I want to throw myself into his arms and inhale him but that might also be a bit strange considering the last time I saw him he was walking away from me, away from us.

'Charlie,' I say and I'm amazed I can even find words. He's every bit as perfect as I remember him. I wondered if maybe I'd been idealising him in my mind since we broke up, but that's not the case. He still has that sandy-brown hair that I want to run my fingers through and grab. He still has that smattering of stubble that I find irresistible. He still has that dimple that I want to stick my finger in.

'Hi, Kits,' he says, a hint of a smile playing on those lips. The lips that used to kiss me goodnight and then kiss me awake again. That used to trail down my thighs until I thought I'd scream.

The lips that used to say my name and make it sound like the most beautiful word that's ever been spoken.

That used to tell me they loved me.

'What are you doing here?'

He's peering at me, his green eyes full of concern. 'Do you think I could come in?' he says. 'I feel like I've been travelling for about half of my natural life.'

I look up at him again and notice the smudge of shadows under his eyes.

'Yes, of course, come through.' He follows me into the living room and immediately flops on the couch. 'Can I get you anything? Water? Food? I'd offer tea but there's only like rose and hibiscus. They can't really get tea right over here.'

Charlie gives me a half smile and reaches into the holdall he dragged in with him and pulls out a turquoise box. Tea bags. 'Fortnum and Mason,' he says. 'I thought you'd be missing them.'

I could cry.

I love this man so much.

I take the tea bags and go through to the kitchen, where I boil water on the stove and make us mugs of tea with oat milk.

'What are you doing here?' I ask again when I take the drinks back through. He's texting someone and I feel a stab of anxiety. What if it's another woman? What if he's telling someone else that he's arrived safely?

I don't think I could cope.

'Tor persuaded me,' he says with that smile again as he slides the phone back into his pocket. 'She seems to think there's something you need to talk to me about?' He gives me an expectant look.

'Oh,' I say. 'Did she?' I have no idea what this means. I haven't told Tor about Antoinette going missing. I haven't told anyone back in the UK.

'Yes,' he says, cocking his head at me in that way I love. 'She made it sound pretty important?'

What is Tor playing at? 'I don't know what to tell you,' I say.

Charlie looks confused. 'Oh. Right,' he says and it feels

awkward between us now. 'Maybe I should have called you first. But I wasn't sure if you'd speak to me.'

'I'm sorry if you've had a wasted trip,' I say, 'but I really don't know what Tor is talking about.'

'That's so weird,' he says. 'She seemed pretty sure when I saw her.'

'You saw her?' I ask. Why hasn't Tor mentioned any of this to me? What's she playing at?

'Yes,' he nods, 'she messaged me and asked me to go to her house.' He sees my expression. 'I was surprised too, but she seemed to really want to talk to me. I was worried something had happened to you.' His voice is softer as he says the last part.

'How was she?'

Charlie looks at his hands. 'Not good,' he says. 'She told me everything that happened. You know with that therapist guy.'

'Aidan Ward,' I say through gritted teeth.

'She seems to think you followed him out here?'

I think about the man in the cellar, the man I was so close to killing just moments ago. I'm not sure how much I can tell Charlie. He knows all about me. But he hates it. Hates it so much that, the last time I saw him, he couldn't even bear to be in the same room as me.

'Charlie,' I say, 'it's great to see you, so great, but now isn't a really good time.'

He frowns. 'What do you mean?'

I sigh. 'Antoinette is missing,' I say.

'What do you mean missing?'

Why does everyone keep asking that?

Is there another definition of 'missing' that's totally bypassed me?

'Gone, disappeared. I think something bad has happened to her.'

I can feel tears scratching at the back of my eyes. I don't want to cry in front of Charlie so I mumble something about water and scurry back through to the kitchen, where I have no choice but to let them fall.

'Kits?' Charlie has followed me. 'What is it? What's wrong?'

There's so much I want to say to him, so much I've practised saying to him in my head, all those imagined conversations late at night.

But I can't say anything.

I'm choking on tears.

And then his arms are around me and he's pulling me into his chest.

'It's okay,' he says. 'It's okay. It's going to be okay.'

My heart sinks and joins the rest of my liquified insides as I think of the last time we were actually together like this. The terror in his eyes that turned to revulsion as he digested what I was, what I am. The back of his head as he walked out of the door, leaving me as crushed as every bone I've ever put through a meat grinder.

'I didn't just come because of what Tor said,' he murmurs into my hair. 'I missed you. Fuck, I missed you.'

'I'm a murderer,' I say because we're so far past trying to sugar-coat any of this or tie it up with a nice ribbon. 'I haven't changed.'

He nods his head gently. 'Maybe I have though.' He lifts my chin so my eyes meet his and I can see the revulsion isn't there anymore. That look that he drove through me like a sword. I don't know what's in its place but it's softer. It's something I want to see. It looks a lot like love. Or longing at the very least.

'Really?' I say. 'You've changed so much that suddenly the thought of even being in the same room as a killer doesn't make you want to throw your guts up? You've changed so much that everything you said to me in France doesn't matter?'

He shrugs slightly, still not breaking eye contact. 'I don't know,' he says again. 'All I know is that I haven't been able to stop thinking about you. And I know it's a horrible cliché but every day there are just new things that I want to tell you. I keep turning around to say something to you and every time I realise you're not there it hits me again.'

'You blocked me.' I say. 'On everything!'

'Because I couldn't stop looking at your socials. And you know I hate socials.' He really does hate socials. 'I was spending every night just scrolling through your photos. My brother had to point out to me how unhealthy it was. And then . . .' He pauses and takes a breath, 'and then Tor called me and I just knew I had to come out here.' He pauses again. 'I still love you, Kitty. I never stopped loving you. Not for a minute. And, honestly, if you want me to turn right back around and get on the next plane home, I'll do it. But I needed to tell you, to your face, that I love you.'

I let my head fall back against his chest. It's so solid and warm that it makes me want to cry even more. He's really here and he's really telling me that he loves me.

He lifts my chin again, putting his hands on either side of my face. 'Do you want me to go, Kitty?'

I shake my head and then his hands aren't on my face anymore, they're in my hair and his lips are on mine and I don't know who kisses who first but he's whispering into my mouth, asking me 'Is this okay?' and it's more than okay.

It's everything.

'Fuck, I've missed you,' he breathes and his hands are on my waist now as he lifts me up onto the table and I wrap my legs around him, pulling him to me, I can't get him close enough. Even when he's deep inside me and we're inhaling each other, it's still not close enough. I sink my nails into his back, trying to drive him even further into me, and he scratches at the skin on my neck with his teeth as we both try to devour each other. It's the most intense fuck of my life. Also maybe the quickest. But that doesn't matter when, minutes later, we're staring at each other again like we can't quite believe the other is real.

'I've missed you too,' I say finally.

'That wasn't supposed to happen like that,' Charlie is saying as he retucks his T-shirt into his jeans and I pull my dress down. 'I wanted to woo you properly.'

'Woo me?'

'Yes, I thought you'd like to be wooed.'

'I think we were just very wooed,' I say.

He smiles and kisses me on the top of my head. 'Can we pretend that didn't happen and can I ask you out for food?'

'Charlie,' I say gently. 'My sister is missing and I'm really worried that something terrible has happened to her. It's not really a good time to be going out for food.'

'Let's get takeout then,' he says. 'When was the last time you had anything to eat?'

I try to think but I honestly can't remember. My stomach gives me away with a growl. But how can I think about something as basic as eating when Antoinette is missing?

'Starving yourself isn't going to help Antoinette,' Charlie says, doing that annoying thing he's always been able to do of reading my mind. 'And you can tell me what's happened.'

I suppose there's not really much I can do until Travis comes back with Antoinette's iPad. And I want to tell Charlie everything.

'Okay,' I say. 'Why don't you take a shower while I order in?'

'Perfect,' he says.

Once I've shown him where everything is I come back downstairs and make sure I've locked the wine cellar door.

54

KITTY AND ANTOINETTE'S AIRBNB, WEST HOLLYWOOD, LOS ANGELES

'So what's been going on?' Charlie asks later when our food has been delivered and we're having an impromptu carpet picnic in the lounge.

And so I tell him.

Everything.

About Ron Wilde and his current location in LV luggage in the wine cellar, about Aidan Ward and how he's rooming with Ron right now, about our surprise housemates. And about the WeHo Ripper and how Antoinette has been determined to hunt him down by posing as a PrivatePool creator.

Charlie's jaw is hanging open by the time I've finished talking.

'Jesus, Kitty,' he says, sipping some water but looking for all the world like he needs something stronger. 'I literally did not predict one part of that.'

'I know,' I say as I shovel fried Brussels sprouts into my mouth.

Why am I so *hungry*?

'It's been quite the trip.'

'And you really think whoever this WeHo Ripper is could have taken her?'

'I can't think of anything else,' I say. 'She wouldn't have gone off alone, she's got no friends here apart from Agnes and Lauren, plus we found her phone outside the house. Smashed. With specks of blood on it.'

'Shit, Kitty, that's awful,' he says. 'But, you know Antoinette. I'm sure she's not giving whoever she's with an easy time.' He gives me a little smile and reaches for my hand, giving it a reassuring little squeeze. 'So what's the plan? What are we going to do?'

'Travis has her iPad,' I say. 'He's going through it to see if there's anything that can help us. If not, we'll have to go to the police.' I grimace at the thought.

'Who's Travis?' Charlie asks.

Oh that's right. I haven't told him that part. An administrative oversight.

'He's a private investigator who helped us find Aidan,' I say. He doesn't need to know that Travis and I went on a date. There's no point in muddying the waters.

'Oh right,' he says as he sucks in a deep breath, puffing out his cheeks, before blowing it out again. 'No wonder Tor thought I should come out.'

Hmm.

I still can't work out what Tor was doing, telling Charlie that I had something to talk to him about.

She doesn't know about any of this.

'How was she?' I say. 'Like, really?'

He chews through a mouthful of food before answering. 'Different,' he says. 'Nervous. Jumpy.'

'Hmm. Well, I guess that's what happens when the man you loved and trusted after an unspeakable trauma turns out to be a monster too.'

Charlie nods. 'She looked so scared and small. Just completely broken. I kept thinking about that night I first met you all. That god-awful party at the V and A.'

I smile at the memory. Tor, Maisie and I had all been at this charity gala that Hen's dad was giving some speech at. The charity was Charlie's and the party was in the John Madejski Gardens at the Victoria and Albert Museum. I remember the first time I saw him, sitting on a wall, rubbing his face and trying to hide his nerves as he went over his own speech. He was honestly the best-looking man I'd ever seen in my life. He'd spotted me staring and gave me a shy smile. I was smitten after that. I look at him now. I still am.

'That was quite a night,' I say and Charlie smiles.

'It was.' We stare into each other's eyes for a couple of beats.

'I'm still going to kill him,' I say. 'Aidan Ward.' I watch Charlie's face closely for his reaction. To my surprise, he doesn't even flinch. 'When we've found Antoinette. I'm going to kill him and I'm going to enjoy it.'

'Good,' Charlie says. 'He deserves it.' He's staring at me now and the eye contact is so intense I have to look away.

'Do you mean that?' I whisper. He leans across the table and takes my hands in his.

'I really do. I've had time to think, as well as miss you. Time to really think about what you said to me in France.'

I grimace. I don't want to be reminded of that awful conversation we had in the kitchen of the house Charlie had been held captive in for days.

The conversation where I told him exactly who I really am.

The conversation where I had to watch myself fall off the pedestal Charlie had put me on.

The conversation where my boyfriend seemed to fall out of love with me before my eyes.

'And I understand why you're out here. Why you needed to find . . . that man.'

'But now I've lost Antoinette,' I say with a sigh. 'I only just found my sister and now she's gone. And it's all my fault.' I hear my voice break on the last word.

Charlie reaches across the table and touches my hand gently. 'We'll find her,' he says. 'I promise you, Kitty. We'll find her.'

I nod, biting back the sob in my throat.

At that moment my phone beeps.

It's face-down on the table and I pick it up and look at it.

A text.

From an unknown number.

There haven't been many points in my life when I've felt absolute and genuine fear.

When the world seems to tilt and everything inside turns to ice.

In fact maybe only once before. Earlier this summer when I was drunk and alone on the beach in Cannes with a man I'd met in a bar.

But even that doesn't compare to how I feel right now.

Because the only person in danger then was me.

I suck in a breath and hand the phone to Charlie, not wanting to look at the words anymore.

Although, even when he has the phone, I can still see them. Like they've been burned into my brain.

I've got your sister. The one who wouldn't stay in her lane.
She's got 24 hours.
Then I'm coming for you.

55

KITTY AND ANTOINETTE'S AIRBNB, WEST HOLLYWOOD, LOS ANGELES

I grab the phone back from Charlie and call the number the text came from. An automated voice answers.

'This number is used for outbound SMS only.'

Fuck.

Fuck.

'It's a burner number,' I say, frustration making tears collect in my eyes. Charlie slips an arm around me. I just want to melt into him and let him hold me.

But I can't.

I need to hold it together.

I need to find my sister.

'Kits,' he says, 'it's going to be okay.'

'I need to send this to Travis,' I say, ignoring his platitudes. 'He might be able to trace the number somehow.' I notice that my hands are trembling as I try to take a screenshot of the text.

'Let me do it,' Charlie says and I let him slip the phone out of my hands before I slump down on the couch.

‘This is all my fault,’ I say. ‘I should *never* have let her come out here with me.’

Charlie sinks down beside me. ‘You can’t blame yourself. You didn’t know any of this was going to happen.’

‘I can absolutely blame myself.’

And I will.

If we don’t find my sister in the next twenty-four hours, she’s going to die. And it’s all my fault.

I should’ve been helping her find the WeHo Ripper, not leaving her to her own devices.

I check my phone again but there’s nothing from Travis.

Not that I expect him to be on-call for me, but this is kind of urgent.

I fire off another text.

Please get back to me ASAP.

‘We should be out there,’ I say to Charlie. ‘We should be looking for her.’

Charlie frowns. ‘Where would we start?’

‘I don’t know,’ I say, ‘but I’ll knock on every door in LA if I need to.’ But as I say the words a wave of exhaustion washes over me, pulls me under.

‘I think,’ Charlie is saying, ‘that the best thing you can do for Antoinette is get some rest. I’ll stay awake in case there’s any news.’

I want to argue but my eyes are already closing. I can’t fight it.

‘Wake me up if Travis replies,’ I murmur as I let the darkness take me and I drift into oblivion.

56

KITTY AND ANTOINETTE'S AIRBNB, WEST HOLLYWOOD, LOS ANGELES

I'm confused when I wake up. I don't remember coming to bed. I sit up and realise it's morning.

The next day.

Like there's not a ticking clock on my sister's life.

Charlie is lying next to me, staring at the ceiling. He turns to face me when he feels me stir.

'Morning,' he says.

'Why did you let me sleep all night?' I pull myself out of bed, shivering when my bare feet hit the tiled floor. 'We need to find Antoinette.'

Charlie reaches out and touches my arm, butterfly soft. 'Kits,' he says, 'you were exhausted. I don't think I could have woken you up if I'd tried. I had to carry you up here.'

'Oh,' I say. 'Did Travis reply?'

Charlie chews his lip and then shakes his head. 'No,' he says. 'I'm sorry.'

I reach for my phone, which is plugged in next to the bed. Charlie really thinks of everything. The screen is irritatingly empty of notifications. I check my text thread with Travis just in case Charlie missed anything. There's nothing since the messages I sent last night.

'Where is he?'

I call him but the phone rings and rings.

What the hell is he playing at?

'Fuck's sake,' I say, flinging the phone away in frustration.

Charlie scoots across the bed and pulls me into his chest. I let my head rest against it, the sound of his heart and the rhythm of his breathing calming my own.

After a moment I pull away.

'Come on,' I say. 'We'd better decide what the next step is.'

In the kitchen, Charlie is making us coffee when Agnes knocks on the door. She has dark circles under her blue eyes that look like she's been smudged.

'Is there any news?' she asks me before she notices Charlie. 'Oh. Hello.'

'This is Charlie,' I say and Agnes raises an eyebrow. 'He's going to help us find Antoinette.'

'Nice to meet you,' she says.

'Shame it's not under better circumstances,' Charlie says. 'Would you like coffee?'

Agnes nods and I fill her in on the text I got last night. She looks horrified.

'And now Travis has gone AWOL,' I say with a heavy sigh.

'What? What do you mean?'

'He's gone complete ghost-mode,' I say. 'Not replying to texts, not answering calls.'

'Shit,' Agnes says. 'I hope he's okay.'

I do too.

But more than that, I want to know what he's been able to find out from my sister's iPad. And I want to know if he can track that number.

I try him again. And again.

I leave a voicemail that's verging on hysterical and another one that definitely is.

My coffee goes untouched. And then cold.

The morning turns into the afternoon and I still can't get hold of him.

'Where the fuck is he?' I scream at no one.

'Kits?' Charlie says, pulling his phone out. 'What did you say his last name is?'

'Truman,' I say. 'Why?'

'Truman with an e or without?'

'Um, pretty sure without. Why? What are you doing?'

'I'm trying to find a website for him. To see if there's another contact number but there's nothing online.'

'What do you mean?'

He holds out his phone and shows me page after page of Google results. 'I can't find anything about a Travis Truman Investigations,' he says. 'How did you find him?'

'Antoinette did,' I say. 'She said that he came very highly recommended.'

'Recommended by who?'

Oh God.

'Reddit,' I say slowly. 'Antoinette got all his details from Reddit.'

Charlie blinks quickly several times. 'Right. But you've

been to his office, right? You know where he works. Where we can find him?'

I blink back. 'Um . . .'

'What? What is it, Kits?'

'His office is a juice bar.'

'I don't understand.'

'We met him in a juice bar on Sunset. He said his office was being renovated.' I slump backwards and hold my head in my hands. Charlie exhales deeply. 'There's no office, is there?'

I'm so stupid.

Why did I not even think to check Travis's credentials myself?

It's not like Antoinette has ever been thorough in her research. My appointment with a middle-aged woman who she thought could be Aidan Ward speaks for itself.

I look over at Agnes. Her lips are pressed together in a thin line.

I know what she's thinking.

'We're going to have to call the police, aren't we?'

But before she can reply, there is a hammering at the front door.

57

KITTY AND ANTOINETTE'S AIRBNB, WEST HOLLYWOOD, LOS ANGELES

It's Travis.

Standing there with a half smile on his face like I haven't just spent the last however many hours stressing my tits off.

'Hey, Kitty,' he says.

'Where the fuck have you been?' I ask as I usher him inside. 'I've been trying to get hold of you! Oh my God!'

I shoo him through to the kitchen, where he and Charlie warily regard each other.

'Charlie, Travis. Travis, Charlie,' I say by way of introduction before I turn my attention fully to Travis. 'Where the hell have you been?' I shake my head. 'Never mind that. I don't care. What have you found?'

He looks blank for a tiny moment.

'Oh right, Antoinette,' he says. 'She hasn't turned up yet then?'

I stare at him. 'No, Travis,' I say. 'She hasn't turned up yet. I texted you about this last night. Did you not get it?'

Travis frowns a little and pulls his phone out of his pocket.

'Oh,' he says. 'So you did. Sorry. Not sure how that slipped past me.' He sucks in a sharp breath as he catches up on my messages. 'Well, that's not good.'

'No shit—' Agnes starts to say but I interrupt.

'We were hoping you might be able to trace the number. Is that something you can do?'

Travis doesn't lift his eyes from his phone. 'Um,' he says. 'I can try. Sure.'

'What about her iPad? Did you find anything on there?'

'Yes,' Agnes says. 'Did you manage to trace the IP address from those messages?'

Travis finally looks up at us. 'Not exactly,' he says. 'I've been following up on some other leads.'

Charlie has been quiet up until this point but he comes over now and stands directly in front of Travis.

'What are these other leads then, mate?' he asks. I give Charlie a glare. He's being rude, which isn't like him. But also, I don't think he needs to be. We're depending on Travis here. But Charlie ignores me. 'They must be good, right? Because Kitty's been trying to get hold of you urgently.'

Travis just stares at him.

'We're waiting,' Charlie says. 'Have you found out anything at all?'

Travis still doesn't say anything but a bead of sweat appears on his upper lip.

'You're not a PI at all, are you?' Charlie says.

Travis sinks into one of the chairs and drops his head into his hands. 'No,' he says in a quiet voice.

What?

What?

I take a step towards him, rage and confusion twisting my hands into fists. I feel Agnes gently grab my arm, holding me back.

Travis looks up at me. 'I'm so sorry, Kitty.'

'What do you mean you're *sorry?*' I spit. 'What do you mean you're not a PI? Of course you are. You've been helping me?'

He shakes his head, which is hanging with shame. 'I'm not. I'm not. And I'm just so sorry. It was never meant to get this far.'

I glare at him. 'You lied? My sister is fucking missing and you've been lying to me?'

He can barely look me in the eye as he mutters again how sorry he is.

'Who the hell are you then?' I ask.

'My name really is Travis Truman,' he says. 'But I'm an actor.'

An actor.

A fucking actor.

'I'm auditioning for a role as a PI,' he's saying as if his explanation means anything, as if it could possibly cut through the red mist of rage that's engulfed me. 'I was trying a bit of method . . .'

'A fucking *role*!' I scream as I shake Agnes off and fly at him.

'That's where I recognised you from,' Agnes says. 'I've seen you at auditions.'

I have never been angrier in my life.

I want to rip his throat out.

I want to scratch his eyes out.

I want to squeeze the life out of him with my bare hands.

But before I reach him, Charlie has wrapped me in his arms and pulled me close into his chest. I struggle a bit to get away but he holds me tight.

'Get out,' I hiss at Travis. 'Get the fuck out.'

'I'm sorry,' he says again as he stands up. 'I really am.' He turns to go but then spins back to face me again. 'I just met you. And I really liked you,' he says. 'So I kept pretending. I'm really sorry, Kitty.'

'We have wasted time waiting for you,' I say, my voice a snarl. 'We thought you were helping us.'

He bows his head.

'I trusted you. And all you've done is waste our time.'

'I don't know what else to say.' He looks cornered. Useless.

'I think you'd better go,' Charlie says.

And he does.

Leaving the rest of us staring after him in shock.

58

KITTY AND ANTOINETTE'S AIRBNB, WEST HOLLYWOOD, LOS ANGELES

Agnes is the first to speak.

'I don't believe it,' she says. 'What the fuck?'

All the rage has evaporated from my body, leaving me feeling light-headed and weak. I pull away from Charlie and sink into a chair.

'He lied,' I say. 'It was all lies.'

'So we're no closer to finding Antoinette?' Agnes says, her shoulders dropping.

No closer at all.

We've got nothing.

No leads.

No location.

Nothing.

We don't even know where to start.

My chest feels like someone is sitting on it. I can't breathe.

'We're never going to find her in time,' I whisper. 'She could literally be anywhere.'

'Give me her iPad,' Charlie says. 'I'm not claiming to be

an expert or anything but I could have a go at locating the IP addresses. My brother knows about stuff like that. I can ask him.'

'Charlie, you are my fucking hero,' I say and look around but I can't see Antoinette's iPad anywhere. 'Fuck. Travis didn't give it back.' I sink down onto the floor and drop my head into my hands. 'I'm such a fucking idiot. My sister is going to die and there's absolutely nothing I can do about it.'

'There is one thing,' Agnes says.

She's right.

It's time.

I pick up my phone and press 'nine'.

Then 'one'.

I'm about to press 'one' again when Lauren comes bursting through the door. Her face is flushed and her hair a mess. She looks like she's been running.

And crying.

But it's not her ungroomed appearance, so different to how I'm used to seeing her, that makes me drop my phone.

It's what she's holding out to me.

A blush-pink silk scarf.

With a savage smear of dark red on it.

Antoinette's scarf.

Antoinette's blood.

'I found it,' she gasps, 'in Cort's car.'

59

KITTY AND ANTOINETTE'S AIRBNB, WEST HOLLYWOOD, LOS ANGELES

'It's Antoinette's, isn't it?' Lauren is saying but I can barely hear her over the blood that is suddenly roaring in my ears. 'I recognised it as soon as I saw it.' She holds the scarf out to me. The delicate pink one I bought for her on our first day here. Lauren's hands are trembling as I take it from her and hold it to my face. It smells like my sister, like the cloyingly rich perfume she wears, like that indescribable scent that is just *her.*

Oh, Antoinette.

Tears sting at my eyes.

The room blurs.

Grief punches me from the inside.

I nod. 'Yes, it's hers.' I slump down into a chair, clutching the scrap of fabric close to my chest. Charlie's at my side, holding my arm, concern tugging at his features.

The room tilts.

'What was it doing in Cort's car?' Agnes says. Her voice is high-pitched with panic and confusion. She looks wildly between us. 'I don't understand. When was Antoinette in Cort's car?'

Lauren swallows and her throat bobs. 'That's not all,' she says, her voice wobbling. She reaches into her pocket and, with shaking hands, pulls out a piece of paper folded into a small square.

What now?

'What's that?' Agnes says as I take it from Lauren.

'A list,' Lauren says as I open it.

It is.

It's a list of names.

Alicia Levy
Sofi Garcia
Ellie Edwards
Juno Blake

I read them out loud.

Agnes's eyes fly wide open.

'Oh no,' she says. 'These are the names of—'

'Of who?' says Charlie.

'Of all the PrivatePool women who have been found dead,' I say, pressing the list into Agnes's hand. Her eyes meet mine.

'Cort's the WeHo Ripper,' she whispers, her eyes widen even more. 'And he's got Antoinette.'

Lauren throws her a look. Her face is pinched. Her voice small as she says, 'I'm so sorry.'

I stand up. 'Where is he, Lauren? Where the fuck is he?'

But Lauren is shaking her head. 'There could be another explanation. Maybe he gave Antoinette a lift somewhere?'

I have to hold myself back from lunging at her. I thrust the scarf into her face. She turns away like she can't bear the sight of it.

'There is fucking *blood* on it, Lauren. Where. Is. He? Tell me!'

Charlie is at my side now and I feel his hand on my arm. I'm not sure if he's comforting me or getting ready to restrain me. I'm not sure what I need more in this moment.

Lauren is still shaking her head in disbelief and I want to shake Cort's location out of her. 'No,' she says. 'Cort would never hurt anyone. Especially not *women.* He's an ally.'

Is she having some sort of breakdown?

Is she completely *fucking delusional?*

Something in me breaks and I'm suddenly on her, my fingers gripping her arms, digging into her flesh, screaming into her face. 'Lauren! Where the fuck is Cort?'

'I don't know!' She sobs as she pulls herself out of my grasp. 'I don't know! He took off. I'm sorry!' And then she's gone, tearing out of the door and towards the guesthouse.

I make a move to follow her but Charlie is holding me back. Tender but firm.

He knows what I'm capable of.

'Kits,' he says, his voice an anchor pulling me back to the room. He turns my head so I'm looking at him. 'She said she doesn't know.'

'She's lying,' I hiss. I turn to Agnes. 'You're their friend. Where is he?' My voice is clipped, almost aggressive, and I clock a flicker of shock in her eyes.

But I don't care.

One of these women must know something.

'I . . . I know where he lives,' Agnes stammers. 'We should go there?' She looks from me to Charlie.

'Yes!' I say. 'Let's go now.' I move towards the table where the hire-car keys are. But as I do, the room tilts again. Spots appear in the corners of my eyes and I have to grab onto the back of a chair to stop myself from falling to the ground.

Charlie is at my side in a flash.

'Kits? Are you okay?'

'I'm fine,' I say but when I try to walk again the same thing happens. 'I just need to sit down for a minute.'

Charlie guides me into a seat. 'You're not going anywhere,' he says.

'I'm fine,' I say, even though my vision is swimming almost as much as my head.

'You're not,' he says. 'You nearly passed out.'

'I'll go,' Agnes says. She crouches beside me and puts her hand on my knee. 'I'll go. I want to find her as much as you do. Believe me.'

And I do.

'You can't go alone,' I say. 'It's dangerous. He's dangerous.'

'He's not going to do anything to me,' Agnes says but Charlie is frowning.

'No, Kitty's right,' he says. 'I'll come with you. Kits, you stay here and rest. Eat something. We'll let you know if we find anything.'

'But I want to come,' I say. 'If he's got Antoinette . . . if she's . . .' I can't finish the sentence. 'I should be there. I'll just wait in the car or something.'

Charlie drops down next to Agnes and they're both looking up at me. 'Let us go,' he says. 'I promise to call you as soon as we get there.' His lovely face is etched with concern. 'Please, Kits. Stay.'

And I hate it.

I hate it so much.

But I reluctantly nod. 'Okay,' I say, exhaustion pressing into me, clawing at my bones. 'Please keep me updated.'

'Of course,' Agnes says, standing and giving my knee a squeeze.

Charlie kisses the top of my head, the tips of my ears. 'Rest,' he says as he and Agnes disappear into the night.

But how am I supposed to rest?

It's an impossible ask with my sister missing, my boyfriend walking into god knows what, and me completely unable to protect either of them.

I collapse on the sofa after Charlie and Agnes leave, clutching a full-fat Coke. I chug half the can and feel the sugar chase the faintness away. I'm still exhausted but not seconds from blacking out anymore.

It's stress.

It must be stress.

I can't stand this feeling of uselessness. I feel so helpless. Completely impotent. I should be with Agnes and Charlie. I should be the one hammering on Cort's door, storming in, demanding to know where my sister is. What's he done to her.

And then . . . what I'll do to him.

Doing nothing feels so pathetic.

Sitting here isn't helping.

I push myself up, ignoring the dizziness prickling my vision, and head back to the kitchen to refill my glass. Caffeine and sugar. That will keep me going until I hear from Charlie and Agnes.

A knock at the back door startles me, even though it's quiet, tentative.

'Kitty?'

It's Lauren.

I don't want to see her now.

'Unless you've got something useful to say about where your fucking psycho boyfriend might be, it's probably best you stay out of my way.'

'I've come to say sorry,' she says, poking her head in and giving me a thin, shame-faced smile. 'Can I come in? Please?'

I want to say no, but I also have a million questions to ask her about Cort. I want to know everything about him now. How long she's known him. Where he's from. How the fuck she didn't notice that he's a murdering lunatic.

I nod and she slips inside, perching on one of the dining chairs, her arms wrapped around her thin frame.

'Where is everyone?' she asks, looking around the room.

'Agnes and Charlie have gone to Cort's place,' I say. 'I'm waiting to hear from them.'

'That was Charlie?' she says. I suppose we didn't really get the chance to do introductions.

I nod. 'Yes.'

I stare at Lauren, waiting.

'I'm sorry,' she says eventually. 'About before. I just can't believe it . . .' She trails off, lowers her eyes. 'I can't believe Cort would do those awful things.'

I frown at her. This is nothing new.

'Lauren,' I say, 'I'm really not in the mood for another

round of you not being able to believe it. So if you've got nothing else to say—'

'Please let me finish.' She looks up at me again and now I can't miss the pain and confusion in her eyes. She takes a deep breath. 'What I'm trying to say is that I can't believe it. But I do. I do believe it.' She sighs heavily and her eyes dart around the room. 'You guys are right. There's no other reason Antoinette's scarf would be in his car. Why there's blood on it. And . . . that list. Handwritten. Cort never writes anything down. It all goes into his phone . . .'

I remember what I said to Antoinette about not leaving a digital footprint.

She rubs her eyes with the back of her hands. 'It's like he didn't want to leave a trace.' She stares intensely at her fingers. 'I didn't want to think that I could've made such a bad choice. I really thought he was one of the good ones.'

Guilt shoots through me. I didn't even consider how hard it would've been for Lauren. Seeing those screaming truths about her boyfriend like that. About the man she trusted.

'It's okay,' I say. 'You weren't the only one he fooled.'

She huffs out a hollow laugh. 'Turns out he's a better actor than me.'

We sit in silence for a few moments, the heaviness of the situation like a presence in the room.

Just then my phone starts to ring.

I grab for it.

It's Charlie.

'Is he there?' I ask, frantic. 'Did you find Antoinette?'

Charlie's voice sounds a million miles away as he says, 'I'm sorry, Kits. There's no one here.' Agnes says something in the background. 'We're going to try to find a way in,' he continues. 'Agnes thinks she can get in through one of the windows.'

'Okay,' I say as I sag with disappointment. 'Keep me in the loop. I love you.'

'I love you.'

The call ends and I turn to Lauren. 'He's not at his place. Can you call him?'

Her brow furrows. 'He won't answer,' she says. 'He raced off in a fury when I asked him about the scarf.'

'Please try.'

She takes out her phone and calls Cort, putting it on speaker. It rings and rings and rings.

'Lauren,' I plead with her. 'If he's not at home, where will he be?' She shrugs sadly, the look on her face pained. 'Please think,' and I'm almost begging. 'If there's anywhere you think Cort could have taken Antoinette, I really need to know.'

Lauren's blue eyes fill up with tears and she makes no effort to wipe them away when they spill and begin running down her cheeks.

'I . . . I don't know. I don't know.'

I grab her hands. 'Please! Think! Lauren, this is important.'

'Wait,' she says, her expression changing from distress to horror and her eyes locking onto mine with sudden, terrible clarity. The colour drains from her face. 'I think I know where he might be.'

60

KITTY'S HIRE CAR, SOME ROAD OUT OF LOS ANGELES, CALIFORNIA

We head east out of LA. I'm driving faster than I should be but I don't care about being pulled over right now. All I can think about is that I hope we're not too late.

As we drive, I notice the landscape changing. The built-up-ness of LA gives way to industrial estates, storage warehouses and sprawling residential developments. I see mountains appear on the horizon.

'How far is it?' I ask Lauren.

'Not far,' she says but I don't really know what that means. This is America after all and don't they happily drive like two hundred miles for a burger? I get stressed out if I have to go south of the Thames. So I keep driving until the mountains are no longer on the horizon, instead they're looming on either side. There are no palm trees anymore, just low, prickly-looking shrubs and the occasional cactus. We're in the desert now.

I hope we're not lost.

'Are you sure you know where you're going?' I ask Lauren.

‘I’m sure,’ she says. ‘Cort used to bring me out here when we first started dating. We used to come here to be alone.’ She presses her lips together like she’s trying to stop herself from crying.

‘Are you okay?’ I ask her.

‘I just feel so stupid,’ she says. ‘If you’re right and I’ve been dating a murderer. What does that say about me?’

‘Nothing!’ I say. ‘Lauren, *if* we’re right about Cort, it doesn’t say a single thing about you. It’s on him. He’s the one who chose to do these awful things. He fooled a lot of people. Everyone who listens to his podcasts and talks. All his social media followers. You’re far from stupid, Lauren.’

She keeps staring straight ahead. ‘But how could I not know? That’s what everyone will be saying, isn’t it? *How could the girlfriend not know?* Oh God, there will be Netflix shows about me!’ She turns to face me now, her eyes wide with panic. ‘And not in the good way.’

‘Lauren, please don’t think about that now. Please. We need to find Cort and hope he hasn’t hurt Antoinette yet.’ My mind flicks to the scrap of fabric, the smear of blood on it, and my stomach lurches. I open the window and take some deep breaths of sticky, warm desert air.

‘Are you okay?’ Lauren asks me. ‘You look like you’re going to barf or something.’

‘I’m fine,’ I say. ‘Just feeling a bit travel sick.’

‘Here, have some water.’ She pulls a bottle of mineral water out of her bag and takes the cap off for me. ‘Drink some of this.’

I take it from her gratefully and swallow down half the bottle.

'Can you check my phone?' I say. 'Has Charlie called?'

'Sure,' Lauren replies and reaches for my phone in the centre console. Out of the corner of my eye, I can see her frowning at it.

'What's wrong?'

'There's no signal out here,' she says, letting the phone slip back into place. 'I forgot about that.'

My gut churns again and I realise how reckless I've been, coming all the way out here to confront a murderer without even a weapon.

And now a phone without any signal.

Lauren notices my distress and she puts a hand on my arm. 'It's going to be okay,' she says.

I'd like to have her confidence.

I've spent so much of this trip rolling my eyes at Antoinette for not being careful. And here I am, doing exactly the sort of impulsive thing I've been warning her about.

I could kick myself.

'Oh, take this exit,' Lauren says. And then we're on a long, desert highway that looks like something out of an old Western movie.

'Where exactly are we going?' I ask.

'Wonder Valley.'

'What's Wonder Valley?' It sounds like a theme park.

'It's just a remote bit of the Mojave out near Joshua Tree. Just derelict cabins, long roads and dust.'

A murder desert.

Cort's taken my sister to a murder shed in a murder desert.

I put my foot down even harder on the accelerator.

We drive for about another hour, the road long and dusty.

It feels ominous and I suddenly remember that Agnes and Charlie won't know where we are. The last thing they need is to think that Lauren and I have vanished into thin air as well.

'Can you text Agnes and let her know what we're doing?' I say. 'Charlie will panic if they get back and find us gone.'

'There's no signal,' Lauren reminds me.

'Please try,' I say. 'It might go through if we find a pocket somewhere.'

Lauren reaches into her pocket, takes out her phone and taps out a message. 'All done,' she says. 'We're almost there. It's round here somewhere.'

I don't even begin to understand how she can tell. All I can see is sand, skeletal shrubs and the odd abandoned building. The whole place is an absolute ghost town, like proper horror-movie vibes. A cold shiver runs down my spine, a ghostly finger tracing the bones.

'Over there.' Lauren points to one of the larger abandoned buildings. 'That's the one.'

I pull over at the place she's indicated. It looks like it was once some sort of homestead, but now it's little more than a ruin. Completely dilapidated. The windows are all smashed in but the glass isn't jagged, it's smooth, suggesting many years of being left to the elements.

'This is lovely,' I say as we get out of the car and make our way towards the building. 'And he brought you here? Did you really not see any red flags there at all?'

Lauren gives a sort of half shrug. 'I don't know. No. It seemed kinda romantic out here.' She looks around the barren landscape. 'Don't you think it's like eerily beautiful?'

I do not think this at all.

I think it looks like something out of a low-budget slasher film.

I think it looks like the end of the world.

But I don't say anything.

Lauren looks like she's in some sort of trance as she makes her way to the front door, or what's left of it.

'There are hundreds of places like this all over the desert,' she says as she pushes the door open and walks inside. 'Cort was always fascinated by them.'

A murderer fascinated by murder sheds.

'Why are they all abandoned?' I ask her as I step over a rolled-up carpet and follow her inside. 'Where did everyone go?'

'Back to civilisation,' Lauren says but doesn't elaborate.

It's dark in the cabin and I feel around on the wall for a light switch. My fingers make contact with something and I flick the switch but nothing happens.

'There's no electricity out here,' Lauren says. 'Hasn't been for as long as we've been coming out here.'

'Right,' I say and reach into my pocket for my phone. But it's not there. It's still in the car.

'Have you got your phone on you?' I say to Lauren. 'We can use the torch.'

'Oh yes,' she says. 'Of course.'

She takes her phone out and turns the torch on. Somehow this makes the whole place even creepier. Now I can clearly see just how rundown it is. There are cobwebs choking every surface, this mixture of sand and dust on the floorboards, a broken-down child's cot shoved against the back wall. It reminds me of a song my dad used to sing to me at bedtime when I was little.

All the crew has gone ashore,
But the ship sails on forevermore.

That icy finger trails down my back again.

'Do you think he's here?' I whisper to Lauren.

'I don't know,' she says. 'Wait here. I'm going to look in the other rooms.'

'Is that safe?'

'Cort's not going to do anything to me,' she says. 'But I can't say the same if we both spring him and he feels cornered. Just stay here, okay? I won't be long.'

She gives my arm a reassuring squeeze and heads to one of the darkened doorways guided by the light of her phone.

The only light in the room now is coming from the moon, which is streaming in through the empty window frames. I look around again. Maybe there is something here I can use as a weapon if I need to. There's an area of the room that looks like it was a little kitchenette and I tiptoe over to it, flinching as the wooden floorboards creak beneath my feet. There's a rusty stove, some battered old pots spilling out of a cupboard and a half-open drawer. I pull the draw out further, slowly, trying not to make any sudden noises. I'm pleased to see a few pieces of cutlery but my heart drops when I realise it's just spoons.

Alanis Morissette would have something to say about this.

I can't believe I came all the way out here with nothing.

I'm about to have another look in the main body of the

cabin but when I turn around, I have to clap my hands over my mouth to contain the scream that I almost scream.

Because a figure has appeared in one of the doorways.

The figure of a man.

A man I recognise.

Only it's not Cort.

It's Travis.

'Kitty,' he says.

But before I can ask him anything, there's a blinding pain across the back of my head.

And then everything goes black.

61

SOMEWHERE, CALIFORNIA?

It's the need for water that wakes me up.

My throat is absolutely parched.

How much did I have to drink last night?

But as I force one of my eyes open, I remember that I wasn't out drinking last night and the pounding head and raging thirst are not a hangover.

I was hit over the head.

'Hey, sleeping beauty. Weren't you supposed to rescue me? You don't look like you're in rescue mode.'

I open my eyes fully and see that I'm not alone, wherever the fuck I am. Antoinette is here too.

She's alive.

And as snarky as ever.

I've never been so happy to hear sarcasm in my life.

'Antoinette!' I say, pulling myself up into a sitting position. It's not the easiest of manoeuvres with my hands cable-tied behind my back. I wriggle my feet. Yep, ankles too. My mind flashes to Aidan Ward in the wine cellar. How the tables have turned. 'You're okay.'

'Well, no thanks to you. But yes. I'm fine.'

I'm so pleased to see her that I think I might cry.

'Where are we?' I ask, looking around for clues.

'In the cellar of Little House on the Scary,' Antoinette says.

'We're still in Cort's cabin?'

She nods. 'Yeah. He brought you down a little while ago.' She peers at me. 'Are you okay? Think you got quite a nasty smack on the head.'

That's right. Someone hit me. 'Where's Lauren?' I say but Antoinette looks at me blankly.

'Lauren?' she says and I explain that it was Lauren who remembered this place, that Cort used to bring her here on dates.

'What a romantic,' she says, screwing up her nose in distaste. Then her face goes serious. 'He hasn't brought Lauren down here.'

Anxiety courses through me. Where is she? What's he doing to her? If he thinks she brought me out here . . . well, I can't even think about how angry he'd be. And what that might look like for Lauren.

'How did you get down here?' I ask and I swear I can *hear* Antoinette roll her eyes.

'That faux-feminist *psycho* offered to give me a lift to find Agnes after I stormed out of the villa,' she says. 'Then he *chloroformed* me and, the next thing I know, I'm waking up and he's dragging me into this abandoned *cabin* in the middle of nowhere. Honestly, I thought it was some sort of hazing thing at first. But no. He is absolutely batshit delulu.'

'Has he hurt you? Has he . . . done anything to you?' I almost don't want to hear the answer.

But Antoinette shakes her head. 'Not physically. But having to listen to that sentient man-bun's deranged yapping has been pretty painful.'

'Deranged yapping! He should rename his podcast that. What's he been saying?'

Antoinette rolls her eyes so hard I can *feel* it. 'Oh blah blah blah, sluts this and yada yada, whores that. Anyway. Good to see you, sis, what's the plan?'

'Plan?'

'Yes, the plan to get us out of here. I'm not really loving basement life.' She shuffles around to show me that her hands and ankles are also cable-tied. 'What's the plan?'

Oh. Right. She thinks there's a plan.

'Um . . . so, the thing is. There isn't really a plan.'

Antoinette blinks at me.

'What do you mean there isn't a plan? There has to be a plan.' Her voice goes up a few octaves. 'Because if there isn't a plan, that means we're just stuck here. In a basement in the middle of the *fucking desert* at the mercy of that unhinged podcast posturer out there.' She sighs. 'Please tell me someone knows where you are?'

'I'm not sure,' I say. 'Charlie and Agnes went round to Cort's to see if he was there. Lauren tried to text them to tell them where we were going but there's no signal out here.'

'Wait . . . Charlie?'

I feel a blush creep up into my cheeks. 'Yeah. We're kind of back together.'

Antoinette's eyebrows shoot up. 'Um . . . how did this happen? Details, please.'

I stare back at her. 'Do you not think we've got more

pressing immediate issues, Antoinette?' I look pointedly at my bound ankles. 'I can tell you about my love life when we've figured out what we're going to do.'

Her brow furrows. 'Okay, but make sure you do. This tea is too good to miss out on.'

Seriously.

This girl has been held hostage by a lunatic for the past few days and she's just casually wanting me to fill her in on what's been happening in my love life.

I'm surprised Cort didn't bring her straight back the moment she started talking.

Then I remember something else.

I remember what I saw before the world went dark and I woke up down here.

'Travis,' I say to Antoinette.

'Huh?'

'Travis was up there. Before someone, Cort I guess, hit me over the head. Have you seen him? Are they in on it together?'

'Wait. What? Travis the PI? Why would they be in on it together? Do they even know each other?'

Of course. Antoinette doesn't know about the whole fake-PI thing so I fill her in. She listens, her lips pressed together and her eyes wide.

'You do realise that is the absolutely last time that I trust a recommendation from you?'

Antoinette thinks about this for a minute. 'Fair,' she says. 'But Travis didn't have anything to do with kidnapping me. Unless he's like a sleeper partner or something?'

'Then what was he doing here?' I say, confused. Nothing makes sense at all.

‘I don’t have any answers,’ she says. ‘Now seriously, how are we going to get out of here? Do you know anything about slipping out of cable ties, by any chance?’

I shake my head.

There must be something we can do.

I look around the room, trying to see if there’s anything useful here but there isn’t. Just some tins of food that have probably been here for years. Maybe even decades.

Then I remember.

The knife.

The little paring knife I grabbed from the kitchen when I was going to kill Aidan. The one I couldn’t find.

It’s in the back pocket of my cut-offs.

That’s where I put it.

I’d been wondering what was digging into my bum in the car.

‘I’ve got a knife!’ I say to my sister. Her eyes light up.

‘Of course you do! You’re Kitty Collins. I knew you’d come through for me. Where is it?’

‘In the back pocket of my shorts,’ I say and I try to reach it. But I can’t. The angle at which my hands are tied is too awkward for me to be able to. It’s a futile mission. ‘I can’t reach it! You’re going to have to get it out.’

Antoinette nods and bum-hops closer to me. Her hands are behind her back too so she’s going to have to feel around for the knife. She moves herself into a back-to-back position with me.

‘So this is awkward,’ she says as she tries to pretzel herself into a position that allows her access to my back pocket. I can feel her twisting and turning behind me but her hands are nowhere near my pockets.

'Lower,' I say. 'You're not even in the right zip code.'

'Well, it doesn't help that you're literally sitting on your butt, you know, the place where the pockets are situated. You need to move too.'

'I can't stand up,' I say. 'In case you hadn't noticed my feet are tied too.'

Antoinette clicks her tongue. 'You're going to have to roll over onto your side,' she instructs me.

'What? I thought you were like the queen of sleight of hand or something?'

'Just do it. Roll over. Hurry up.'

I grumble as I slide down onto my back and roll over onto my side. The floor is made of stone and it's cold and hard. 'This is the least fun I've had since losing my bag at the airport,' I say. I'm sure I hear Antoinette stifle a giggle. I'm not certain that she's taking our kidnapping as seriously as she should be. 'Are you laughing?'

'No. Okay, a little. But you've got to admit this is kind of funny. I've got it!'

'Great,' I say. 'Now cut through the cable tie on my wrists.'

Again this is not as easy as it sounds. And having Antoinette poking around near my skin with a blade while she can't see what she's doing isn't exactly ideal.

'This knife is useless,' she hisses as she attempts to saw through the plastic tie. 'Could you not have sharpened it?'

'I'm sorry,' I say. 'Next time I find a knife I've stashed in my shorts and forgotten about, I'll make sure I sharpen it first.'

'There's no need to get snippy. It hurts my feelings,' Antoinette says.

As if she has any feelings.

I'm not sure how long it takes her to cut through the cable tie. It might be ten minutes, it might be an hour. Time becomes something of an abstract concept when you're lying on your side, cable-tied on a cold, stone floor with your sister blindly stabbing near your butt with a knife. But she eventually gives a cry of triumph and I feel the tension in my wrists slacken.

I'm free.

'Now do me,' Antoinette says and I'm only tempted to leave her bound for a split second.

Once our hands are liberated, we cut our ankles free too.

'That feels so good,' Antoinette says as she stretches her arms high above her head, wiggling her fingers.

'How often does he come and check on you?' I ask.

'A couple of times a day usually. To give me some water and crackers. The refreshments here are extremely mid.'

'Okay, we need to think smart and be prepared. Here's what we're going to do.'

And I tell Antoinette my plan.

Because she's right. I *do* always have one.

Eventually.

62

THE ROOT CELLAR, CORT'S ABANDONED CABIN, WONDER VALLEY, CALIFORNIA

When the door of the cellar opens after an indeterminate amount of time, we are ready. Antoinette and I have positioned ourselves like we're still tied up.

The plan – if it can even be called that – is actually very simple.

Ambush.

I'm pretty sure the pair of us can take him down. Especially when one of us has a knife and we also have the element of surprise.

The footsteps sound heavy.

'Cort,' I mouth to my sister.

She nods.

And then Cort slides into view. He's wearing a pair of track pants, a white T-shirt and his bun looks like it's been freshly styled.

It takes all my self-control not to launch myself at him right away.

'Ladies,' he says. 'I hope you're enjoying your stay?' I

notice that he's carrying two pale green Stanley cups, one in each hand. 'I've brought you some refreshments.'

'We didn't order anything,' Antoinette snarls.

Cort shoots me a look. 'I hope you're going to be a better guest than your sister. She's been nothing but a giant pain in the ass.'

I give him a sweet smile.

'You drink some first,' Antoinette says to him.

Cort rolls his eyes. 'Do we have to go through this every time I bring you water? I told you already. Why would I bother drugging you when you're already tied up in the cellar?' He gives Antoinette a little smile and takes a sip out of each of the cups. 'Happy now?'

'Just delighted,' she says.

Cort gives me a look like he's saying *what is she like?* Then he squats down to place the drinks in front of us. And that's when we strike. Antoinette leaps up and claws at his face while I use my new signature move and bring my foot up to his crotch. He yowls and falls to the floor, not knowing whether to clutch his face or scrotum. I immediately straddle him, holding the knife to his throat.

'How does this fit into your theories of fake feminism, Cort?' I say.

He's winded but, unfortunately for me, I seriously underestimated Cort's strength and he manages to push me off. I fly backwards, the little paring knife scuttering across the floor.

He laughs as I land on my back with a thud. It's cold and brittle.

'When will you sluts learn your place?' he says with a

shake of his head. 'Now I'm going to have to hurt you, aren't I? I really didn't wanna do that. I was going to get rid of the two of you quickly. But I've changed my mind after that little display.'

He lunges at me and suddenly his hands are around my throat. They feel rough and dry, which surprises me because I thought Cort would be the type of guy who takes care of his hands. I guess the brutal business of murder has roughed them up a bit.

He holds my eyes as he throttles me and I can see that he's enjoying it. It's always sexual for male killers, isn't it? Perverts. I try to gasp for breath but he's gripping me too tightly. I start seeing stars in my peripheral vision, but just as I'm preparing myself to black out I see Cort's eyes glaze over and he slumps heavily on top of me.

'What took you so long?' I ask Antoinette as I wriggle out from underneath him. 'I was on the verge of unconsciousness there.'

'The knife went under one of the shelves, couldn't reach it,' she says as she inspects the knife, which is now covered in Cort's blood. 'What *is* this anyway? A vegetable peeler?'

I stand up and look down at Cort, who now has a puncture in the side of his neck that he's bleeding out of.

'Let's get out of here,' I say and Antoinette nods her agreement.

We stumble up the steps and into the main body of the cabin. I'm not sure how long I was knocked out for but the rooms are now bathed in a dim smoky light, which suggests it's somewhere in the early hours of the morning.

'We need to find what he's done with Lauren and then—'

I don't finish my sentence because I've spotted a bundle in the corner.

A bundle that looks very much like an injured person.

I edge closer towards them and can see a puddle of blood spreading out from what appears to be a stab wound in their abdomen.

I lean in closer.

It's Travis.

Travis has been stabbed.

63

CORT'S ABANDONED CABIN, WONDER VALLEY, CALIFORNIA

'Travis,' I say rushing over to him and sinking down beside him. There's blood everywhere. Antoinette follows me but I hold a hand up to stop her. 'No,' I say. 'Stay there. You don't need to see this.'

He's clutching his side, a sticky red stain leaking over his fingers. 'What happened?'

He looks at me and tries to smile but the pain turns it into a grimace.

'Got sliced,' he says, pulling his hand away from the wound and looking at the blood. He's losing it fast.

'What are you doing here?' I say. 'I don't understand.'

He fixes me with those brown eyes. 'I figured it out,' he says and, despite the massive blood loss, there's a hint of pride in his voice. 'The IP address from Antoinette's iPad.' His voice is raspy, his breathing becoming increasingly shallow.

'And you came all the way out here? Alone?'

'I fucked up, Kitty,' he says. 'And I wanted to put it right. I wanted to find Antoinette for you.'

'You're an idiot,' I say, but what I really mean is *thank you. Thank you for trying to fix your mistake.*

'I couldn't live with the thought of you hating me,' he says as I reach for his hand. It's cold but, somehow, still clammy.

I squeeze it.

I've seen lots of men die.

And I've wanted it every time.

But not this time.

I don't want this.

'You shouldn't have come out here alone,' I say, holding his hand in my lap. 'What were you thinking?'

He coughs. Something dark and liquidy slides out of his mouth. 'Can you forgive me?'

I've seen enough men die to know that he hasn't got long.

His skin is already slick and waxy, the colour has drained from his face. He stares up at the ceiling as if he's watching something play out on it.

'Kitty . . .'

I grip his hand tighter. 'Of course I forgive you. Of course I do.'

He's trying to say something else but his voice is so raspy now that I can't make it out.

I lean my ear against his mouth.

'What is it, Travis?'

'Lawman,' he says, his eyelids fluttering. I can feel him fighting to stay with me. Fighting and losing.

'Police? You want me to go to the police?'

His eyes flutter again. 'No . . . lawman . . . Kitty.'

'Okay, no police. No police. It's okay. It's okay. I've got you.'

His eyes flutter closed and I pull his head into my lap, gently stroking his hair as he lets out his final breath.

64

CORT'S ABANDONED CABIN, WONDER VALLEY, CALIFORNIA

Antoinette comes over to where I'm crouched, cradling Travis's head in my lap. She puts her hands on my shoulders.

'Is he . . . ?'

I look up at her, nodding through my tears. 'Yes.'

'Oh fuck,' she says. 'I'm so sorry.'

I wipe my eyes roughly with the back of my hand. 'Poor Travis.'

'Poor Travis,' Antoinette echoes.

Just then a noise from what was once the front door startles us. It's Lauren.

Alive.

Unharmed.

Thank God.

She looks flushed, dishevelled, like she's been running.

'Lauren!' I say. 'You're okay?'

She stares at me before running at me and wrapping her arms around me. I'm a little taken aback as I've never seen her this tactile before. I awkwardly hug her back.

'So are you!' she says. 'God, I was so worried.'

'What happened to you?'

'I ran,' she says. 'After Cort hit you over the head. I just ran and ran. I thought I'd be able to find someone else. Get some help.' She shakes her head. 'There's nothing. No one.' She looks around, her eyes wide with fear. 'Where is he?' she says. 'Where's Cort?'

'In the basement,' I say. 'You don't need to worry about him.'

'I got him good,' Antoinette says and Lauren's eyes widen even more.

'You mean . . . he's dead?'

'Dead as fuck. Completely cooked. I got him right in the jugular.' I wish Antoinette didn't sound quite as delighted with herself as she does. He may have been a murdering psychopath but he was still Lauren's boyfriend. A little sensitivity wouldn't hurt here.

Lauren's hand shoots to her mouth and I can see that it's trembling. Lauren collapses like she's been shot. Her legs give out from underneath her and she falls to the floor, gasping. She crawls into child's pose and I can see huge sobs shaking her body.

'I need to see him,' she whimpers. 'I need to see him.'

An image of Cort and the huge gaping hole in his neck pops into my mind. She really *doesn't* need to see him. That's the kind of thing that'll land her in therapy for years.

'Lauren,' I say carefully as I kneel beside her, putting a hand on her back. 'You need to breathe. You're having a panic attack.' She doesn't stop sobbing and gasping and I look to Antoinette for help but she just shrugs, helpless. I rub her back like I've done for Maisie and Tor in the past. 'Come on,' I say to her. 'Sit up. It's okay.'

She pulls herself into a sitting position and stares at me. Her mascara has bled around her eyes. The effect would be funny if the situation wasn't so awful. She looks like a Tradwife who's had a 2010 emo Tumblr makeover.

'It's not okay, Kitty,' she says. 'He's dead. Cort's dead.'

That image again.

That stab wound and all that blood.

Yeah.

Cort's very much dead.

'You cannot feel bad about that,' Antoinette snaps from her corner, wiping the blood from the knife on her sleeve. 'You know what he did. To those women.'

I glare at her and shake my head. She might be right, but Lauren won't want to hear that at the moment. Whatever Cort was, she loved him. And that's not just going to go away.

I turn back to Lauren. She looks too fragile to touch right now. Like she might break if I try to offer physical comfort.

'I'm so sorry,' I say. 'I can't even begin to imagine how hard this is for you.'

She keels forward, pressing her fists into her eyes harder than can be good for them.

'He was mine,' she says between sobs. 'I loved him. I really did.'

'You loved who he was *pretending* to be,' Antoinette says. And then, under her breath so only I can hear, 'And that was a prick as well.'

I glare at her again.

Lauren folds over again, shaking violently.

'Lauren, you need to get it together.' Antoinette's patience has run out now. 'You can't fall to pieces. We need to get out of here.'

Lauren's head shoots up and she fixes my sister with a look so cold it makes me shiver. 'You!' she says. 'You killed him.'

Antoinette lets out a sharp breath. 'Yes. Because he would've killed all of us.'

'He wouldn't have hurt me.' Lauren is shaking her head. 'He loved me.'

My sister snorts. 'He was a psychopath. He didn't love anyone. You were just useful to him. An accessory.'

'Antoinette!' I say. 'That's enough.'

Whatever their relationship was like, Lauren has lost the man she loved and Antoinette's blunt truths are not what she needs right now.

'You could've just . . . I don't know . . . called the police or something.' Lauren's voice is high-pitched with distress now.

'He'd have gone to prison,' Antoinette says.

Lauren's body shudders. 'I'd rather visit him in prison than in a fucking cemetery.' I risk putting my arms around her, half expecting her to shake me off. But she doesn't. She sort of melts into me. I can feel the fight, the anger leaving her body as the truth sinks in.

'I didn't know him,' she whispers. 'All that time we were together and I didn't know him at all. How could I not know?' She pulls back again and looks at me. 'That's what everyone is going to want to know, isn't it? How could I not have known what he was up to? But I didn't. I swear.'

'It's okay,' I say, stroking her hair as she collapses back into me. I can feel her tears soaking through my top. 'It's okay.'

'Kitty? Antoinette?'

It's Charlie's voice.

Relief floods through me as he appears in what's left of the door, Agnes at his side. They both stop in their tracks when they see the chaos of the cabin. The blood, Travis, Lauren trembling beside me.

Charlie hurries over to me and I throw myself into his arms, breathing him in like he's clean air and I've been deprived.

'Thank God,' I whisper into his chest.

He pulls back and cups my face, his eyes searching, looking for any sign I've been harmed.

'Are you okay?'

'I'm fine,' I say.

His eyes linger on my face for a beat then, seemingly satisfied that I'm all right, he turns to Antoinette. 'You?'

'Hello, stranger. Nice to have you back on board. We can talk about the appalling way you treated my sister later,' she says. But then the bravado evaporates and I see her shoulders sag. 'I'm okay. I'm alive.'

Agnes moves towards my sister, relief all over her face, but then Lauren lets out a broken whimper from behind me. Agnes stalls, her eyes flicking between them. She's torn and doesn't know who to go to. Lauren, her best friend of years. Or Antoinette, whom she's hardly known for any time at all but obviously cares about. Lauren, who's just discovered her boyfriend is a violent serial killer. Or Antoinette, who's been kidnapped and held hostage for days.

Lauren makes the decision for her in the end and throws herself into Agnes's arms, where she crumbles again.

'It's okay, honey,' Agnes says. 'I've got you.'

Lauren lifts her head and looks at her friend, her expression is raw grief.

'He did this,' she says. 'It was him. Cort.'

Agnes strokes Lauren's head. 'I know. I know.' Her eyes flick to Antoinette and they have another one of their wordless conversations. Then she looks back to Lauren. 'I'm here. It's okay. You're going to be okay.'

'Let's get her out of here,' I say.

We make our way out to the cars. I look back, one last time, at Travis. A fist squeezes my heart.

'I'm so sorry,' I whisper before Charlie takes my arm and leads me to the SUV.

'I'm driving,' he says. I'm not about to argue.

Agnes is leading Lauren to her car but Lauren stops and pulls away.

'Wait,' she says. 'I need a moment.'

Agnes nods and steps back to stand near Antoinette. She places a hand on her arm and my sister leans into her.

We watch as Lauren walks back towards the cabin, to the place where the man she thought she loved will rest forever. She takes something out of her pocket and stares at it for a few moments.

And then a small flame flickers in the barely there morning light.

A lighter.

She crouches down and picks something up off the dry desert floor and holds the flame to it before flinging it into the wooden cabin.

The tiny flame takes hold and then the wind catches it too and, in a heartbeat, the whole place is engulfed in fire.

Lauren watches it for a few moments. Then she turns her back on it and walks towards us, flames billowing behind her, as the cabin burns and burns.

'Can we go home now, please?' she says.

'Yeah,' I say. 'We can.'

65

KITTY AND ANTOINETTE'S AIRBNB, WEST HOLLYWOOD, LOS ANGELES

Charlie wakes me up several hours later with breakfast in bed, including avocado on toast, coffee and – the best thing – my iPad with the Flightscanner app open.

'You,' I say to him, 'are the best man that has ever existed.'

He laughs. 'Thank you. Although I suspect the bar is low.'

I kiss him on the cheek. 'It's on the floor of the basement in hell. But I think you single-handedly raise it up a few notches.'

'I know you're keen to get home,' he says.

And I am.

I so am.

I want to get back to London.

I want to get back to my apartment.

I miss everything about it.

I want to get back to Tor and help her on her healing journey.

I want to see Maisie and put my hands on her swollen belly, feel those tiny babies kicking her from the inside.

I want to get back to my life. My life with Charlie.

'What happens when we get back?' I ask him as I take a big bite of my breakfast. 'With us? Where are you going to go?'

Before we went to Cannes earlier this year, Charlie was living with me in my Chelsea apartment. I loved everything about co-habiting. Eventually. It took me a little while to get used to sharing every aspect of my life with someone else. Well, almost every aspect. Keeping my nocturnal activities hidden from my live-in boyfriend had proven quite challenging. I look at Charlie now and I honestly don't think he's ever looked more handsome. The morning sun is peeping through the blinds and making the golden bits in his hair shine. He smiles and I reach out and touch his face. I loved waking up to his face every single day and I want to go back to that. I want to live with him again, this time with no secrets. But Charlie moved back into his flat in Clapham Junction when we split up. Maybe he's going to want to take things slowly.

I really hope he doesn't.

'Let's see,' he says, but not in the kind of way that a parent says it to a child when they really mean 'absolutely not'. He smiles at me and I put my finger in the dimple in his cheek. 'I mean, you want to go back, right? There's no one else here you want to go after?'

I laugh and bury my face into his chest. 'No,' I say, 'I'm done.'

And, the thing is, I really feel like I mean it this time.

I've always enjoyed my work.

The kills usually leave me feeling alive, like I'm absorbing some sort of life force and power from the men.

And, of course, the feeling that I've done something good is unbeatable. The knowledge that I've pre-emptively stopped something terrible from happening to a woman who doesn't even know I exist is intoxicating.

I get why Charlie enjoys charity work so much.

But I just haven't had the same sort of highs out here. Even though the men we've killed have been some of the worst I've ever met. It's all just felt a bit . . . flat. I mean, it still feels good. I'm just so tired. I think I like having killed much more than I like killing.

Maybe I'm just getting too old for it.

'Kits,' Charlie is saying, 'did you hear me?'

I look at him again and realise I'd totally zoned out.

'Sorry,' I say, 'what were you saying?'

'There's a flight home the day after tomorrow,' he says. 'Shall I book it? Will that give you enough time to tie up the loose ends?'

'Loose ends?'

He cocks his head, his brow slightly creased. 'Yes, the loose ends.'

'What do you mean?' I ask.

'Well, I might be mistaken but don't you have a man in your wine cellar? One you were particularly keen on killing? And a couple of suitcases you need to get rid of?'

Oh, that's right.

I still need to kill Aidan Ward.

How did *that* slip my mind?

66

KITTY AND ANTOINETTE'S AIRBNB, WEST HOLLYWOOD, LOS ANGELES

So here it is.

The moment I have truly been waiting for.

The moment that I can wipe this repugnant piece of excrement off the face of the planet.

The kill that I've been looking forward to the most.

Like, literally, the most ever.

No other kill has made the blood pump through my veins in quite the same way it's doing now.

I feel so completely full of life.

Maybe I was being a bit hasty earlier when I said killing no longer gave me the buzz it used to.

Maybe.

Antoinette has recovered from her near-death experience and has been sharpening knives in preparation.

'I love that sound,' she purrs as the beautiful metallic clink of steel on steel echoes around the kitchen, where we've been prepping. 'I'm going to enjoy this one. Thanks for waiting for me.'

‘Of course,’ I say. ‘As if I’d go ahead and kill him without my little apprentice to help me.’

Antoinette considers my words for a moment. ‘Don’t you think,’ she says, ‘that after what happened in the desert, that I’ve maybe graduated from being your apprentice at this point?’

I look at my sister, who’s looking back at me hopefully.

She’s right.

Of course she’s right.

She’s more than shown how far she’s come since we first arrived out here.

We haven’t just found Aidan, we’ve also closed the loop on the WeHo Ripper. And that’s down to my sister. My infuriating sister who planned it, baited him and walked right into danger for it. I want to shout at her for being reckless but I can’t.

I’m not angry at her.

I’m proud.

I smile. ‘Okay, you’re no longer the apprentice.’

‘Do I get to make the first cut then?’

‘Don’t push your luck.’

She gives me a grin and we gather up our supplies before making our way into the wine cellar. Aidan is huddled in a corner, shivering. It’s always cold down here but I cranked the thermostat down a few more notches before I went to bed, just to make his last night extra special. It’ll probably spoil a few of the wines but they’re necessary collateral.

I’m sure Agnes’s parents would understand.

‘Cold?’ I ask as we make our way down the steps. Aidan looks up at us but doesn’t say anything. ‘Don’t be like that,’

I say. 'I think I've been really nice, welcoming you into our home like this. Providing you with bed and board.'

Aidan eyes Antoinette and the bundles of glinting steel we're both carrying.

'Is this it then?' he says. 'Are you finally going to put me out of my misery?'

Antoinette gives him a smile that is somehow both devilish and dazzling. 'Yes,' she says. 'But we're going to make sure you have even more misery first. A few days in a freezing cellar will seem like an absolute spa break by the time we're finished with you.'

'You'll be begging for death,' I add, in case he doesn't understand that we're about to torture him horribly.

'Can we possibly just get it over with quickly?' he asks. 'I'm sure you've got things you need to be doing.' He casts a pointed glance over at the LV cases in the opposite corner. 'I won't even struggle,' he promises. 'Just shoot me or something.'

'Oh no,' I tell him. 'That would take all the fun out of it. I'm sure you understand that, right? Like you *could've* chosen to just give Tor one quick slap. Or you *could've* chosen not to lay a finger on her at all. But you didn't, did you?' He swallows hard and I see his Adam's apple bob. Why has he got such a prominent Adam's apple? I'll be cutting that out. 'Antoinette,' I say. 'Have you got the list there of all the injuries Mr Ward inflicted on my friend?'

Antoinette nods. 'I have, Kitty.'

'Could you read it out, please?'

'Of course.' She clears her throat like she's about to make an important speech. 'Three broken ribs, a fractured cheekbone, a lacerated spleen thanks to one of the broken ribs poking it.

That caused internal bleeding and needed surgery. Then there was the nasal fracture, the collarbone fracture from where she hit the floor and the traumatic brain injury.'

Aidan's eyes widen.

'You did that to her,' I say. 'Because you lost your temper. Because she wasn't ready to sleep with you. Are you proud of that?'

He has the decency to lower his head in shame. 'Of course I'm not. I'm appalled that I did that to her.' He raises his eyes to mine. 'I don't expect you to believe me, Kitty, but I hate myself for what I did to Tor. I really cared about her.'

I narrow my eyes at him. 'So bad that, even though you did all that to her, you packed up and fled the country. Yeah. That screams deep shame and remorse.'

'I panicked,' he says. 'Let me go and I'll go back to the UK. I'll turn myself in.'

'You're a coward,' Antoinette hisses as she stalks over to him and kicks him in his side. He lets out a howl of pain.

'You're right,' he says. 'I'm a horrible coward. But I promise you that I will make this right. I'll get on a flight today if you let me. I'll go right to the police and tell them everything I did to Tor. I deserve to be punished. I do. But I don't deserve to die.'

'That's where you're wrong though, Aidan,' I tell him. 'Even if you're actually telling the truth and you go back to London and turn yourself in, which I highly doubt, you know as well as I do that your prison time would be short, if at all. I'm guessing this would be your first offence as you were a practising psychotherapist and allowed to work with people. Your first offence on record, that is, because I'm guessing this wasn't the first time you've been violent to a woman?'

'It was!' he protests. 'I've never hurt anyone before.'

'I find it very hard to believe, Aidan, that you went from being a peaceful, nonviolent man to beating a woman half to death.'

'I was under a lot of stress. And you don't know what it was like. You weren't there. Tor provoked me.'

I glare at him and Antoinette gives him another kick.

'Anyway, the point is that a judge could be lenient with you. First offence, a respected member of society up to this point. You'd do maybe four or five years in prison. Maybe none at all. Maybe you'd just be handed some community service and told to do a fucking anger-management course.'

'The prisons are horribly full,' Antoinette says. 'So it's possible he wouldn't even get a custodial sentence.'

'See,' I say to Aidan. 'Do you think that's fair? Do you think it would be fair on Tor to know that you were still out on the streets after what you did to her?'

'I wouldn't go near her, I swear to you. I'd move away.'

I pretend to think about this for a moment. 'But then how would I keep an eye on you, Aidan? How would I know that you're not hurting another woman? Only worse this time. Because that's what happens, isn't it? When men like you get away with it once. You wouldn't stop until you killed someone.'

His breaths are coming out in gasps now.

I love it when fear makes men hyperventilate.

'No,' he says. 'I could never.'

'Sure you could,' Antoinette says as she squats down so her face is at the same level as his. 'It's incredibly easy. Right, Kits?'

'It really is,' I agree.

'And addictive,' Antoinette says and I nod. 'It's actually really hard to stop once you get a taste for it.'

'So you see,' I continue, 'I couldn't, with a good conscience, let you go.'

He's almost sobbing now. 'You can. You can trust me. I'll never even speak to a woman again. I won't even look at one. Just please don't kill me.'

I drop down next to Antoinette and hold his eyes with mine. 'But I trusted you once already, didn't I, Aidan?'

I can tell he's remembering the same moment I am. When I went to see him at his clinic in London. I was concerned when Tor told me she'd fallen for her therapist. I mean, it's not great, is it? I was convinced he was taking advantage of her. She didn't even realise how vulnerable she still was after her attack in Mykonos. What sort of a man makes a move on a woman who is entrusting him with her emotional health? The red flags were flapping all over the place. So I paid him a visit. And he convinced me that he had fallen in love with my best friend. Why wouldn't he? She's incredible. Turns out Hollywood is the perfect place for Aidan Ward because he's one hell of an actor. I'll never not trust my instincts again.

'I meant every word I said to you that day, Kitty,' he says now.

'No,' I say. 'You didn't. Because if you meant even one single word, you never would have done this.' I take my phone out of my pocket and scroll through to the photos Tor sent me of her injuries. I hold them in front of Aidan's face. He tries to move his head so he's not looking at them but Antoinette grabs it and holds it still. 'Look,' I say. 'Look what you did to her.' I scroll through the photos, knowing he's seeing images of Tor's broken face, of the deep, angry bruises on her torso, of the drain in her skull removing fluid from her brain. I watch his face as he looks at the pictures. 'This is the woman you told me you loved. This is what you did to her. And you're seriously trying to argue that you don't deserve to die?'

Aidan's eyes are wet when they meet mine.

'I'm sorry,' he says to me.

'You're sorry I caught up with you, that's all.'

'Anyway,' Antoinette says in a sing-song voice. 'Do you remember that list of injuries I read to you?'

Aidan's eyes widen. 'Yes?'

'Which one first?'

His brow puckers a little. 'What do you mean?'

Antoinette fixes him with one of her hard stares. 'It's not a complicated question, Aidan. Which. One. First?'

I decide to help him out as it's clearly challenging his brain. 'Antoinette wanted to go straight to throat slicing,' I say, 'but I thought it would be more fun for you to experience some of what you put Tor through. That's why we made that list for you. Think of it as a kind of menu.' His eyes widen even more. 'Time to pick your starter, Aidan.' His eyes don't leave mine. 'What?' I say. 'Did you think that just because we bonded a bit while I was going through a crisis that I was going to spare you?'

I laugh in his face.

No chance.

Antoinette hops up and starts unravelling the tarpaulin sheet. 'This will make it easier to clean up when we're done,' she says cheerfully.

I stand up and start unpacking the bundle of tools I brought down with me; the knives, the kettlebell, the electric meat tenderiser. 'You're awfully quiet, Aidan,' I say. 'I guess it's chef's choice?' I pick up the kettlebell. 'How about we start with that cheekbone?'

Antoinette has finished rolling out the tarp. She looks up. 'That's Agnes's,' she says. 'Be careful not to get too much head gunk on it.'

'I can't promise that,' I say as I make my way over to Aidan.

67

KITTY AND ANTOINETTE'S AIRBNB, WEST HOLLYWOOD, LOS ANGELES

Some time later, I'm not sure exactly how long because time sort of loses itself when you're torturing a man in a wine cellar, the door creaks open and I hear feet on the steps. I look up and it's Charlie, holding a tray of what looks like lemonade.

'Lauren made drinks,' he says. 'I figured you'd be getting thirsty by now?'

'Oh God, yes!' Antoinette says, dropping the hammer she's been working with and skipping over to the steps and Charlie.

I want to stop him from coming any closer. Charlie is so pure and, even though he says he's accepted who I am and what I do, I worry that seeing me in action might give him the ick. Aidan isn't looking great at the moment. His face alone would be enough to make even the strongest stomach quiver.

'Thanks,' I say. 'You can leave it up there.'

But Charlie is already making his way into the cellar.

He puts the tray on the floor before standing up and tilting his head and looking at Aidan.

Aidan is, remarkably, still conscious even though we've gone to town on his cheekbone and ribs. I'm half-impressed that he didn't pass out when we fed his right hand, the one he used to hit Tor, into the meat tenderiser.

That was Antoinette's idea.

The girl is beautifully sadistic.

He sees Charlie and his eyes, which had begun to deaden with each menu item we served up to him, suddenly brighten.

'Help me,' he croaks. I haven't gotten to his Adam's apple yet. It will be one of the last things I do. I want to hear every single utterance until he takes his last breath. 'Please. They're killing me. Slowly.'

I look at Charlie, expecting a haunted look in his eyes, but he just stares at Aidan with an expression I can't make out.

'It's Aidan, right?' he says after a moment. 'I don't believe we've met.'

'Help me, man, they're crazy.'

Charlie lifts a hand to his face and rubs his stubble. 'Are they?' he says. 'Or are they justifiably fucking furious about what you did?'

Aidan's left eye is a pulpy mess but his right eye widens. 'You've gotta help me, bro?'

Charlie lifts a shoulder. 'I'm not sure that I do.' He crouches down so he's eye level – pulp level – with Aidan. 'You see, I know Tor as well. And like Kitty and Antoinette, I think she's pretty great.' He peers at the other man's face then stands up again. 'I've seen what you did to her. How you turned a woman so full of life into a shell. So no, I am not your *bro* and I'm not going to help you. You deserve everything you get. In fact, I'd help but I don't want to deny Kitty the joy of killing the man who hurt her friend, *our* friend, so badly.' And then he comes over to me and kisses me on my forehead. 'Let me know if you need anything else, okay?'

God, I fucking love this man.

'I will,' I say as Aidan begins to sob.

Charlie makes his way back up the stairs with all of us staring after him.

'Wow,' says Antoinette. 'You know how I feel about men, but you have got yourself a king there, Kits.'

'I really do, don't I?'

I want to bask in Charlie's words and how much they mean to me but Antoinette and I need to get back to work. It's getting late and I don't want to spend the whole night down here.

From somewhere in the darkness behind me I hear the unmistakable and exquisite clink of steel hitting steel. Antoinette is sharpening her knives.

This has been a long time coming.

'Have you got any last words?'

Aidan just stares at me.

'Oh, come on,' Antoinette says, 'you've been super chatty up until now. This is your legacy. There must be something you want to share?' She's looking at him with narrowed eyes.

'Just do it,' he croaks. 'Just kill me.'

Antoinette hands me one of the knives.

'I told you you'd be begging for death,' I say as I hold the tip to his Adam's apple.

I watch it bob one final time.

Afterwards, when Aidan is packaged up in suitcases like Ron Wilde, Antoinette and I go back upstairs. I'm impressed to see that Lauren, Charlie and Agnes have been busy making dinner. No one mentions what we've been doing in the cellar.

'It's roast chicken!' Agnes says brightly as she wraps her arms around Antoinette. She doesn't even flinch that my sister's sundress is covered in blood spatter.

'There's cauliflower for you, Kitty,' Lauren says as she gets a tray of roasting vegetables out of the oven.

'Oh, can someone go and get Lana Del Gay from the guesthouse?' Agnes says. 'She'd never forgive me if I ate chicken without her.'

I look around the room. Lauren is dishing the food up. Charlie is pouring drinks. Agnes and Antoinette are curled around each other on a chair.

'I guess that'll be me then,' I say.

'Lana,' I call as I let myself into the guesthouse. 'Where are you, you little menace?' But the dog doesn't come running out of wherever she's been snoozing like she usually does. 'Lana? There's chicken waiting for you.'

Still nothing.

That's weird.

She's usually like a little furry tornado at the mention of chicken.

Where is she?

I stop and listen for a moment.

And then I hear it.

A quiet whining, coming from Lauren's room.

I find her in there, her little paws scrabbling furiously at Lauren's closet door.

'What's in there, you little gremlin?' I say, pulling the closet open.

Lana gives a yelp of delight and launches herself at a half-chewed slipper. I pull it out for her and she snatches it from my hand, carrying it out, her tail wagging frantically with joy.

I almost miss the notebook that dislodged when I reached for the slipper.

Almost.

68

KITTY AND ANTOINETTE'S AIRBNB, WEST HOLLYWOOD, LOS ANGELES

Back in the kitchen, Antoinette, Agnes, Lauren and Charlie are waiting for me before they start eating.

Lauren has made another round of lemonade.

She pours me a glass.

'It's my own special recipe,' Lauren says. 'Cort used to love it.'

'Thank you,' I say as I pull out a chair next to Charlie. 'So I guess the question is, what are we going to do with . . . you know.' I gesture towards the cellar.

'Actually,' says Charlie. 'We've just been talking about that. And Agnes has an idea.'

Antoinette looks at Agnes and I'm not lying when I say that she absolutely glows. My sister is totally smitten. I wonder if I look like that when I look at Charlie.

'What's your idea?' she asks.

Agnes smiles shyly. 'Well, you know how my parents still live out in Newport Beach? That I grew up there?' Antoinette nods. 'I thought maybe we could swing past and say hi before Kitty and Charlie fly back to London.'

Antoinette looks puzzled. 'While I would absolutely love to see where you grew up,' she says, 'I don't really understand what that's got to do with our body problem in the basement.'

Agnes leans in closer. 'My parents own a yacht,' she says. 'And the Pacific gets pretty deep out there. Like seven, eight thousand feet.'

'Ahhh,' Antoinette says with a smile. 'You're so clever.' She kisses Agnes on the cheek.

'So, what do we think about a little day trip?' Agnes asks.

'I think that sounds incredible,' I say.

Agnes claps her hands together. 'I'll give my parents a call and let them know we want to take the boat out.' She turns to myself and my sister and adds, 'You'll love Newps. I can't wait to show you.'

'I'll make more lemonade,' Lauren says.

69

AGNES'S PARENTS' YACHT, CATALINA CHANNEL, OFFSHORE FROM NEWPORT BEACH

The sun is beating down on my skin and I stretch out luxuriously on the sun lounger on the upper deck. I've got to hand it to Agnes, this is a much better idea than dumping the body parts all around the Hollywood Hills with the hope that the mountain lions find them before the police. I take a deep, happy breath. It's actually going to be okay. I feel a hand snake up my inner thigh and I open my eyes to see Charlie looking at me, his pupils dilated.

'I like you in this bikini,' he says, leaning in for a kiss.

'Oh really?'

'Very much. I think I'd like you even better out of it though. Want to disappear below deck for a bit?'

'Get a room, please!' Antoinette's voice drifts over to us, ruining the moment. I sit up and look at my sister, who's peering over the top of her sunglasses at us. 'We're here to do a job, Kitty, it's not a jolly.' But there's a smile on her face. It's good to see that being held hostage in a basement for three days hasn't fazed her at all.

We loaded up the SUV first thing this morning and arrived in Newport Beach just over an hour later. Agnes's parents were delighted to see us and only too happy for us to take their cruiser out for a spin.

'They're boat people,' Agnes warned us before we arrived. And she wasn't kidding. Her mum, who looks exactly like Agnes but with silver-blonde hair instead of golden, greeted us wearing a T-shirt saying 'nauti but nice'. Charlie, king of dad jokes, appreciated the pun. 'They made me get a boating licence when I was like sixteen. I could steer a boat before I could drive a car.'

I love yachts and as soon as I saw the sleek white vessel glistening like a crystal in the harbour, I knew that today would be a great day. The wind is splashing saltwater on our skin and we can see the faint silhouette of Catalina Island in the distance. I'm really into this body-disposal-but-make-it-luxe vibe we've got going on here. Maybe I should get a yacht. It's a lot more pleasing than feeding hacked-up lumps of flesh through a mincer.

Suddenly the engine cuts and the only sound is the slap of waves against the hull of the boat.

'This is it,' Agnes calls from the flybridge. 'The deepest part of the channel.'

I stand up, the wind whips my hair around my face and I can taste sea salt on my lips. The Pacific Ocean stretches out around us and I suddenly feel very small, like how you sometimes feel when you look up at the huge expanse of night sky and realise how tiny and unimportant you really are in the universe. I look over the side of the deck and have to catch my breath. The water is so deep here that it looks black, bottomless. I can't even imagine what lies beneath the surface, what secrets those depths hold. And I'd really rather not know. I love the ocean, but I mean the blue, shimmery surface of it. What goes on down there is none of my business.

'You ready?' Agnes skips down from the flybridge with a smile on her face, like we're about to go for a refreshing little paddle rather than dump two dead bodies into the water.

I nod and Charlie takes my hand as we walk carefully around to the saloon where the cases are waiting for us. We put a kettlebell in each case along with the body parts, just to make sure they reach their ocean-bed destination.

'The water is about seven thousand feet deep here,' Agnes tells us as I continue to peer into the depths. Seven thousand feet of cold, black water. Deep enough to swallow anything and keep it in its bowels forever. I grip the railing so tightly my knuckles go white. You would not want to go overboard here.

'Let's do this thing,' Antoinette says and she heaves one of the cases into her arms before letting it slide from her grip and into the water. It hits the surface with a splash before sinking deep down into the infinite blackness. 'Rest in pieces, Ron.'

My turn.

I pick up one of the cases containing some of the remains of Aidan Ward and drag it to the side of the boat. It's heavy but I'm strong enough to haul it over the railing and let it drop into the water. I watch as it sinks and feel relief wash all over me.

It's done.

He's gone.

Tor can feel safe now. She can stop hiding away. Stop being terrified that he'll come back and finish her off.

She's free.

And it's this feeling, the feeling that – because of me – a woman can feel that little bit safer when she's walking alone at night, that makes it all worthwhile.

We all work together to dump the rest of the cases overboard, sending the rest of Ron to his watery grave.

I glance at Lauren to see how she's holding up.

I know this can't be easy for her.

Ron Wilde and Aidan Ward are getting a more dignified final send-off than Cort did.

'I'm going to take a moment,' she says, catching me looking at her. 'I just need to clear my head.'

'Of course,' Agnes says and she gives Lauren a reassuring rub on the arm. 'I'm so proud of you, bestie. I know how hard this has been for you.'

Lauren gives her a sad smile before pulling a kaftan over her bikini and walking around to the other side of the boat.

'I hope she's gonna be okay,' Agnes says quietly as she watches Lauren leave.

'She will,' I say. 'It will take time and she'll need to do the work. But she'll heal.'

Antoinette is looking visibly uncomfortable with all the attention we're giving to Lauren. 'Let's try to enjoy the rest of the afternoon,' she says. 'Kitty and Charlie are leaving tomorrow.' She looks up at the sun, which seems even brighter out here in the middle of the ocean, a never-ending golden hour. 'Let's get some vit D. God only knows what the weather is like back in London.'

Charlie and I head up to the top deck and I watch as he stretches out on a lounger. God, he looks good. Agnes and

Antoinette are nowhere to be seen, so much for spending some time with us. Oh well. I take the opportunity to kiss Charlie, long and deep.

'Hello, you,' he says. 'That was nice.'

'It was, wasn't it?' I breathe him in. 'You smell good.'

'It's Tom Ford.'

'No, it's definitely you.'

He sits up and cups my face in his hand. 'I missed you, Kits. I know I've said it a hundred times already, but I really need you to know how terrible I've felt about how I left things in Cannes.'

'I know,' I say. 'I missed you too. Unbearably.'

He kisses me again and then lies back, hands behind his head. 'I could get used to this, you know?'

I stare at him. 'Really?'

He shrugs. 'Yeah. I could be a boat person.'

I laugh. 'Well, I can't wait to get back to London.'

'I'm glad you said that. I was worried I really would have to be a boat person.' He wraps his arms around me and I let myself sink into them.

70

AGNES'S PARENTS' YACHT, CATALINA CHANNEL, OFFSHORE FROM NEWPORT BEACH

I'm so wrapped up in the delicious bliss of just lying in the arms of the man I love that I stop paying attention to anything else. When I finally glance up, I notice that Agnes and Antoinette have materialised and are sharing a lounger on the top deck, they're both asleep.

Charlie is gently snoring next to me.

I look around but can't see Lauren anywhere.

I haven't seen her since she said she needed a moment to herself.

A jolt of concern flashes through me.

I stand up and wrap a sarong around my waist. There's a breeze coming off the sea now that makes me shiver. Goosebumps prickle on my arms.

I find Lauren staring over the side of the boat, into the dark, swirling water.

She's holding her lighter, flicking it on and off as she stares at the waves.

I cough to alert her to my presence.

She spins around and stares at me in surprise. 'Kitty! I thought you were—'

'Asleep?' I say, moving closer to her. 'Like the others?'

She nods and smiles at me. 'It's been an exhausting few days.'

'It has,' I say, joining her and looking into those black, black waters. 'It really has.'

She peers at my face, her eyes searching it for something. 'Aren't you tired?'

I shake my head. 'Too hyped up over finally getting rid of those bodies,' I say. 'That and the fact I didn't drink any of your drugged lemonade.'

Lauren stares at me.

There's silence for a moment or two before she regains her composure.

Another smile, saccharine sweet.

A little shake of her head.

She's good.

I have to give her that.

I totally underestimated her.

'I'm sorry,' she says, her brow furrowing in confusion. 'I'm not sure I quite follow.'

I lean in closer. 'It's quite simple,' I say. 'I didn't drink any of your drugged lemonade. That's why I'm not unconscious on deck like the rest of them.' I take another step towards her. 'So what was the next part of your plan going to be, Lauren? Because it was you, wasn't it? The WeHo Ripper. It's been you all along.'

Her face folds.

* * *

It was Travis who told me.

I didn't really think he was talking about the police when he was gasping 'Law-man' as he bled out. I knew he was trying to say 'Lauren', that she was part of what had been going on with Cort.

I just hadn't realised how big a part she'd played.

I was given another clue on the way home from the cabin.

'I'm so glad Agnes got Lauren's message telling you where we were,' I'd said to Charlie as we drove through the desert. We were following Agnes and Lauren in Agnes's car. Antoinette was asleep in the back seat.

Charlie glanced over at me, his face puzzled. 'What message? We didn't get a message.'

That didn't make sense. 'How did you find us then?'

He gave a sheepish smile. 'Location sharing,' he says. 'I didn't turn it off. I liked seeing where you were.'

But Find My Friends doesn't work without a signal.

And Lauren had told me there wasn't any.

The smoking gun, though, had been the notebook.

The one that Lana Del Gay accidentally led me to. I pulled it out and flicked through it. Imagine my surprise when I found pages and pages of that list of names Cort had supposedly written. Pages and pages of Lauren trying to perfect his handwriting.

She planted the note.

She stole Antoinette's scarf.

She wanted Cort to take the fall.

For *her* murders.

The only thing I don't know is why she did it. Why was she killing women?

She's staring at me now, a look of confusion on her face that I'd totally buy if I didn't know she was a killer.

'Me?' she says. 'Kitty, I have no idea what you're talking about. It was Cort. We all know that. And why would I drug the lemonade? I made that to distract myself. Hello. My boyfriend just died, remember?' There's no hint of fear or desperation in her voice.

'You're actually a really good actor,' I say. 'It's a shame you didn't apply yourself in school as much as you did in plotting and killing.'

'I'm not acting,' she says but a muscle twitches at the corner of her mouth. That's her tell.

'You set Cort up.'

And, just like that, the mask drops.

She blinks at me and lets out a cracked laugh. 'That idiot? Kitty, I didn't set him up. He knew exactly what I was doing. He might not have actually killed anyone, but he was still complicit. He brought them to me. He might have been an annoying motherfucker but women *flocked* to him.'

'He charmed them so you could murder them?'

'I didn't murder them,' she says, sounding almost outraged. When I open my mouth to tell her to tell the truth she holds a hand up to silence me. 'I *saved* them.'

'They're fucking dead, Lauren,' I say. 'That doesn't scream *saved* to me.'

She laughs but it's a horrible hollow noise. 'I saved them from themselves, Kitty. Don't you see?'

'No. I really don't. All I see is four dead girls. Four families who will never see their daughter, their sister, their cousin again.' I pause for a moment. 'Is it four? Are there any more?'

She shakes her head. 'Just the four. For now. When I've got rid of all you nosy little gremlins, there will be more.'

That's when I notice the bottle at her feet is actually a fuel cannister.

'You're going to kill more women?'

'Kitty,' she says, shaking her head as if she's disappointed in me. 'I'm going to *save* more women. Once I've got rid of y'all snoopers.'

'Lauren,' I echo her tone. 'How is strangling these women and leaving their bodies by Hollywood landmarks saving them exactly? You're really going to need to walk me through that one because I don't understand.'

The only thing I understand is that she's a fucking lunatic and that I should push her overboard now.

But I'm curious.

She clearly believes in her mission as much as I believe in mine.

'Is this a trick?' she's saying now, narrowing her eyes at me.

'How would it be a trick?' I say, holding my hands up and showing her that I'm not carrying anything in my bikini. 'Tell me. I want to know.'

Her brows pinch. 'Isn't it obvious?'

I shake my head. 'Not really, Lauren, no.'

She sighs and shakes her hair out. 'You saw all those comments. Online,' she says. 'You said yourself that they didn't even let the bodies get cold before they were calling those women sluts.' Her voice cracks a little on the last word. 'That's what the world thinks of women who sell their bodies. The saving grace is that they didn't have to read any of it themselves. Now they don't have to worry about any of their sins.'

'Their *sins*?' I repeat. 'You mean making their own choices about their own bodies?'

Lauren just stares at me. 'You have no idea, do you? No idea what it's like to be called a slut. For it to be the one thing that defines you. To be the biggest skank in the world. To get anonymous death threats on Myspace. For your own father to call you a whore. To disown you.'

Ah.

So there's a personal story here.

There usually is.

'What happened to you, Lauren?' I keep my voice low and level. A trick that I learned from my time in the cellar with Aidan Ward. Guess it wasn't a total waste of time after all. 'Tell me.'

She stares at me for a moment as if trying to work out whether I'm being genuine. 'I've lived it,' she says eventually. 'I know what the future looks like for those girls.'

I take another tentative step towards her. 'How?'

She sighs. 'I was thirteen,' she says. 'There was this house party. I was going through my pushing-boundaries era so I snuck out of the house and went.' She stares back out to sea. 'Where I grew up, it was small, my dad was the local pastor. I didn't know that some of the boys had a bet on to see who could nail the pastor's daughter.' Her gaze turns watery.

'Lauren,' I say but she holds a hand up to stop me.

'Anyway, I was young and wanted to show the other kids that I wasn't just this prim little princess. So when this guy offered me a drink, I took it. I'd never had alcohol before. He thought it was funny and, when I finished it, he got me another. And then another. I guess I blacked out at some point.'

She pauses to take a deep, shuddery breath. 'All I can really remember is coming round in a bedroom and my dress was all bunched up, my underwear off. I couldn't find them so I had to go downstairs without them. Everyone was looking at me.'

'You were assaulted,' I say but she's not listening to me. She's still staring out at the horizon, flicking the lighter on and off.

'The next day at school, everyone was talking about me. The guy went to our local high school and had been bragging about what he'd done to me. Some kids from school had seen me come down the stairs all crumpled and confused. The story spread like wildfire. I was a slut for the next three years. Until my dad threw me out. That's when I came to LA.' The tears that have been pooling in her eyes finally fall down her cheeks. She wipes them away with the back of her hand like they're an embarrassment. 'That's when I saw how many girls out here needed my help.'

'Killing them is not helping them, Lauren.' It's Antoinette.

I was wondering when she was going to make an appearance.

Of course I didn't let my wing woman drink drugged lemonade either.

Even if it was watered down.

'About time,' I say to her. 'No rush. Just a lunatic with a lighter and a cannister of fuel.'

'Sorry,' Antoinette says. 'I think I *did* actually drift off for a bit. It's really soothing, isn't it? Being rocked by a boat in the sun. I think I'll buy one.'

'That's great,' I say. 'But maybe you can share your Amazon wishlist with me some other time.'

‘Oh,’ she says. ‘Of course.’ She side-eyes Lauren. ‘Are we doing this then?’

I shake my head. ‘No,’ I say.

Antoinette looks confused. ‘What do you mean no? We agreed. Get her confession, then throw her overboard.’

Lauren is looking back and forth between us, watching a verbal tennis match.

‘I’ve changed my mind,’ I say. ‘We’re not killing her.’

Antoinette stares at me as if I’ve checked out of reality. ‘She is literally standing there with a lighter and a cannister of something I’m willing to wager isn’t fucking Mountain Dew. She was going to kill us.’

‘She’s not a monster,’ I say. ‘She’s a *survivor.*’

My sister still looks baffled. ‘What? How is she a victim? A victim of what exactly?’

‘Of men,’ I say. ‘Of the patriarchy. Of violence starting in the mouth. Of having her body policed from the age of *thirteen*.’

Antoinette rolls her eyes. ‘Yes, I heard her little story. How do we even know that’s true though, Kits? She’s already proved to us that she’s a better actor than we realised. It could all be lies.’ She folds her arms across her chest. ‘The only thing we know for sure about her is that she’s killed women. A lot of women.’

‘Because of the *patriarchy*,’ I say. ‘Because of how it uses words like slut to control women.’ I shake my head. ‘No. We’re not killing her.’

‘What are we going to do with her then?’

‘We’re going to recruit her,’ I say and Antoinette stares at me so hard that I think her eyes might actually eject from her skull.

‘*Recruit her?*’ she hisses. ‘What the hell are you talking about?’

‘She can help us,’ I say. ‘She can help us get rid of the real enemy. The men who assault women. The men who hurt women.’ I smile at my sister. ‘She’s already pretty proficient in killing.’

‘Have you totally gone off the deep end? She’s a killer. Of women. She was going to kill me. *Us*.’

I take a step towards my sister. ‘I know,’ I say. ‘But *we* don’t kill women. Not when we can help them. Lauren’s just been damaged by the patriarchy and shame and everything that goes with being a woman. We can help her. I know we can.’

Antoinette presses her lips together. ‘Kitty . . .’

But I haven’t finished. ‘No, listen to me. I know it won’t be easy but we can train her up. She can head up operations over here when we go back to London!’

Antoinette holds her hand up. ‘No, Kitty. She’s completely unhinged. She can’t be trusted with something like this. Absolutely not.’

‘But—’ I start before I’m interrupted by a scream.

I spin around and stare at the spot where Lauren was just standing but she’s not there. I look around. She isn’t anywhere.

And then I hear it.

The crash of something hitting the water.

Something that sounds like a body.

Antoinette and I run to the railings and stare over into the black water.

There’s no sign of Lauren.

But Agnes is standing there, her eyes full of flame and fury.

71

KITTY AND ANTOINETTE'S AIRBNB, WEST HOLLYWOOD, LOS ANGELES

It's almost dark by the time we get back to the villa. Four out of the five of us who left this morning.

Charlie, when he woke up, radioed the Coastguard about twenty minutes after we watched Lauren disappear into the depths of the Pacific Ocean.

She didn't really stand a chance out there.

'It's really cold in there,' Agnes had said, her voice like ice. 'Even in summer. Sharks too.'

We let the boat drift a bit before we threw in the life ring.

The Coastguard sent out a helicopter and a couple of boats with spotters, but they didn't find anything.

We had to answer some questions and Agnes took charge. She explained that we'd lost two people. Lauren – and her boyfriend Cort – who'd dived in after her because she couldn't swim.

Genius really.

Now we don't have to worry about explaining Cort's mysterious disappearance.

It was a silent road trip home.

I think we're all in a bit of shock.

We're sitting around the kitchen table now. Charlie has poured everyone brandy, but my stomach is still rolling from everything that'd happened and mine sits untouched.

Finally, Antoinette says the words none of us has so far dared to. Once words are out in the world, they can rarely be taken back.

She turns to Agnes, a tiny furrow between her brows, and says, 'You pushed her.' It's not accusatory. It's just stating a fact.

Agnes nods, once. 'She was going to kill me,' she says, again just voicing a fact. Then she looks up at my sister. 'She was going to kill all of us.'

They look at each other for a long minute, having some sort of conversation without actual words. I can't tell what Antoinette is thinking. I know that she believed Agnes was kind and good. I don't know what her being a killer means for them.

'You saved us,' Antoinette says eventually.

Agnes looks down at her hands and lifts one shoulder in a half-shrug. 'Then we're even,' she says. Then she looks up. First at Antoinette. And then at me. 'For Richard Stone.'

Ah.

So she worked that out.

I suppose it wasn't too hard to join the dots.

'Are you okay?' I ask Agnes. 'She was your best friend.'

Agnes thinks about this for a moment before giving me a watery smile. 'She was *pretending* to be my best friend,' she says. 'I guess she was a better actor than any of us gave her credit for.'

We sit in silence for a few moments longer, each of us caught up in our own thoughts.

I can't help but feel bad for Lauren and how she died. My thoughts battle each other. Could I have helped her? Or was she too damaged by everything she'd been through? She was so earnest when she was explaining to me why she killed those women. She really believed she was saving them. Her logic, although completely fucking twisted, kind of makes sense.

Like me, she just wanted to protect women.

'We should think about getting to bed,' Charlie says after a while. 'It's been a long day.'

I kiss him on the cheek. 'Yes,' I say. 'There's just one thing I need to do first. I'll meet you upstairs.'

He gives me a puzzled look as I grab my phone and take it through to the living room, closing the door behind me.

72

KITTY AND ANTOINETTE'S AIRBNB, WEST HOLLYWOOD, LOS ANGELES

'Hey, Kits.' Tor sounds and looks tired when she answers my FaceTime call. 'How's it going?'

This is the moment I've been waiting for. The moment this whole LA adventure has been for. The moment I can tell my best friend that she doesn't need to be scared anymore. That the monster under her bed is gone for good.

When I was very little, I was scared of monsters. I thought they hid under my bed at night, waiting for a chance to slip out and eat me up. I remember hiding under my duvet, breathing as quietly as I could, hoping that they wouldn't hear me. Then, when I heard my parents come upstairs to bed, I'd race across the hallway into their room and snuggle into bed with them. I believed that they would keep me safe. They tolerated this when I was a toddler but by the time I was four my father evidently decided enough was enough. He gave me a spray bottle of water that he told me was a monster spray.

You spray it all over your room and your bed, Kitty, and it will keep you safe from the monsters.

He thought he was a genius but all it taught me was that I had to fight my own monsters now. That I was on my own.

And, of course, as I got older I began to learn that the monsters aren't under the bed at all. Sometimes they're in it with you.

I made a promise that I'd never let a woman fight her monsters alone if I could help it. Killing Aidan Ward wasn't just for Tor, it was for every woman who has had to fight alone.

I swallow hard. What I say next is going to change everything.

'It's done,' I say.

There's a long beat of silence before I hear Tor breathe out. It's a breath she's been holding since she came out of her coma. She closes her eyes as she exhales and I can see the beginnings of a smile dance at the corners of her mouth. She looks like the sun has just come out and shone on her.

'Are you sure?' she says eventually.

I nod. 'Oh yes. I'm very sure,' I say. 'Couldn't be surer.'

And then she *beams* and it's like the sun has come out and shone on me.

'You,' she says, 'are a fucking angel.'

'Thank you.'

'No, better than an angel. What's better than an angel?'

I think for a moment. 'An archangel?'

'A *guardian* archangel,' Tor says. '*My* guardian archangel.' There's another little beat of silence. 'Kitty. I can't thank you enough for this. I will forever be in your debt.'

'Shut up,' I say. 'It was my pleasure.' It absolutely was. Wiping that man off the planet was a complete pleasure. 'Besides, I owed you—'

'No.' Tor snaps her fingers. 'No, you did not. If I'd just listened to you, to your warnings about him in the first place, none of this would have happened. You wouldn't have needed to . . .' She trails off. She doesn't know what I needed to do. Or how I did it. And I don't think she'll ever ask. She shakes her head and smiles again. 'Anyway. You can come home now?'

I smile back and I can feel it's huge and goofy on my face. I'm so excited to go home.

'I can!' I say. 'I absolutely can.'

'Let me know when you'll be back. I'm going to arrange a brunch for us. With Maisie. Even if we have to take it to her house. Even if . . .' She trails off again and moves out of view of her camera. I wonder what's going on but then I hear her crying. Big gulping sobs. The soundtrack of relief. After a moment or two, she appears back on the screen. 'Did he know?' she says, dabbing at her face with her sleeve. 'Did he know what was happening?'

I nod. 'Oh yes. He absolutely knew what was happening. And why.'

'Did he suffer?'

I think for a second. Is she asking me because even though she wanted him dead, she wanted it quick and painless? Or is she asking because she wants me to tell her that he suffered for every single second of suffering he put her through? For every minute she was in the hospital. For every panic attack she had when she came home. For the physical pain he inflicted on her body. And the emotional pain that has kept her broken and housebound ever since his brutal attack.

'He suffered,' I say. 'He spent his last minutes hoping for death. Knowing it would be the only relief.'

She beams again. 'Good,' she says. 'I'm glad.'

'He deserved every bit of it,' I say.

'And you're absolutely sure he's definitely gone? There's not going to be some weird encore to this where he pops up again somehow?'

I laugh. 'You watch too many slasher films. He's gone. Do you want me to bring you a finger to prove it?'

Now she laughs. 'Have fun explaining that at customs.'

There's silence again, the kind of silence you can only ever have with someone who knows you inside and out. Someone who has seen every single one of your flaws and dark moments and loves you, not in spite of them, but because of them.

'So, have you told Charlie you're pregnant yet?'

And my world spins off its axis.

'What? What are you talking about?'

Tor lets out a bark of laughter. 'Oh come on, Kits. You don't need to play dumb with me. I've been with Maisie day in and day out. I think I can spot a pregnant queen when I see one.'

I stare at her. 'I'm not pregnant . . .' Am I?

But then I think about the last few weeks. The sickness and tiredness I put down to jet lag. The irritability that I put down to forced proximity with a Gen Z-er. The aversion to alcohol. The literal vomiting at a murder scene.

'Wait,' I say to Tor and I swipe on my period tracker app on my phone. When was the last time I bled? Shit. I haven't had a period in almost two months. How have I not realised that? My hand shoots down to my abdomen. Could I be?

'You didn't know?' Tor says but I can barely hear her. This can't be happening. This isn't part of the plan. I don't even know if I want kids. How could I be a mother? I am not a creator of life, I'm a taker of it. No, no, no.

I look at my best friend again, who is staring back at me, her eyes huge with concern.

'Fuck.' I say. 'Fuck.'

73

MUSSO AND FRANK, HOLLYWOOD BOULEVARD, LOS ANGELES

'Thanks for coming,' Antoinette says after we've been seated in our booth and handed our menus. 'I've always wanted to come here.'

It's lunchtime, Charlie and I fly home later today and my sister begged me to come for lunch with her before we do, just the two of us.

'You don't need to thank me,' I say. 'I'm your sister. I love having time just the two of us. I know I've been sort of glued to Charlie since he arrived but I'll always make time for you. You know that.'

Antoinette smiles. 'That's great to know,' she says, 'but I meant thanks for coming *here*. It's not exactly the restaurant of choice for vegans.'

She's right.

As soon as I walked in I could smell the steak fat and my stomach contents tried to yeet themself out of my body. I'm trying not to think about what Tor said. But it's there, niggling away right at the back of my mind where I keep all the things I don't want to think about. Locked away in a box. For now.

'That's okay,' I say. 'I was craving a bowl of mashed potatoes and a side salad anyway.'

She laughs.

'Anyway, I'll pay you back by taking you to the most vegan place that ever veganed when we're back in London.'

Antoinette is suddenly very focused on the menu. She doesn't say a word. Which, I've learned, is very not like my sister.

Something's wrong.

'Antoinette?' I say. 'What is it?'

'Hmm?' she says, still not looking at me. Her eyes are intently looking at the menu.

I reach over and grab it out of her hands. 'What's going on?'

'I don't know what you mean,' she says.

'Don't give me that, Antoinette,' I say. 'You clammed up the minute I mentioned London.'

Her cheeks flush. 'Okay,' she says. 'I was going to wait for the food to get here, but seeing as you're so persistent with your interrogation.' She picks up a napkin and starts ripping it to shreds. I want to take that out of her hands as well.

'Spill already,' I say, my patience getting thinner by the second.

'I'm not coming back,' she says. 'To London.'

I stare at her. 'What?'

'I'm not coming back to London.'

'I heard what you said, Antoinette. I meant "what" like what are you doing? And why not?'

She shrugs. 'There's nothing for me there. Not really.'

'I'm there,' I say. 'And there are loads of bad men there. I don't want to work alone anymore.'

'You'll be fine,' she says. 'And anyway, you've got Charlie. You've got Maisie and Tor. You've got Carmella and Gabriel. I don't have any of that. My mother barely acknowledges my existence. She never has. That's not going to change.'

'What about me?'

'You don't want me hanging around. You've got a whole life you've been wanting to get back to. I'm not part of that.'

'Of course you are!' I say. 'You're my sister. And we've only just found each other.' I reach across the table for her hand. She lets me take it, but it's limp.

She shakes her head. 'I just don't want to go back, Kits.'

'What are you going to do then?'

She shrugs. 'I've got enough money to do anything I want. Agnes and I are going to travel for a bit. And then, I don't know, come back here. I like it here. It suits me.'

I look at her over the table.

Her eyes are shining, she looks tanned, relaxed, happy.

It really does suit her.

I just hadn't noticed before.

As usual I've been too busy thinking about myself.

'What about us?' I say. 'What about, you know, business.'

She gives me a little smile. 'Well, I never said I was giving that up. Just think of it as more of an international enterprise now.'

'Wow,' I say. 'Killers Without Borders. You've made up your mind, haven't you?'

She smiles but her eyes soften. 'You don't need me,' she says. 'You never have. And, you know, I want to see where things go with Agnes. I really like her.'

'You've just met her,' I say and Antoinette gives me a slightly admonishing look that makes me feel bad and childish. I realise then how much she's grown in the few weeks we've been out here. 'You've only just met me too,' I say, my voice quieter now. 'You know, properly.'

She squeezes my hand back now. 'I'm not leaving you, Kits,' she says. 'You'll still see me all the time. I promise. I just need to choose something for me.'

'I get it,' I say eventually. 'But that doesn't mean I like it. I've only just found you. I'm not ready to let you go.'

'You're not letting me go,' she says. 'Because I'll still be your sister. Nothing will change that.' She lets go of my hand and pours herself some water. I watch as she swallows it, wishing there was something I could say to her that would make her change her mind. I need her in London with me. Not just for the killing but for other things too. I touch my hand lightly to my stomach.

Maybe.

I open my mouth to tell her, but then I close it again.

No.

She's made her choice.

I can't make this about me.

It's not fair.

Antoinette puts her glass back down on the table and raises her eyes to meet mine. There's a small, uncertain smile on her lips. 'So, we're good then?'

I smile back. 'We're good.'

She laughs, sits back in her chair, the moment too charged for her comfort zone. 'Anyway,' she says. 'It's not goodbye. Not really. It's just see you later.'

‘Yes.’ I nod as the waiter comes over to take our orders. Even though I have no appetite now.

‘Come on,’ Antoinette says to me. ‘Don’t take too long. You’ve got a flight to catch.’

My fingers flutter to my stomach again.

There are a few things I need to do today.

74

TOM BRADLEY INTERNATIONAL TERMINAL, LAX, LOS ANGELES

I've left Charlie in the lounge, claiming that I need to do some last-minute retail therapy to decompress. He offered to come with me but I told him that this is something I need to do alone. Which isn't a lie. I just need to find a shop selling what I need.

We said goodbye to Antoinette and Agnes with lots of hugs and promises to be back to visit soon.

'Look after her,' I said to Agnes as the Uber pulled away.

'She's in good hands,' Agnes had replied and I believe her.

I hate goodbyes so I was almost grateful that I had something much bigger on my mind when I gave my sister a final hug.

Now I just need to find out, one way or another.

I scurry past some of my usual go-to shops with barely a second glance. Although I might have to pop back in and check out that dress in Bvlgari in a minute.

No, no, no.

Stay focused, Kitty.

Ugh, why are there so many duty-free shops and clothes shops? This isn't what I need at all.

Why isn't there a Boots or a Superdrug?

God, I can't wait to get home.

I suppose I could wait until I get back to London. But I can't. The thought of spending eleven hours on a plane and not knowing would be torture.

I spot a Hudson store and hurry over to it.

Please, please, please.

I see what I'm looking for and think I say 'Oh my God, yes' out loud because I'm getting some funny looks from other travellers as I make a grab for the item and rush to pay. I stuff it in my bag.

Now I need to find some toilets.

Okay. So this isn't exactly how I ever thought this moment would go. Not that I've particularly thought about it. But it's not really every little girl's dream to take a pregnancy test in an airport loo. Especially when whoever is in the cubicle next to me is making noises – and smells – that truly belong on a farm. Forget all that *we listen and we don't judge* crap. I am being forced to listen and I am very much judging. Anyway. Whatever is going on in that cubicle is none of my business. My business is here. In my hands. All I need to do is pee on this stick, wait three minutes and then I'll know.

Turns out that peeing on demand is easier said than done though. It's never been something I've excelled at, in all honesty. I've had to give samples to the doctor before and it's like I just totally dry up from the inside. I don't understand it. It's not like I'm not well hydrated. Is it stage fright? I squeeze and squeeze but not even the smallest drop of pee is playing ball. This is ridiculous.

'Come on,' I whisper to my bladder. 'What are you playing at? This isn't the time to go all shy on me.'

After what feels like several lifetimes I feel a small but determined stream of pee finally leave my body.

I hope I'm not missing the stick.

That would be beyond frustrating.

I pull the stick out from underneath me to check and am relieved to see that I've hit the spot.

So now I wait.

God.

This is awful.

What if it's positive? How will I tell Charlie? We've only just got back together and we've never even spoken about kids. Not in any real depth anyway. I know he's not opposed to the idea, in theory. But theory is a hell of a lot different to reality. Particularly when the mother of your potential child has a sideline in serial killing. And how do I feel about motherhood? I'm not one of those women. Not like Maisie, who played with baby dolls the moment she could walk. Who started any conversations about our futures with the words *when I'm a mum*. Who goes all funny when they walk past the baby section in a shoe shop. Like I can appreciate that teeny-tiny Chloé sliders are cute, but Maisie gets positively gooey. And the shoes might be cute but what about the thing that goes inside the shoes? Babies are loud. And they sleep like shit. And they excrete stuff from every single orifice. Plus how the hell would a baby fit into my lifestyle? For one, serial killing when I'm the size of a penthouse and my centre of gravity has left the chat would not be easy. And what about when it's born? Then I'll be the one excreting stuff from every orifice. For *months* after I pop the thing out. And serial killing isn't exactly known for its generous maternity package. What would I do? Stop mid-slaughter and whip out a breast pump? *Sorry, sir, would you mind waiting a few moments for your imminent painful death? I just need to hook myself up to this milking machine before my tits explode.* It's just not practical. And this is before we even consider the fucking issue of genetics. My father was a psychopath and both of his daughters have uncontrollable bloodlust. One more than the other though. Let's hope Antoinette never decides to procreate. There's no way that's not a family trait. What if this baby doesn't get the memo that killing is only acceptable if the *killee* is an absolute abhorrent monster? What if I birth this generation's answer to Jack the Ripper. Or Jacqueline the Ripper? How would I ever be able to live with myself if I unleashed something like that into the world?

God, I'm having a panic attack.

Okay, Kitty, breathe. It's okay.

I take some deep breaths.

I close my eyes.

My heart begins to slow down.

My thoughts don't feel like they're racing ahead of me.

This baby would be half Charlie. So there's no way it could be all bad. Charlie is the best person in the world. He's kind and he's funny. He's generous and loyal. He's the smartest person I know. Admittedly the bar there is pretty low, but still. And he's just got so much love. It emanates from him. It flows through his veins. I'm pretty sure if I ever cut Charlie open –

not that I would without very good reason – he'd bleed glitter and rainbows or something. For all of my darkness, he is light. Would that cancel out all that's bad from me? I can't believe anything that is half Charlie's DNA could ever be fully bad. And our kid would be pretty cute. Beyond cute. Whichever one of us it looked like, it would be a knockout. Suddenly there's an image of a little girl in my head with Charlie's sandy hair and my blue eyes. My rosebud lips and Charlie's dimples. My olive skin and Charlie's freckles.

My hand slips down to my belly.

This is the longest three minutes of my life.

If I *am* knocked up then I'm only a few months behind Maisie. I wouldn't have to go through the horror of new motherhood alone, one of my best friends in the world would be right by my side. Maisie would be thrilled. And my baby would have instant best friends.

My baby.

My baby.

The three minutes are surely up now.

I open my eyes and look at the little window on the stick.

Oh.

Oh.

75

TERMINAL FIVE BAGGAGE RECLAIM, HEATHROW AIRPORT, LONDON

It's early hours of the morning in the UK when we land. The flight was bumpy and I promise with my soul that I am never flying economy again. The back pain is just not worth it. Charlie managed to sleep for almost the entire ten-hour flight, but I did not. And now I'm tired and grumpy.

But the moment we step onto the tarmac, my bad mood dissipates. The sun is shining and there is a crisp autumnal coldness in the air. I take a deep lungful, closing my eyes, drinking it in. It even *smells* like London. None of that sticky sweetness that hangs in the LA air. It's all fumes and pollution and I love it. God, I have missed this place so much.

'Come on,' Charlie says, tugging at my sleeve. 'Or are you planning to stay here all day smelling the plane fumes?'

I roll my eyes at him. 'I was having a moment,' I say. 'A spiritual one. I was becoming one with London again.'

'Would you like me to hold your handbag while you kiss the tarmac?'

I give him a tight smile. 'No, thank you. I'm ready to go now.'

Just then my phone buzzes with a notification.

'Who's that?' Charlie asks as he slips an arm around my shoulder.

I laugh and show him the text.

> *Miss K Collins. This is a message to let you know that your luggage has been located at LAX. Please contact us at your convenience to arrange collection.*

'There's your bag,' I say to Charlie but I'm not sure he's heard me so I lean over and grab his battered holdall from the carousel. He really needs to get a new bag. Maybe I'll go shopping for one for him when we're home. A 'happy getting back together' present. It's so old and gross. In fact, it's so old that it's barely survived its time in the luggage hold and as I hoist it off the baggage belt the zip gives way and half the contents spill out onto the terminal floor. I drop to my knees and start gathering up his belongings.

'Oh fuck,' Charlie shouts when he sees me on the ground. He drops down next to me. 'You don't need to do this,' he says. 'Keep an eye out for your bag.'

'What's this?' I say as my fingers close around a small velvet box that's fallen out of his bag along with all his other crap. It's a jewellery box. Specifically, a ring box.

'No! Give that to me,' he says and tries to swipe the box out of my hand, but I move it out of his reach and stand up. I open it and am suddenly staring at the most stunning ring I've ever seen. It's a cushion-cut diamond and has to be at least three carats. The main diamond is framed by other little diamonds and it sits on a delicate platinum band that looks like it shouldn't be able to hold all the bling. It's absolutely stunning.

'What's this?' I say, barely able to tear my eyes away from the huge sparkling rock. Is this what I think it is?

'Ugh,' Charlie groans from the floor, rubbing his hand across his face. 'This wasn't how it was supposed to be.' He looks up at me. 'Can you give that to me, please?' I frown down at him, pass him the box. 'At least I'm on one knee,' he says. 'That's something.' He looks at the ring sitting in the box and then holds it out to me. 'Kitty,' he says and I can't believe this is happening.

People at the baggage carousel are turning and looking at us.

I think I see someone get their phone out.

'Kitty Collins. I have loved you since the day I met you. And, while I didn't envision I'd be doing this in baggage reclaim at Heathrow, I suppose nothing about our relationship is conventional.' Someone makes an *awwww* sound and Charlie takes a deep breath. 'Will you marry me?'

I feel like I'm going to pass out. My head swims and I swear I can see stars in my peripheral vision.

This is really happening.

Charlie is down on one knee at my feet, asking me if I'll be his wife.

How can this be real?

Just a few weeks ago he'd blocked me from everything and I thought I'd lost him forever.

I'd think I was dreaming if I had ever had a dream based at an airport before.

But it's real.

It's really real.

My mind skips ahead of me and I see myself walking down the aisle in a white dress – probably a Danielle Frankel – into the arms of a man who loves me more than anything else in the world. Then the two of us are somewhere hot and exotic, maybe the Maldives, getting couple's massages and staying in the honeymoon suite. Then a beautiful house, obviously in Chelsea still, near good schools.

Maybe we'll get a dog.

Maybe we could get two dogs?

But, urgh, marriage.

Isn't that going against everything I stand for? It's one of the foundations of patriarchy, isn't it? Literally invented so women become property. Ownership and obedience dressed up as romance.

That rock is *really* nice though.

'You need to give him an answer, love,' an older lady standing at my shoulder says.

Oh, right, yes. I suppose I do.

I look down at Charlie, patiently waiting for my answer. My Charlie. Who sees me exactly as I am. Who knows my darkness. Has *seen* my darkness. And still wants me. Still loves me. How could my answer be anything other than yes?

'Yes,' I say and a look of pure relief washes over Charlie's face as the small crowd that has gathered around us erupts into cheers and whoops and cries of 'congratulations'.

'Thank God for that,' he says, pulling himself up to standing as a man slaps him on the back. 'You were quiet for so long I thought you were going to say no.'

I pull him into my arms. 'As if,' I say and he takes the ring out of the box and slides it on my finger. It's so gorgeous I already can't imagine my finger without it. I pull him towards me and rise up on my toes so I can kiss his mouth.

'Sorry about the venue,' he mutters. 'I was obviously planning to do this somewhere else. Somewhere romantic.'

'Shh,' I say. 'This is perfect.'

'You're perfect,' he says and grips the back of my head as he kisses me deeply. The crowd around us whoops again and someone wolf-whistles.

'Get a room,' someone shouts and we break apart laughing.

'That,' says Charlie. 'Sounds like a good idea. Ready to get out of here, Mrs Chambers?'

'There's no way I'm taking your name,' I say.

'I know,' says Charlie. 'I'm still going to call you that though.'

We walk, arm in arm, through the terminal towards the taxi rank, Charlie waving to the crowd like he's a celebrity.

I'm engaged.

I'm fucking engaged.

76

BLUEBIRD CAFÉ, CHELSEA, LONDON

'Show us the rock!' Maisie squeals in excitement. We're having brunch and I'm delighted that it's warm enough today to sit outside.

I hold my left hand out and she and Tor make lots of OOOH and AHHH sounds over the ring.

'Fuck, Kits,' Tor says. 'Did he rob the Tower of London for that or what?'

'How are you even able to hold your hand up under the weight of it?' Maisie says.

'Oh stop it,' I say. 'It's very pretty though, isn't it?' I gaze lovingly at the diamond. For all my feminism, I've been remarkably impressed by a man down on one knee, holding a ring out to me, asking me to love him forever.

'Very,' Maisie agrees. 'I can't believe one of us is actually getting married. Like, how grown up is that?'

I laugh. 'Maisie, you're literally about to be a mother of two. I think that wins Grown-Up Top Trumps.'

But Maisie shakes her head and runs a hand over her belly, which is huge. I stare at it with mixed emotions. 'Nope, it's definitely being someone's wife. I'm still waiting for Roo to pop the question. I'd love a fuck-off massive diamond. I hope he gets me one as a push present?'

'Maisie, you're having an elective Caesarean. You aren't going to spend a second pushing anything,' Tor says.

'That's not the point,' Maisie says with a pout. 'I think I deserve something nice for all this work.'

'Wait,' I say. 'Didn't he literally just splash out on a new car for you?' Maisie told me the other day about the Mercedes G Wagon that had been delivered to her at home, fresh from the manufacturer.

She rolls her eyes. 'Sorry, did I not specify *something nice for me*? That car is purely so we can transport the babies, the dogs and all their paraphernalia around easily. You have no idea the amount of stuff that comes with babies just for them to survive a day.'

We laugh and I pick up my mimosa – virgin – taking a long sip as I lean back and let the sunshine hit my face. It feels so good to be here. In a place I love with people I've loved all of my life. I've decided to take some leave from killing bad men. I look at my friends and realise I've made the right decision. There are things in life that are more important now. Anyway, it's not like I'm bowing out completely, I've simply passed the baton along to my sister and – I have a feeling – Agnes too. There's actually such a sense of peace in knowing I don't have to get my hands dirty anymore. I steal a quick glance at my ring again, at the promise Charlie has made to me, to love me forever.

I simply don't have time for killing anymore.

I've got a wedding to plan.

And a few other things too.

Tor and Maisie are talking about Maisie's birth plan and Maisie is telling a very graphic story about tearing – 'literally flaps to butthole'. I zone out and spot a couple walking on the street. I can't hear what they're saying but I can tell from their body language that he's admonishing her for something. He's towering over her with a thunderous look on his face while she's shrinking away from him, her eyes big and afraid. I hold my phone up and snap a picture of his face. He doesn't notice, too deep in whatever he's saying to the woman cowering at his side. I save the photo and make a mental note to do a reverse image search later, try to find out who this man is.

But then I feel the tiniest of flutterings in my stomach.

Different from the feeling of rage unfurling inside me.

It's tender, kitten-soft and I want to protect it forever.

So, instead, I forward the picture to Antoinette.

And then I delete it.

Epilogue

THE FOUR SEASONS, TAORMINA, SICILY

Sicily is drop-dead stunning, there's no doubt about it. And The Four Seasons is exquisite. Much better than that battered old 'Chateau' Kitty had me staying in.

How is it even a fucking Chateau when it's not in France?

Everything here is white limestone and bougainvillea. And waiters appear the minute you even *think* about feeling hungry or craving a limoncello spritz. It's a shame Kitty isn't here, but she says she's got too much to do with the wedding planning.

The last person I expected to become a Bridezilla.

Agnes is adjusting to our new nomadic lifestyle pretty well. I look over at her now. She's bronzed and beautiful in a gold lamé bikini. She's staring out at the infinity pool that we've been lounging around, contentedly sipping her cocktail and sighing with happiness occasionally.

I pick up my phone and swipe through to the LA gossip site that I check daily. Ron Wilde is still missing, presumed drunk. Apparently someone 'spotted' him living like a hobo in Alaska. Someone else says he's working at their local 7-Eleven in Kentucky. And someone else thinks they see him on Skid Row. As long as his fans remain creepy and parasocial, no one seriously thinks he's lying at the bottom of the Pacific Ocean.

Life couldn't be more perfect.

I slip my sunglasses down and glance at the terrace below. A couple is sitting at the bar overlooking the water. A couple I've been watching. To the untrained eye they look like any other loved-up pair out here on vacation.

But not to me.

I know who he is.

He's older than she is by about twenty years. That's my first clue. The power imbalance. She doesn't look like she's much older than me. Pretty in the way all the young women here are. I sit up and peer closer at them. They're not tan enough to have been here very long. I haven't seen them around before. And there's definitely something off. The body language. She's cowed and he's talking to her, quietly, not loud enough to let anyone hear, but I can take a bet.

You embarrass me.

I saw you looking at those men.

You dress like a whore.

And then I see it. How she flinches when he lifts his hand too quickly. She's used to that hand.

And not in a good way.

That familiar little flicker in my chest ignites.

The one that speaks to me.

The one that hasn't been wrong yet.

This is a bad man.

A very bad man.

Agnes nudges me with her foot. 'What are you staring at? And why isn't it me?'

'I'm not staring, I'm observing,' I say.

She sits up on her lounger and looks at my face, inspecting it. 'You're plotting,' she says finally. 'What's going on? Why have you got your murder face on?'

I nod towards the couple. 'She's scared of him,' I say and Agnes squints over at them. She stares down at them too.

'He's old enough to be her dad,' she says. 'Gross.'

'So gross,' I agree.

The man's voice gets louder, only slightly, but enough for the occasional word to drift up towards us.

'Disrespect.'

'Attention-seeking.'

'Slut.'

The woman murmurs something to him, trying to placate him, but he cuts her off, grabs her wrist. And not lightly.

Agnes is still watching. 'He's awful,' she says.

'Yeah,' I say, unable – and unwilling – to drag my eyes away.

'Do you think she's okay?'

'No.'

'Do you think—' Agnes lowers her voice. 'Do you think we should do something?'

By 'something' she means kill him.

Make sure he never hurts this woman, or any woman, ever again.

He gets up and storms off towards the steps that lead to the private cabanas. His girlfriend stays at their table. It looks like she's crying. Silently and secretly but it's body language that I can read.

Agnes's eyes are on me. 'I know that look,' she says. 'How are we doing this?'

I'm not sure yet.

Maybe an accident on a jet ski.

Maybe he slips and falls in the shower, the tiles are lethal when wet.

Maybe he falls overboard, he looks like the type who'll charter a yacht at some point.

There's no rush.

That's one thing I've learned.

There's time to plan this.

Like my sister would.

Someone needs to keep an eye on the bad men of the world while she's on maternity leave.

I lean back on my lounger. The sun hits my skin, hot and delicious. The sea glitters beyond the pool.

Anything feels possible here.

Acknowledgements

I always say what an absolute privilege it is to write these when I reach the end of a book, and this one is no exception. Maybe even more so, because this book was not birthed easily. Everyone says it's the second novel that's the tricky one, but I take your 'second novel' and raise you 'the third in a series'. It's not for the faint of heart.

Thanks, as always, to Euan Thorneycroft for being a brilliant agent and for metaphorically holding my hand through the darker days.

Big thanks to everyone at HQ and HarperCollins who has had a hand in making Kitty's third outing her best yet.

Huge, huge thanks to Caroline Lakeman for the cover design. I say it every time, but I think this one might be my favourite. I will absolutely be making lime green my whole personality this summer.

And of course, thank you to my friends and family, who have been endlessly patient with me while I wrote (and rewrote) this book. Thank you for understanding and still liking me when I cancelled at the last minute. So. Many. Times. I appreciate you all. Annaliese, shall we grab the other half of that bottle soon? No plastic cups.

Thank you to my gorgeous *teenagers*, Seb and Sophia.

But most of all thank you, yes *you*, dear reader. You consistently make my dreams come true. I love your posts, your messages, your little words of encouragement, and your support and love for my books. You're the best. Truly.

Find out where Kitty's journey began. . .

Meet Kitty Collins.
FRIEND. LOVER. KILLER.

He was following me. That guy from the nightclub who wouldn't leave me alone.

I hadn't intended to kill him of course. But I wasn't displeased when I did and, despite the mess I made, I appeared to get away with it.

That's where my addiction started . . .

I've got a taste for revenge and quite frankly, **I'm killing it**.

Available in audio, ebook and paperback.

Something bad happened last night.

I've woken up with the hangover from hell, a stranger in my bed, and I've gone viral for the worst reasons. My best friend Posey is dead. The police think it was a tragic accident.

I know she was murdered.

There's only one thing stopping me from dying of shame. I need to find a killer.

But after last night, I can't remember a thing…

'A whip-smart whodunnit, this will keep you guessing' *Red*

Available in audio, ebook and paperback.

Dear Reader,

We hope you enjoyed reading this book. If you did, we'd be so appreciative if you left a review. It really helps us and the author to bring more books like this to you.

Here at HQ Digital we are dedicated to publishing fiction that will keep you turning the pages into the early hours. Don't want to miss a thing? To find out more about our books, promotions, discover exclusive content and enter competitions you can keep in touch in the following ways:

JOIN OUR COMMUNITY:

Sign up to our new email newsletter: http://smarturl.it/SignUpHQ

Read our new blog www.hqstories.co.uk

X: https://twitter.com/HQStories

f: www.facebook.com/HQStories

BUDDING WRITER?

We're also looking for authors to join the HQ Digital family! Find out more here:

https://www.hqstories.co.uk/want-to-write-for-us/

Thanks for reading, from the HQ Digital team

HQ